LockeStep

LockeStep

A JOHN LOCKE MYSTERY

Jack Barnao

CHARLES SCRIBNER'S SONS/NEW YORK

Charles Scribner's Sons
Macmillan Publishing Company
866 Third Avenue, New York, NY 10022
Collier Macmillan Canada, Inc.

This is a work of fiction. Names, characters, places, and incidents either are the product of the author's imagination or are used fictitiously. Any resemblance to actual events or persons, living or dead, is entirely coincidental.

Library of Congress Cataloging-in-Publication Data

Barnao, Jack.
LockeStep.

I. Title.
PR9199.3.B3717L6   1987   813'.54   87-13035
ISBN 0-684-18782-5

10 9 8 7 6 5 4 3 2 1

Printed in the United States of America

For my daughter, Liza Lawson

LockeStep

one

I tracked Dee Sade, a.k.a. Billy Purvis, to the Victoria dining room of the Prince Albert Hotel. It's one of the best-known places in the city. That figured. Dee was the latest in a line of rockers that stretches all the way back to Liverpool. They were raised on fish-and-chips, and whenever one of them is in Toronto and leaves his suite to play with a steak, you can count on his doing it at the Prince Albert, where the reporters lie in wait to show the world that its idol has learned how to use a knife and fork.

Dee's fans had followed him to the hotel. A dozen policemen were holding the fort against a bunch of kids who should have been doing their homework instead of freezing their ears off in the February sleet. I was dressed for it, wearing a camel's hair overcoat on top of one of my two Savile Row suits. At the door I made a point of looking snooty, so the cops assumed I was a guest, and nobody tried to head me off as I walked into the dining room, leaving my topcoat with Maria, the Filipino hat-check girl.

The maître d' in the Victoria Room owes me one. I was eating dinner there once when a drunk punched a waiter in the eye and started explaining what the-trouble-with-you-bastards is.

1

He was drowning out the spell I was trying to cast on a super-cool lady lawyer, so I put a come-along hold on him and whisked him out through the kitchen before the remaining female guests could reach for their lorgnettes to see who was doing all that swearing.

Now I called my marker. "I'm here to see Dee Sade," I told Maurice, and he shrugged so wide you'd have believed him that he hailed from Paris, instead of the Christian quarter of Beirut.

"He says no visitors, but for you, M'sieu Locke."

I winked and walked by, pulling the Dee Sade Enterprises check out of my top pocket. Sade was sitting with his bodyguard, the one I'd been called in to replace three days ago when he overloaded his nose with Colombia's answer to the blahs and had to spend a little time wrapped in wet sheets.

The job had been relatively easy. I'd spent most of the time sitting on a hard chair outside the Star Suite, rereading *The Conquest of Gaul* and turning down offers of chemical refreshment while Dee Sade and the Marquises broke up furniture and enjoyed female companionship inside.

He was no more depraved than any other sex god. He seemed heterosexual and preferred his girls nineteenish and blond. A few underage hopefuls had turned up, but I'd sent them home. I wasn't sure how fussy his drummer was about age. Sentiment on my part, the girls all looked hard enough to go the distance, but I've been in too many countries where children are for sale. It goes against my grain, if not the intended victim's. One of them had expressed her gratitude by calling me an interfering old asshole. I resent that. I'm only thirty-two.

Dee looked up from his Mousse Saumon de Maison. I noticed he was avoiding the capers. Maybe somebody should tell him they were chips. "This bounced," I told him and dropped his check in the middle of the plate.

The bodyguard jerked in his seat, but Dee shook his head and he subsided. "Sorry about that, mate," he said. "I'll get George to write you out another one."

"No, thanks, I've played enough handball for one contract.

2

Why don't you reach into that bag you keep under your left armpit and peel me off three neat thousands."

The Liverpool sharpie shone through the mascara he was still wearing, a souvenir of his last gig, twenty-four hours ago. " 'S the ma'er, wack, don't you trust me?"

"Right in one." I smiled at him, like an uncle beaming at a backward boy. So far our voices had been low enough that the diners at the next table wouldn't have overheard. People would have thought I was asking for an autograph for my niece.

The bodyguard growled at me now like a well-trained Dobe. "Listen, Mac."

I beamed at him now. "Oh, hi, Freddy. They got the straw out of your nose, did they?"

He flashed an angry look at Dee, who was still playing it cool. When you're used to being under hot lights with a thousand screaming girls throwing their underwear at you, I guess you develop your own built-in refrigeration system. He said nothing. It was time to up the ante. I slapped my hands together jovially. "So, in honor of the fact that your road manager has tried to stiff half the people who've worked for you this trip, why don't you pay up before you're wearing that mousse?"

That was too much for trusty, loyal, helpful Freddy. He swore and lunged with his steak knife.

I moved outside the thrust and chopped him across the nose. He crashed backward, tipping his chair and splaying his feet up in the air until he rocked sideways and lay still. Somebody screamed. I turned to the door and nodded to Mahomet, alias Maurice, beckoning with one finger. He flew to my side.

"This gentleman seems to have fainted," I said, "Perhaps you could take him outside to get some air."

He stayed in character. "M'sieu! We cannot 'ave violence."

I picked up Freddy's napkin from the table and dropped it on his face to cover the blood. Then I reached into my top pocket and came up with my emergency fifty. I tucked it into Maurice's hand. "Cause him to disappear," I said.

3

He did. "Oh, *mon pauvre*," he cooed. "Come this way," and he propped Freddy up on his wobbly legs, out through the kitchen, away from the high-priced diners.

I turned back to Dee Sade. "It's about my three grand."

He laughed. Not a disarming, hands-raised chuckle, like a rock star fending off compliments. This was a street brawler's guffaw at a coup. " 'Ard-nosed sod, aren't you," he said. But he was reaching past his gold crucifix and Scorpio sign, in under his left armpit.

He pulled out his money bag and extracted two thousands and a handful of hundreds. I counted them. There were twelve.

"What's this, a bonus?"

"Naaaoh, that's for makin' me laugh," he said. "I 'aven't 'ad a chuckle like that since me mam caught 'er tits in the mangle."

A class act.

I folded the cash and stuffed it into my pocket. Maurice came back. "The gentleman is 'urt," he said.

Dee cut me off before I could apologize. "Tell 'im to go see George, get 'is money, an' go 'ome. 'E's bleedin' useless."

I unfolded one of the hundreds. "And make sure he gets this." Maurice looked at it greedily. "Make good and sure," I said, and his shoulder sagged. "Of course, m'sieu."

He picked up the chair and went back to the kitchen, holding the hundred ahead of him, like a Freddy-finder that was switched on. Dee frowned at me. "Are you the one was an officer in the SAS?"

I nodded. "Lieutenant Locke, at your service."

He wasn't smiling. Under his mascara and the ravaged leanness his eyes were intelligent, I noticed. When he spoke again he had shed the working-class Liverpool accent. He sounded like any north-country British actor. "I had a cousin in the Paras. The IRA killed him and seventeen others in an ambush."

I nodded. "Yes, we got the man who set that bomb. The news was never in the papers. He was run over by a truck, a terrible accident."

4

Dee pointed to the chair that Maurice had straightened. "Have you had dinner yet?"

"Not yet."

He waved his hand, a gesture that would have plucked a million female heartstrings if he'd done it onstage, and when he spoke, his accent was back full-blown. "For Crissakes, wack, siddown an' eat. An' if we can get that bleedin' camel jockey back, I'll start agen on one o' them pink things."

I ended up earning my extra two bills by taking him to the airport in a limousine. We got there at nine, and I remembered my other appointment. As soon as Dee was safely through security, off my hands, and teamed up with his sidemen, I rang my downstairs neighbor, Janet Frobisher.

She answered, her voice diluted by Handel's *Water Music*, pouring down the receiver at me. "Hello."

"Hi, Janet, it's your friendly neighborhood pest, John Locke."

"Hello, John. You can't make bail, right?"

"Wrong. But if you look outside your back door pretty soon, you're going to see a moose with a big Irish face muttering to himself about my letting him down. I wondered if you could tell him I'll be there in forty minutes, I'm out at the airport."

She laughed. Her laugh is one of the nicer things about her. There are several. "Is he a friendly moose?"

"A pussycat. His name is Martin Cahill and he's a Mountie. But don't expect the red tunic, he usually wears a greenish tweed suit. Could you give him my message, please?"

"I'll do better than that. I'll pour him a drink on your behalf," she said. "If he's an Irish moose, I'm sure that will cool him right out."

"Do that for me, and I promise never to propose."

She laughed again. "You're on," she said and hung up.

5

two

I live in the top flat of a triplex in Moore Park, the upper-middlebrow middle of Toronto, old enough that it's still largely WASP—the landlords anyway. Most of my neighbors are yuppies. They include the usual number of whiz kids, Chinese doctors and computer magicians, Korean accountants, German architects, all those people who made their parents proud. Then there's the exception, a free-lance bodyguard, me.

My neighbors wouldn't approve. Most of them have antinuke bumper stickers on their Porsches. By their lights, anybody who spent ten years in the British Army, seven of them with the SAS, is an obvious candidate for Fascist of the Month. They're wrong, as it happens. Seven years of fighting terrorism has taught me that right and left are labels that don't mean a thing when a guy has a grudge and access to an AK47. I guess I've found out the hard way that nothing is as simple as a cocktail party theorist can make it sound. In the meantime, I ply my trade, guarding bankers and lawyers and rockers and rich Arabs in town to turn oil revenues into Canadian real estate. All I want out of life is good food and beautiful women and excitement enough to scratch the itch I developed over those years in Northern

Ireland and the Falklands and on the scene at a number of hostage situations, including the Iranian Embassy in London.

I paid off the cab and walked around to the rear stairway. I can get as far as the second floor by going through the front door, but there are a few outstanding grudges against me on the part of the IRA and the PLO. The boys may not be on to me yet, but if they are, they'll come up the back stair. That's why I always check for myself.

It was clear but noisy. The ground floor is occupied by a pair of gays who fight six days a week and reconcile on Sundays. This was Thursday, and the battle of the stereos was raging. One of them was hammering out the soundtrack from *A Chorus Line* in the front while the other was playing Chopin in the bedroom. From outside their back door it sounded like a boiler factory.

Fortunately the place is well built. From Janet's apartment on the second floor all I could hear was "Sheep May Safely Graze." If ever I do propose to her, it will be to get my hands on her record collection. I think too much of her to want to lay casual hands on her handsome body.

She opened up on my first tap. "Right on cue," she said. "I was just going to get us both another drink."

I kissed her on the cheek, glad of the chance. She's a striking woman, hair the color of good English ale, green eyes, clear skin.

"Thanks, Janet. By 'us' I hope you mean yourself and Martin."

"In person and punctual. He was outside within a minute of your phone call."

That probably meant this was not the first refill she had organized. Martin has an Irish thirst. I glanced at the bottle of Scotch she was pouring from. Glenlivet. Most likely the same one I had brought down here at Christmas. Normally it would have lasted her a year. Now it was looking peaked.

"Thank you for taking care of him. Can I help, or can I go on through?"

"Go on through," she said. "You'll have yours on the rocks, right?"

"Thank you." I went through to her living room and found Cahill on the couch, eyes closed, his head nodding pleasurably to the music. But he's a policeman through and through. He must have sensed my aura. Without opening his eyes, he asked, "What the hell kept you?"

"Dee Sade and the Marquises. A little payment trouble, all cleared up now."

He opened his eyes and looked at me thoughtfully. "Is that one of the Limey coats you bought when you were in their army?"

I beamed. Rough hewn he may be, but the guy knows quality. "Sure is. Right from Savile Row. Why'd you ask?"

"Makes you look like a bloody great fairy," he said and closed his eyes again.

I slipped out of the coat and sat down across from him. "If I wanted to get hissed at, I could have stopped off downstairs."

He opened his eyes as Janet came in with the Scotch and reached up for the glass that had no ice. He raised it to her. "May your shadow never grow less."

"A little thinner, maybe," she said. "But cheers anyway."

We drank and I waited. He'd called me that morning, saying it was about a job. Period. I could see he liked Janet, but he was too good a copper to break security for a friendly face. So we sat and sipped and listened to Bach until Janet laughed. "Listen, if I promise you that this place isn't bugged by the KGB, and if I slip out to the milk store for a pound of butter, would you two care to discuss business? The tension is making me nervous."

Martin finished his Scotch in one decisive swallow and stood up. "I wouldn't want to put you out, Janet, you've been very kind. But I'm under orders to keep tight security. And what with your working for CBC Radio . . ." He made a "What can I say?" shrug.

She held up her hands. "I know, a man's gotta do what a man's gotta do." She reached for his glass. "Why don't you two head up and talk things over and come back for coffee later?"

"I'd like that a lot. Thank you," Martin said. He hooked his head at me. "So would the dude here. Only why don't you come up and drink some of his coffee? He owes you."

So we left it like that, and I led the way up the back stairs to my place. My discreet little indicators were all in place. Nobody had come in while I was out, and I had alarms on the windows that would have warned me if a cat burglar had come to call, so I opened up and brought Martin in for a drink. He had a Bushmills and sat and sighed over it. "Scotch is only a poor substitute," he said. "I wish people would remember that."

I got myself a glass of water. I'd already had the equivalent of eight ounces of booze that evening, and I wanted to stay bright-eyed if Martin had business to discuss. Mountie business was something I had never run into before. "So what's on your mind?" I asked him.

He lowered his glass to his knee. "The name Greg Amadeo mean anything to you?"

I shook my head. "Sounds Italian, that's all."

"It is. He's ex-bush-league muscle for a Montreal loan shark. Only he has one advantage most of his buddies don't."

"What's that?"

"His mother's Mexican. Seems that Poppa Amadeo was low enough on the totem pole that nobody objected when he married outside the language."

"Okay, so his dad's a social climber. What else?"

"What else is that the guy speaks good Mexican Spanish. His mother made him learn and he kept it up."

I thought about that one while Martin sipped his Irish, frowning pleasurably. "I have a feeling you're going to tell me he's become the man in charge of their Mexican drug operation, right?"

He nodded. "True's you're born. Five years now. He heads down there four, five times a year. Comes back. We jump on him. Nothing. Mr. Clean. Only a few weeks later there's coke to burn all through town, and friend Greg is driving a different car or living in a ritzier address or layin' better-looking women."

9

"Envy is one of the deadly sins," I said, and Martin waved his drink, dismissing me, without spilling a drop.

"He's welcome. No, the thing is, he's the number one go-between of the coke trade in Ontario."

He was grinning, waiting for my question. "And?"

"And we've got the bastard, dead to rights. After years of searching him at the airport, taking his luggage to pieces, his camera, his radio. We got him with a kilo of coke at home."

"And you're sending him away for ten years. Good. I love happy endings."

"Better than that." He swirled the whiskey in his glass and swallowed it as if it were medicine that he had to get out of the way before he could talk business. "We've got him scared enough that he's opening up on his bosses, the people who really control the traffic in town. Like, all he is is the bagman."

"An even happier ending. Just as long as you don't expect me to go to jail and guard his greasy little body against all those love-starved weight lifters."

Martin set his glass down and looked at me. "In a way we're looking for something even tougher."

"Like what?" Excitement is my drug, but I have no intention of letting some large Irish copper talk me into an overdose.

"Well, he's made a deal with the inspector. He's ready to fink on the whole Canadian operation, at a price."

"What's the price? Immunity, what?"

"More than that." Martin picked up his glass again and examined it thoughtfully, the way an archaeologist might if one ever digs out the ruin of this apartment. I handed him the Bushmills, and he poured himself a slug and set the bottle down. I waited. When he gets into this kind of trance, it's dangerous to wake him.

At last he looked up. "The price is, he wants one last week in Mexico. He has a Mexican wife down there. That's in addition to the wife and kids he has up here. He also has some cash stashed away. He wants to make sure his wife gets the cash so

10

she can hide herself someplace. Because when he spills his guts up here, nothing he ever cared about is gonna be safe."

"That's romantic as hell," I said. "But where do I come in?"

He looked at me very straight. It was like locking eyes with a gargoyle. "We can't send a copper to Mexico with him. The lawyers would have a field day when it came time to prosecute the other bastards."

"Besides which, if he gives you the slip, the egg will be all over the front pages."

"That, too." He put his drink down, untasted, and stood up. "What it boils down to is, we need a civilian hard-nose to travel with him."

"Skipping all the fine print, what will you pay me?" The job sounded interesting. I like Mexico anyway, and this assignment would be unusual.

"We can't pay you anything. We don't know anything about this, you understand," Martin said, and as I opened my mouth to protest, he grinned. "But our boy is plenty scared. If you can keep his ex-workmates off his ass, he'll pay you ten grand."

"How long is the job?" I was never good at arithmetic, but I'd just picked up a thousand a day for three days. Ten thousand was nice, if I didn't have to take six months earning it.

"One week. There are package tour flights every day from Toronto, but the first one we can get you on is Sunday. If you need to get out, we'll arrange for you to come back on the first available. But, meantime, you're booked to go down this Sunday, come back the next."

"That makes the pay worthwhile. But I need to know some more things first. Like how many buddies has he got down there waiting to back-shoot me and help him onto his horse to ride away into the sunset?"

"It figures he's got organization down there. No doubt of that," Martin said. "He's gotta have all kinds of donkeys bringing in the dope from Colombia, and I gotta admit those boys play rough."

11

"You're a real comfort," I told him, standing up. I think better on my feet, a fighter's reflex, maybe. "Okay, next question: Where is he going?"

"The tour plane is going to Ixtapa," Cahill said. "Ever hear of it?"

I nodded. "Yes, I know it, but that's not where he's going. It's one of the tourist ghettos, like Cancún, a strip of North American hotels and watered lawns and swim-up bars, every Mexican there goes home at night to Zihuatanejo."

"Never heard of it." Cahill shook his head. "You sure 'bout that?"

"Certain. It's the original fishing village, typical Mexican small town, clustered around a bay where you can swim without having a fifteen-foot wave fall on your head like a wall."

"You been there?" He looked up at me over the lip of his glass.

"Several times. Used to go there with my family, back before there was even an airport. Used to come in by boat from Acapulco, which is a couple of hundred kilometers down the coast."

"Wish I was going," he said wistfully. "All them *señoritas* in their bikinis."

"Gringos in bikinis. The Mexicans are modest."

He shook his head sadly. "Figures. Anyway, you gonna go?"

"What about backup? You have any contacts down there? I mean, somebody must've tipped you off about Amadeo. You've got to know someone down there."

"There is a guy. He's not with us, he's with the Americans, one of their undercover antidrug people. Name of Jesus Soto."

"That's 'Haysoos,' not Jesus. Good, how do I get in touch with him? I'm going to need somebody watching my back while I watch Amadeo."

"I'll make sure he's at the airport the day you get there. It'll be discreet, though, don't expect him to run up and kiss you on both cheeks, or whatever the hell it is they do down there."

"I'll need a picture or a good description. It would help if I had the license number of his car—something, anyway, to identify him for sure, I may need him."

"All right." Cahill straightened up. "You go on Sunday, a six o'clock flight from Lester B. Pearson Airport, Terminal One. I'll fix up the tickets. Now, whyn't you put the coffee on and bang on the floor for Janet to come on up. I've seen enough ugly for one evening."

three

Sunday was three days away, which was fortunate, since Friday was my mother's birthday and I was needed for my annual walk-on part as family black sheep. Sometimes I get the feeling that if I didn't exist, they would have invented me to flatter my elder brother the geologist, and my sister the shrink. Both of them waltzed through school the way most kids waltz through summer camp, married the right people, had the correct number of kids, one of each, and settled down. I didn't. School was a pain, and though my family finagled me into first Harvard and then Cambridge by pulling strings most people never get their hands on, I didn't finish either one. What little education I have has come from the army or from books, mostly history, that I've read to pass the time.

In the meantime, my family is gritting its teeth and waiting for me to grow up. They like to get me in corners at parties and ask who is going to take care of me when I get old. Except my father, of course. Old age is something that has never crossed his mind. He's sixty-three but looks fifteen years younger and is usually off in some windblown corner of the world drilling for

14

minerals, coming home once a month to let my mother resharpen her claws on him. She's an undisclosed few years younger than he and spends her time doing committee work and looking regal.

I had picked her up a silk scarf, with a little guidance from Janet, who has made it a hobby to try to civilize me, and I was as ready as I get to sip tea and nibble cucumber sandwiches in the family's twenty-three-room shack in Rosedale.

My three-year-old Volvo fitted into the circular driveway behind my brother's Audi, my sister's Porsche, and my brother-in-law's camper van. I grinned when I saw that. He had probably come direct from the operating theater. He's a good head, a surgeon at Sick Kids' Hospital, where he pioneered a new technique for transplanting kidneys. He's explained it to me twice and I still haven't got it, but people bring their children from all over the world to get him involved. His name is Jake, short for Giacomo. His last name is Valenti, which made my mother sigh when he first came home with Susan. Italian! Catholic! I'm lying. She groaned, twice.

Walter met me at the door. He's worked for the family since I was born, the year he smashed up his leg on one of Dad's drilling operations. I give the old man marks, he's loyal. Anyway, Walter is a buddy of mine in a quiet way. He's a veteran of Korea, and I guess it was his quiet suggestion that sent me off to join the Grenadier Guards after I was sent down from Cambridge, finally giving me the direction I'd been missing so far. "Good to see you, John," he said and we shook hands.

"How's the atmosphere?" I asked him.

He looked around conspiratorially. "Chilly, you ask me. Your mother's on the warpath."

I winked at him and walked on through. The Matriarch was standing with her back to the fireplace, with my brother and sister making like bookends. My father was on the telephone, Jake was helping himself to tea, and the four grandchildren were sitting in a row on the couch wondering how soon they could go home. My brother's wife was sitting, sipping tea and practicing to look like her mother-in-law when Robert inherits this house.

I waved at the kids first and they all squealed, and my sister's boy peeled off the couch and hung around my leg. He's dark like his dad and full of Italian enthusiasm that survived being diluted by the ice water he inherited from my sister. I picked him up and kissed him. "Hi, Champ."

"Hi, Uncle John." He clung on tight, a sure sign that Mother was indeed on the warpath. I wondered if she had discovered another of my father's adventures. For a guy his age he has a highly developed roving eye. I went up to her and kissed her. She turned her face at the last moment and spoke to Jake as I planted my dutiful peck on the cheek.

"It doesn't really need milk," she said, "It's Darjeeling."

"I thought it might put some heart into it," Jake said cheerfully. "If I had a patient as weak as this, he would be in intensive care."

"Happy birthday, Mother," I said, and held out the parcel. She didn't take it. She was too busy wiping young Andy's nose with his napkin, leaving me with my arm out for thirty seconds. Then she said, "You got here at last."

"I thought zero hour was four," I said. It was four minutes past by my watch.

"It was," she said.

I set Andy down and handed him the package. "Put that on the table for me, Andy; then come and see what I brought you."

He pattered over to the table and came back, this time with the other three in tow. "In my pocket," I told them and bent down so my brother's eldest boy could reach in for the bag of candies.

"Don't eat them now. They'll spoil your dinner," my mother said, beating my sister to it by a microsecond.

I winked at the kids. "Share them out. If there's any left over, I'll have them. No fighting."

They went back to the sofa and sat happily grubbing in the

bag while I bussed my sister and sister-in-law and shook hands all around.

My father hung up the phone and said, "You're looking pale. You need some fresh air."

"Up in Baffin Land maybe?"

"Ellesmere Island," he said, "We're on to an oil prospect. I'm flying back on Monday."

"I'm heading to Mexico on an assignment the day before that. Should get some fresh air down there," I told him.

My mother said, "What kind of assignment?"

"Plying my trade, guarding bodies." I gave her the opening; after all, it was her birthday.

"That's not a job for a gentleman."

"Well, my officer-and-gentleman phase is over. It's John Locke, civilian and prole, these days."

Now my brother took the relay baton off her. "You'd be welcome in the company, John. With your experience in the service you'd do well in management."

"I like my own line of work," I explained. "It's like crime. It doesn't pay, but the hours are good."

Jake was the only one who laughed out loud, although my father grinned until he got a lightning strike from my mother's eyebrows. Jake said, "Have some tea, John. It'll remind you of the army."

I accepted a cup. "Thanks. Why? Is it laced with saltpeter?"

His wife asked, "Saltpeter? Why would they put saltpeter in your tea?"

"The Raj believes it takes the sex drive out of the men. It's part of the folklore of any army. Ask Walter, he'll tell you the same thing. Ask Dad."

My sister looked at me through narrowed eyes, as if I were paying her fifty bucks an hour for her opinion. "You do set an enormous importance on your sexuality, don't you?"

For a tightass she is remarkably discerning. "Most guys do," I told her.

Apparently they didn't in headshrinking circles. Only patients ever mentioned the dirty word. "More than anybody I've encountered outside my practice," she said.

I frowned at Jake. "Are you letting the side down, Giacomo?"

He laughed. "I just don't ever mention the word," he said, ignoring the flash from my sister.

She kept after me. "Think about it. Of all the things you might have said about the tea, you had to bring the topic around to sex."

"Sorry, Doctor, I'll change the subject before you send me a bill."

"Most men of your age have finished the promiscuous phase of their lives. They've matured and settled down."

"You can prove anything with statistics. If you're a believer in statistics," I said. "When I come across the right woman, I'll settle down to a life of pot roast and diapers and dutiful lovemaking twice a week, like all the other boys on the block. But for the moment I'm still shopping around. Now, can we change the subject before you traumatize the youngsters?"

She wasn't going to, but my father was uncomfortable enough that he did it for me. "So, what are you going to do in Mexico?"

"I'm working with the RCMP."

Even my mother looked impressed for a heartbeat. The Mounties are right up there with the Queen and cucumber sandwiches in her book. "Doing what?" she inquired, almost kindly.

"I'm sorry, I can't discuss it. I just wanted you to know that I'm carrying the flag on this assignment."

My father managed a gruff chuckle. "If I know the government, it means you're getting paid next to nothing, right?"

I owed him one, so I nodded. "Pretty much. But there's a bonus for performance, so the rent still gets paid."

From that we managed to get the conversation turned around to governments and politics, and Jake was able to make the standard doctor's speech about government regulations in Canada driving most of his colleagues to Texas, where the money, if not the grass, is far greener. After about twenty minutes of it my mother even deigned to open her gifts and be gracious about them, study the lopsided handmade card Susan's kids had drawn for her, and listen while Andy and his sister explained what everything was meant to be. As long as she was holding court, it was almost pleasurable, and I was lulled into accepting the invitation to stay on for dinner, after my brother and sister took their families home.

Dinner was an honest pleasure. We've had the same cook for thirty years, and she had prepared my mother's favorite, Beef Wellington with mushrooms Bordelaise, one of the few things on which my mother and I agree. With a robust burgundy it was perfection. Then, off the same Anglo-Saxon gastronomical wall she had made blueberry crumble, with fruit my mother had bought from the Indians up at what I refer to as the summer palace in Muskoka. Afterward we all adjourned to sit around the fire with our coffee.

My mother excused herself after half an hour to prepare for a meeting she had the next day to put the squeeze on some construction company for the building fund for Sick Kids' Hospital, leaving me with my father and our Calvados. She was relaxed by now and maternal. She kissed me good-bye and told me to take care of myself in Mexico. After she had gone, my father and I sat down again and relaxed.

Times like these are the only real communication we ever have. There's something about drinking with your father that transcends the normal relationship. You don't have to get out of shape. Just having a bottle on the table between you gives you an equality that doesn't exist during the day while he's running the world and you're scrambling to find yourself a place on board. Times like these I even like the old bastard.

Just to break the silence, I said, "You're the only man I know who always drinks Calvados in preference to Cognac. Why's that?"

"It reminds me of the war," he said, reaching for his pipe.

"The locals turned out, did they, when you landed?"

"We didn't see them on D day. The Germans had cleared everybody out, but once we got through Bernières and into the open country and regrouped, we found ourselves in orchards.

Hard fighting, still, but that evening, as the men dug in, the farmer came around with a pitcher of Calvados. It was his best, too." He puffed on his pipe. "A barrel he'd been aging before the war. He'd buried it under the hay in his barn for the duration, saving it for liberation. God, it was like velvet. I can remember it now. And the pitcher, big, coarse china thing with flowers painted on the side. We drank to victory first, and then to all the friends we'd left on Juno Beach."

I sat and looked at the fire, enjoying the aroma of his tobacco and my own more recent memories until he prompted me, out of kindness, I guess. "Did you ever get a drink in those kinds of circumstances?"

"Not quite so memorable, because it wasn't home-grown liquor. But I was with the Paras when they liberated Goose Green in the Falklands, and one of the locals had a bottle of Bushmills. Just one bottle, among the survivors of the whole company, so it didn't do more than wet our lips, but I've preferred Irish to anything else, ever since."

I'd never thought of him as sentimental but he stood up now and went over to the liquor cabinet for the Bushmills and a fresh glass. He poured me a tot, then topped up his Calvados and handed me my glass.

"*Sláinte*," he said, Gaelic for "Good Health."

"*Sláinte va.*" I toasted him in return, and we drank as friends.

four

I reported to Cahill the following night at a hotel near the airport. He was in room 880, next door to the room where Amadeo had been on ice for almost a week.

"How come you've kept him here this long? There had to be flights sooner than this," I said as I dumped my flight bag.

"It's the first charter flight we could get you onto. There are regular flights, of course, but all of them go by way of Mexico City, changing planes. Apparently that's a big airport, lots of chance for him to disappear on you. This one only stops at Manzanillo, and we've arranged for you to stay on board."

"How about weapons? You're sure this guy of yours will have a piece for me? Or can I take my own? I'd be happier carrying that."

"I know you would." He held up one hand, apologetically. "We can get you aboard with it at this end, but you'd never get it out of the airport at that end. We don't have any connections."

"Not with the police?"

"A couple, near the top. But there's a whole lot of corruption in Mexico. Hell, the chief of police of Mexico City was staging bank robberies, running drugs, murdering guys. He built him-

21

self a palace someplace on the proceeds, right before they got on to him and chased him out." He stopped and scratched his head absently. "So, that's a long way of saying we can't give you a whole lot of backup."

"Just so's I'm not standing there bare-handed if some of Amadeo's Mafia buddies come looking for him, that's all."

"Don't worry. Our guy will be there with a package for you. It'll be a basket of fruit with a gun in it."

"Where's he going to deliver?"

"You'll get it at the airport, but don't count on pressing the flesh. He wants to stay low. Drugs is big business in that state, Guerrero. Hell, the growers shot down a couple of government helicopters in the mountains there last spring, guys who were out to spray the marijuana crop with Agent Orange."

"Not very friendly."

"The spraying, I guess you mean." Cahill humphed. "Dumb way of controlling it, I think. Some bastard'll always find a place to grow it. What they oughta do is legalize grass anyway, lean on the other shit."

"Legalization doesn't work. Didn't in Britain, anyway. They still have a runaway heroin trade despite that prescription business. Addicts don't like anybody to know they're hooked."

"Spare me the philosophy," he said. "I just try and enforce the law. Doesn't matter how they write the goddamn thing, they'll still need coppers."

"Okay, so you're off the unemployment rolls. Now tell me the good part, where are we staying and where's my expense money?"

He opened the dressing table drawer, took out a brown envelope and tossed it on the bed. "We've got a thousand bucks, half of it is already changed into pesos. Apparently it's not expensive, living down there, and your hotel accommodation is prepaid. You're with a tour group, Sunbird International, staying at Cuatro Vientos."

"The four winds. Yeah, I know the place. It's one of the big new spots they've built over at Las Ropas."

"What's that mean?" Cahill was tired. He'd been part of the security team watching Amadeo and hadn't been out of the hotel for a week, except to call on me on Thursday night. He had no patience left but was still pro, still looking for hints that might be useful.

"It's the trendy end of the beach inside Zihuatanejo Bay. it means the beach of the clothes. Apparently a shipwreck washed up a bunch of clothing there. Recently they've started building hotels over there for tourists. It's about a mile out of town."

"I'll keep it in mind if I ever get a vacation," he said. "Now, sign for the cash and I'll introduce you to the boyfriend."

He took me next door, where two other RCMP men were playing chess while Amadeo lay on the bed watching a movie on television. He was younger than I had expected, around twenty-eight, fit-looking, handsome in a loose-lipped Travolta-ish kind of way. Cahill switched off the TV and told him, "This is John Locke, Greg, he's going to look after you."

Amadeo lay back on his pillow and stared at me disdainfully. "He sure don' impress me," he said.

The feeling was mutual, but I said nothing. Cahill did it for me, snapping at Amadeo, "Nothing impresses you unless it's got big tits or a shotgun poking up your nose," he said. "This guy is the best in the business. Don't give him any trouble, or he'll break your head."

"Him'n who else?" Amadeo asked. "Now, can you get your fat ass away from the TV, I was watchin' that movie."

Cahill switched it back on. "Fill your boots," he said, and hooked his head outside. I followed him and he shut the door behind us. "Nasty little prick. Since we offered him immunity, he's been figurin' he was royalty. Wouldn't bother me any if his buddies wasted him after he's talked."

"They may do that. They've got long arms, those people."

When we got back in our room, I went over the projected plan of action a few times with Cahill. Apparently Amadeo had been tight about details. All he had said was that he would be picking up his cash from some hiding place and spending some time with his Mexican wife. The room at Cuatro Vientos was just a cover. We wouldn't be staying there the whole time.

"That's not a hell of a lot to go on, Martin. The way I read it, he's going to be looking for a chance to bolt. He's got enough friends in the drug trade that he could have me shot in the back without too much trouble, then pick up his money and run. Hell, even if he was in Dutch with the Mafia, they'd never find him in Mexico. If he's got cash stashed somewhere, he could vanish."

"I know. The way I see it, you're in danger if you're away from the town," Cahill said. "So you insist that he see his wife someplace where you can keep him holed up. The only dangerous part is when he takes you off somewhere to pick up the money. I figure that's when his business partners from up here will jump him, and you with him. They must know he's been turned around. We busted the door down on his house to get in."

"They know, all right. And he knows it—that's why he wants to pay me ten grand to cover him. Probably didn't know anybody in his line of work he could trust to make the pickup with him."

I had thought about this job a lot during the three days of waiting. It promised to be one of the harder assignments I'd ever taken on. I guess Cahill agreed; he sucked his teeth. "I wish I could go along with you. It's a tall order for one guy."

"All in a day's work," I said. "I've had to to watch my back before and stay on top of guys."

"Right. I want you in lockstep with him, everywhere. If you want, I can get you some cuffs, you can handicap him a little while you're going anywhere suspicious."

"It won't take cuffs. I can cover it."

"Yeah, I think you can, that's why I volunteered you for the job." He reached out his hand and we shook solemnly. "Take care of yourself. If it's you or him, make sure it's you gets out."

"Every time," I assured him. "Now let's crash, that flight leaves at six, we're going to have to be out of here around three forty-five."

24

• • •

It was snowing when we left for the airport, a thin, mean snow that promised to turn into the biggest blizzard of the winter. I was wearing my British overcoat on top of light summer gear, a cotton windbreaker and blue jeans, ideal for Mexico or for the airplane but inadequate for February in Toronto. I gave Cahill my coat and asked him to bring it back when he picked me up the following Sunday. "You just get back here with the prisoner an' I'll buy you dinner," he promised.

"I'll be looking for something more than fish-and-chips. But if the government's picking up the tab, I'll take you someplace."

"You're on," he said. Then he got serious. "One of our guys is taking care of Amadeo until you get through security. Go right to the gate, and he'll be there. After that, he's all yours."

"Just what I always wanted, a hood of my very own."

Terminal One is about thirty years old and is crowded to the walls when a charter flight leaves. I got in the lineup with several hundred people at the Sunbird counter and kicked my bag ahead of me until I got my boarding pass. My seat had already been chosen, the girl told me. I was on the aisle in the smoking section, which meant that Amadeo would be between me and the window. I thanked her and checked the bookshop but it was closed. I'd anticipated that and packed my copy of *The Reason Why*, by Woodham Smith, the story of the Charge of the Light Brigade, one of the British army's more spectacular screw-ups. It would pass the flight for me, and I didn't count on having time to read once we touched down in Zihua.

The only personal weapon I was carrying was my clasp-knife. It's big enough to set off the metal detector and get security people in a flap, so I had stuck it in my toilet bag and had to hope that my luggage made it onto the flight, something that doesn't always happen even in the best regulated airlines. In the meantime I got through security without any problems and walked around the corridor that circles the concourse until I reached Gate 32, where I found Amadeo sitting smoking next to one of the RCMP men from his room. There wasn't space next to them, so I just nodded to the Mountie and tapped my watch. He nodded in return, and I stood by the window watching the activity around our aircraft until they called the flight. Then I went over and joined the pair of them, and when we reached the gate, the Mountie nodded to me and I was officially in charge.

Amadeo looked at me and said nothing, just held out his boarding pass to the attendant and walked through the gate and down the boarding tunnel. I fell in behind him, checking how many of our fellow passengers were already wearing the sun visors they'd been handed by the Sunbird representative in the departure lounge. They all looked excited and were chatting about how early they'd had to get up, or how much they'd drunk the night before. They ran heavily to middle-aged moms and pops, with a few younger couples and one or two wistful pairs of young women who were flicking the occasional covert glance at Amadeo and me, probably wondering if we were gay.

Amadeo had a carry-on bag with him. I assumed the Mountie had gone through it ahead of time, but when we reached our seats I nudged him in the back and said, "In the overhead compartment, Greg."

"Don't you trust me?" he sneered.

"Would you?" I asked him, and smiled politely at the hostess who was pushing upstream against the flood of passengers, like a spawning salmon making the run upriver.

The same stew came back with a salver of candies and he waved her away. I took one and unwrapped it and sat back, waiting for him to talk. He looked like a talker. He had the self-importance of the middle-management hood, used to holding court to a bunch of mouth-breathers. I figured the best way to find out his plans was to listen for a while. Questions would only make him cunning. If that didn't work, I would be more direct.

After a couple of minutes he squirmed in his seat. "Couldn't you guys afford first class? This is the Chinese way to travel."

"You generally fly first?"

"Always," he said. "First cabin all the way."

"Which way is that?" I dropped the question in and got the expected response. His face pulled up into a sneer and he said, "You wanna know my route?"

"There's no first class on this flight, and it's the only direct flight to Zihua."

"It sure as hell ain't the only way to get there."

"Not if you want to stop off in Mexico City. I've always found the smog a bit unpleasant." I'd decided to milk the one advantage I had over him. He figured me for a lightweight, so I cultivated the image, slipping into the languid officers' mess drawl used by the Eton and Sandhurst upper crust in the British army. I'd never cared for them particularly, but they all had one thing in common, they were a lot tougher than they appeared.

"If a little smog gets to ya, you'd never last in my line of work. We live hard," he said.

"You just told me it was first cabin all the way. Which is it?"

"You some kinda Limey?"

I just snorted as if he'd amused me, closemouthed, not telling him one way or the other. I had no doubt he thought that anybody with an English accent was a wimp. Leslie Howard has a lot to answer for. They should never have rereleased *Gone with the Wind*.

"I worked with an English crowd for a while."

"Oh, you did?" He was bursting with contempt now, mocking an English accent. If he'd had a silver dollar in his pocket, I'm sure he would have screwed it into his eye like a monocle. "What work you do? Offer candy t' little kids?"

"I'm more interested in the kind of work you do. I understand it pays well."

"Don' worry. You couldn't handle it. It's men's work."

"Really? You need to be a man to push nose candy to high schoolers?"

Now he looked at me, his face stone cold. "Did anybody ever tell you you're an asshole?" he hissed.

27

"Plenty of people." I beamed at him like an English vicar. "One time each."

"Well, listen, asshole," he whispered, but before he could complete his sentence I caught his hand and rolled his fingers back. He bent, reflexively, trying to minimize the pain, and smashed his head against the padded back of the seat in front of him.

The man whose seat he'd bumped looked back at him in alarm. "You all right, Mac?"

"Cramp," I explained over Amadeo's head. "It happens sometimes, he'll be all right now."

I let go of Amadeo's fingers, and he sat up, rubbing them with his left hand. "Cute," he sneered. "You won't catch me like that another time."

"I don't need to, do I? Now, what were you going to say before you hit your head?"

"It'll wait," he said.

"I don't think so. You're not paying me ten long ones for nothing. I assume you're counting on your business buddies to play rough. I can do a better job of taking care if I know what to expect."

He thought about that, but he was still smarting from the shock I'd given him, and besides that, he had another five hours of safety ahead of him before we deplaned, so in the end he said, "Jus' relax, okay? I'm the guy's in danger, not you. I'll tell you when you have to get excited."

"Fine. Then I'll go on with my book." I smiled politely and opened *The Reason Why*. Amadeo glanced down at it once or twice, then looked away; books weren't his kind of action. He proved it when the stewardess came around with magazines. He told her, "Yeah, gimme *People*," and took it without even a nod of acknowledgment, flipping through it until he came to a shot of a girl in a swimsuit that he fixed on, staring at her as if she were a talisman, while we rolled down the runway and into the sunshine that lay five thousand feet above snow-covered Toronto.

28

As soon as the no-smoking light went out, he lit a cigarette and started chain-smoking. When the drinks trolley came around, he ordered rye. I had a Scotch and set my book aside. His magazine was still open at the same place, and I asked him, "She a friend of yours?"

It gave him a chance to sneer, and he took it. "Don't you know who that is?"

"Should I?"

"Should you? You might say. That's Debra Steen, she's the girl in all the swimsuit commercials, hair, diet pop. Hell, you can't watch TV, you don' see her five times a night."

I had a quick vision of him playing house in Toronto, being the thoughtful hood, sitting around his big plasticky palace with a wife with lacquered hair, watching TV on the nights when he wasn't out peddling coke. A funny mixture of a man.

"I guess I've missed her," I said.

"Yeah, well, you're missin' a real treat. I wanna tell you, she's got everythin'." He held the photograph up admiringly.

I studied it. The girl was pretty, dark, and slender, almost boyish, and there was a hint of mischief in her eyes. She didn't smolder, she twinkled with promise, and the camera had a love affair going with her. She looked to me as if she would be a disappointment in the flesh.

"Good-looking girl," I said politely to humor him.

"Don' she get you goin'?" He was astonished.

"That's just a photograph. She might surprise you if you bumped into her on the street."

"How's 'at? You crazy, what? Look at her."

"I guess she's not my type. I like more curves, don't you?"

"Oh, sure, curves is nice." He frowned at the girl. "Only this one looks like she'd really be special."

"They're all special, each one in her own way." There, the Locke philosophy.

He shrugged. "What I wouldn't give to take a run at this one."

"Thought this was going to be a family visit," I said carefully.

"You'll make your wife jealous, and Mexican women can be really fiery."

He looked at me coldly. "Not Maria," he said. "She knows better'n that."

A typical Latin macho male, not above laying down the law with a well-timed slap or two. Still, Maria had probably known what she was getting into.

"Says here that this girl is in Mexico for an extended fashion shoot this month," I read.

"Here, lemme see that." He grabbed the magazine and read the page through, painfully slowly. "Hey, yeah. How about that? Shit, wouldn't it be somethin' to run into her?"

"Don't hold your breath, it's a big country."

He waved me down. "Not that big when you're talkin' swimsuits."

Mexico must have three thousand miles of coastline, but I didn't want to burst his grubby little balloon, so I sipped my Scotch and then said, "I need to know a little something about your plans, Greg. The way I see it, your friends in Toronto must know you've been picked up. But there's been nothing in the papers, so they're starting to think you've been turned around. They could be feeling unfriendly. If I'm going to watch your back for you, I need to know what's happening."

"Nothin' tonight. We check in, have a few laughs, take a swim maybe, then tomorrow, my wife gets there. I go see her, like where she's at."

"Where's that going to be, the same hotel?"

"I'll tell ya when it's time."

"It's time now. If the boys you're in business with in Canada know where you're headed, you could be in real trouble."

"They don' know. Hell, you think I tell guys where I'm gonna be the whole time? I come, I go, I'm my own man."

He was expanding again, recovering the face he had lost when I slowed him down. And, in fact, he held all the cards. No matter what he told me, I would not be able to trust him. It was going to be a sleepless week anyway, so I might as well let

30

him think he was being clever. "Okay, but remember you're paying for protection, and I can protect you better when I know what's going down."

"You already know what's goin' down. I've gotta pick up a package, an' I wanna see Maria because she's gonna have to dig herself a hole to hide in for a while, an' she'll need bread. Okay?"

"Okay." I finished my drink and set the glass down. "How about seconds on your rye?"

We had another drink and then they served lunch, typical airplane food, and typically, he sneered at it. I didn't, but then, I've been in the army. Once you've eaten their food for a few years, airlines seem luxurious, even to a moderate kind of gourmet like myself.

After the meal he snoozed most of the way to Manzanillo, waking up to fill out the entry form the stewardess handed him. I did, too, listing my occupation as geologist. It's a precaution; bodyguard sounds menacing, and the last thing I needed was attention. I've even got a few of my father's business cards with my name on them. Locke Explorations, John Locke, BSc. As long as nobody wants me to talk in detail about pre-Cambrian rocks, I can wing it.

The aircraft landed at Manzanillo at eleven-thirty local time, and it was already hot, thirty-two degrees Celsius, the captain told us. We were given permission to stay on board if we wished, but I didn't want to draw attention to us, so we de-planed into bright sunshine and the unmistakable spice-and-cigar-smoke smell of the tropics. The sun was almost overhead, and a few lazy turkey vultures were circling on stiff wings, riding the thermals that rose from the runway. After a couple of months of cramping chill in a Toronto winter, it was blissful.

Amadeo said nothing, didn't look around or up at the birds, just stumped across the hot concrete to the airport concourse. We went in and lined up with the other passengers to have our entry forms stamped and the duplicate filed. Amadeo spoke in rapid Spanish to the immigration man, too fast for me to follow. My own grasp of the language is rudimentary, tourist Spanish, heavy on nouns, light on verbs, and very slipshod on tenses, but I can get around. Whatever he said didn't seem significant; we went through the gate and into the concourse, where we found ourselves mixed in with the returning Sunbird crowd, all of them brown against the pallor of this week's crop.

Amadeo asked, "You wanna beer?" and when I nodded, led the way to the lounge upstairs. Here I was back in my own language level. Amadeo took a table overlooking the runway while I went to the bar and said, *"Buenos días, dos cervezas, por favor."* I think *cerveza* was the first Spanish word I ever learned.

I went back to the table with a couple of Superiors, and Amadeo said, "This all they got? It's the worst beer in Mexico."

"They didn't have any Bohemia. Figure they don't need anything in here, there's no competition."

"You been here before?"

"Yes, I was in Zihua a few times. I like it."

"It's deader'n hell," he said, and sipped his beer. "Me, I like Mexico." He pronounced the *x* as an *h*, and I knew he meant the city, he was talking like a Mexican now.

"That where you generally stay?"

"Except when I see Maria." He didn't volunteer anything else and I didn't pump him. I'd already proved to myself that questions shut him up. I branched out onto an oblique track.

"I didn't realize Mexico was big in your line of business. I thought it was all grease and hash oil produced here."

He looked at me, and his face was expressionless. "Contacts," he said.

So that was it. A Colombian connection. Certainly it would be no trouble to bring coke in here, and since Zihuatanejo was a port, it must be a staging stop on the run from the Andes to Yonge Street in Toronto. I said "Oh," round-mouthed and polite, and he said no more until we had finished our beer and been called back onto the flight.

five

The passengers beside Amadeo had got off in Manzanillo, and he had a girl sitting next to him for the twenty-minute hop to Zihua. He used the time well, chatting to her about the country and her trip, pouring on a kind of gutty charm, full of growly chuckles and dry comments. She was sorry to see him get off when we reached our destination.

We came down the ramp into the sunshine, and this time I was working, not watching the vultures but scanning the balcony around the top of the terminal for any sign of a gun barrel. I didn't really expect one; any enemies of Amadeo's would have better chances to kill him in town, where they could melt away while a crowd gathered, but I was here to bring him back to Toronto, and I started earning my keep.

A bored official with a luxuriant mustache checked our entry forms and waved us through to pick up our bags. The other Sunbird passengers were milling about, excited by the atmosphere and the warmth, clustering around the Mexican hostess in her orange Sunbird costume, making inquiries about buses. Amadeo was cool, he went and stood by the baggage carousel and I went with him, waiting for our bags. Mine was down early, and I opened it and discreetly transferred my knife to my pocket. His must have been the first bag aboard, it was one of the last off, and then we walked out past the customs men, who waved us by. Outside there was a smell of good cigar smoke overlaying the tropical flower-and-dust smell, and you could see all the pale Canadians stretching and expanding like flowers in the warmth.

In front of the concourse there were buses lined up. Two were for Ixtapa, the other for Cuatro Vientos. I glanced around, looking for my contact. At the airport, Cahill had said, and I was here, on schedule. The sound of Spanish everywhere and the languid warmth of the early afternoon were reminding me that I was a long way from home and I had a job to do.

The perky little hostess called out, "All Sunbird guests, please," she waited, then added *"Por favor,"* and there was a chorus of giggling and we moved in closer to her. "All of you who are going to Cuatro Vientos, take the first bus, those who are going to Ixtapa, you take either one of the others, okay?"

We went to the first bus and handed our bags to the driver, who stuffed them into the open belly on the side, and then I saw what I'd been looking for. A boy, about ten years old, carrying a basket of fruit.

I moved out to the back of the crowd, keeping Amadeo in my peripheral vision. *"Quiero las frutas, yo soy señor Locke."* Not classical Spanish—I want the fruit, I'm Mr. Locke. The boy looked at me, no doubt comparing me with the description he'd been given, then said, "Hola," hello, and stuck the basket into my hands. It felt heavy, and he looked at me knowingly for a moment as I took the weight. *"Bueno,"* I said, and gave him a thousand pesos. He nodded and left. I watched him, but he didn't get into a car, just wandered away. Pro, at ten years old.

A large pale woman who looked as if she might teach music in a Toronto high school said, "Did you get that lovely basket of fruit for just a thousand pesos?"

"Not exactly. I'm an agronomist, these are samples."

"How interesting." She was sizing me up. Her left hand was free of rings, and she was fortyish and handsome, wondering

34

how lonely I was feeling, maybe. I smiled at her. Manners cost nowt, as a Lancashire corporal of mine had been fond of saying.

"Are you staying at Cuatro Vientos?" I asked and she nodded. "Good, perhaps we'll meet in the bar," I said and ushered her aboard ahead of Amadeo.

He was looking at me contemptuously. "You're a genuine goddamn *turista*, eh? Can't wait to get off the airplane an' you're buyin' a buncha crap."

"These are special," I promised him.

"Like hell." He sighed. "This is gonna be a great week."

The bus was air-conditioned, and there was a babble of comment from our fellow tourists as they chuckled about having come all this way from home to get cool, and then we settled down for the twenty-minute ride into Zihuatanejo. It took us past a few poor homes, typical farm community places with parched fields and orchards of palms and trees I didn't recognize. It was the wrong season for the jacaranda trees to be in bloom, but there were bougainvillea bushes everywhere and a few trees of the red and orange flowers that my father had called Flame of India on my first trip here, back when I was twelve and you had to come in by boat from Acapulco.

The little mountains reached down right to the highway, covered with a sparse brush, leaves wrinkled and dusty in the heat. If a man had to fight over this land, his first and biggest need would be water, I decided.

We slid into Zihua at the big highway roundabout, past the town's monument, a big phallic symbol made of fiberglass and plywood, a modern thing painted garish colors. It had developed a crack halfway up and was scaffolded with the irregularly shaped tree trunks they use for props and a couple of sheets of plywood. It looked like a Martian prepped for major surgery. Nobody was working on it. I guessed it was a mañana project; they would get around to it some tomorrow as yet unspecified. And anyway it was nearly 1:00 P.M. now, siesta time. Only the farmers were working; nobody with an hourly paid job was out in the heat.

35

Cuatro Vientos is a big terraced hotel. You get to it by driving the road around Zihua Bay, with a view over the town if you want to crane and look back. The rocks and sand and few rich people's homes are down to your right, hanging on the cliffs. Beyond them is the width of the bay, possibly three-quarters of a mile to a narrow, quarter-mile gap and beyond that, the Pacific, with nothing of importance between you and Japan. To the right, where very few of the tourists bothered to look, was the local landmark, the Parthenon. It was built as a copy of the original by the crooked copper Cahill had mentioned, in his last days before the new president of the country made his attempt to clean up the corruption. Now it was deserted except for a crew of security men with war-surplus American M1 rifles. On a previous trip I had met an American Viet Nam avoider, married to a local girl, who claimed to have been to a party there. A swinging party, he had assured me, while his wife was out in the kitchen of their little restaurant, all the coke a nose could hold. I glanced up as we passed; the same chains were in place across the driveway, still off limits, I guessed.

The bus swung to the right, through the flower-draped gateway of the hotel and down the steep little run to the office, located at the topmost level of the building. We got off the bus and filed inside. There was the usual excitement at the check-in counter. People were promising to meet one another on the beach when they had freshened up, bellboys were lugging suitcases and the first-time guests were oohing and aahing over the view. The pale woman smiled at me as she went off with a clone of herself, saying, "In the bar, remember." She was looking at Amadeo a little doubtfully, and I realized that two guys traveling together are going to narrow the eyes of any normal woman. He was not doing my reputation any favors, but there wouldn't be time for any romantic interludes anyway, I was going to need all my faculties, all the time. Ah, well, man must work sometimes.

We checked in and were given the keys to room 612, on the top level, the best view but the farthest distance to climb up and down to the beach. I was glad of that. I wouldn't have any chance to run, but I could keep in shape by doubling up and down the steps while Amadeo picked his way to the beach and back.

The room was huge, stretching the width of the building, from the narrow access balcony at back to the broad, luxurious front balcony with its hammocks and potted plants and chaise longues. The room was typical for the region, tile floor, with the beds and cupboards built in, out of concrete. It sounds like hell, but it's cool and enables the chambermaid to wipe the floor down with a mop, the most efficient way of keeping a place wholesome and free of *cucarachas*, the big brown cockroaches of Latin America.

Amadeo threw his bag down on the bed nearest the front balcony. "I need a drink," he announced.

"Yeah, in a minute." I dumped my own bag on the other bed and started lifting out the fruit. There was a pineapple surrounded by oranges, and a prickly guanabana, like a huge green gooseberry to look at, but perhaps the most delicious fruit in the world to eat.

The basket had a false bottom, and underneath that I found my gun, a snub-nosed Colt .38, and a box of shells.

The gun was a disappointment. The barrel is too short for accuracy, and I don't like revolvers anyway, it takes time to reload them. I prefer an automatic where you can slam in a second magazine and carry on firing.

Amadeo didn't have the same preferences. "Shit, you got a piece?"

"Yeah." There was a lightweight holster with it, again, not my choice, a shoulder holster, painfully slow. I would be better with the gun in my pocket.

I tried the action on the gun; it was hard, a new weapon usually is, but the double-action worked perfectly, turning and presenting a new round after every firing. Then I loaded it and slipped it into the pocket of my cotton windbreaker.

"Now I'd like to shower first, then have that drink," I said.

"I'll shower later. I'm gonna have me a tall margarita an' a swim," he said.

"So kick back for five minutes," I told him. "And now we're on our own, let me give you the rules. If I'm going to stop somebody hitting you, it needs cooperation. Your job is to listen when I tell you something and not make any moves I don't know about, okay?"

"Yeah, sure. Why'd ya think I'm payin' ten grand? I'm gonna buy a dog an' do my own barkin'?" He waved me away. "Go shower, I'll wait here."

He sank down on his bed, arms behind his head. I took my clean shirt and shorts and the windbreaker with the gun in it and went into the bathroom, leaving the door open.

The bathroom was typical. The whole room was tiled and had no divisions, no shower curtain. I put my clothes in the sink and slipped quickly under the shower, then dried and changed. Amadeo was still on his bed, arms behind his head, eyes closed. After all the arrogance he had shown on the plane, I was waiting for the other shoe to drop, but for the moment I relaxed and put on a pair of white socks and my running shoes. When I was ready, I said, "Okay, you gonna change into your swimsuit?"

"Yeah." He rolled off the bed and changed. I looked him over as he did; his body was lean but not well muscled. He must have played soccer as a boy, he had good legs still, but there was a puffiness to him that would turn into real fat before he reached thirty-five. He looked up and caught me watching him. "You queer?"

"Sorry to disappoint you, no."

"I figured you was a Limey, you'd be queer."

"You'd be surprised how many of them aren't," I told him.

His swimsuit was skimpy, and when he picked up his towel and headed for the door, I stopped him. "Listen, I know it pays to advertise, but you can't go into the bar like that. Stick your pants back on or the locals are gonna think you kick with the wrong foot."

" 'S matter with the swimsuit?" He looked down at himself in surprise. "I wear it all the time."

"If you're going to make it through this week with your head still on, you're going to have to be inconspicuous. Put your jeans on and a shirt."

Surprisingly, he did it, sighing but not complaining. While he zipped up, I transferred my passport and cash to a plastic case I always use overseas and stuck them into the left-hand pocket of my shorts. It's a good trick, either you leave your valuables in the hotel safe or you keep them with you at all times. Even a trained man can have his pocket picked, but I'm right-handed, and a pickpocket would go for the right-hand side. I don't think even the best of them could hit a second pocket before I caught him, so I always keep small bills in the right-hand, heavy duty valuables in the left.

Amadeo didn't bother. He watched me and shook his head. "Don' trust nobody, do you? I've stayed here before, it's safe as a church."

"Good, then your gear will be okay. Let's go."

We went out the front way, onto the wide balcony that faced southwest and was flooded with brilliant sunshine. Amadeo walked to the rail and looked out over the bay. It was the first casual move he had made, and I watched him as he leaned on the rail, I glanced all around, seeing only an elderly couple at the far end of the balcony, sitting in the shade of the overhang, sipping tall drinks and reading pocket books. They were burned mahogany-brown, and the woman looked up and waved. I waved back, then joined Amadeo and looked down on the bright beach and the gentle rollers breaking on the sand. Pelicans were gliding along the crests of the waves, moving laterally with them as they rolled up the beach, rising every now and then to gain height for a quick plunge, coming up again with their bills convulsing as they swallowed their catch. Long-tailed frigate birds were floating high over the water, looking for boobies and gulls they could bully into dropping their fish. Out on the water lay a clutter of yachts, most of them with American flags at the stern, courtesy Mexican flags on the mast.

"Why the hell would anybody live where we do?" Amadeo asked. "This place is heaven."

"Great for a few weeks, but you'd go crazy living here, no books, nobody to talk to, no choice of food."

"I got plenny o' people to talk to. I speak Spanish." He straightened up, turning away from the rail, "So let's get that margarita."

We walked back around the end of the balcony and took the steps down to the ground floor. The bar was set up outside, under an awning of banana leaves. It had stools all around it, but most of them were vacant, it was still siesta hour, and the guests were up in their rooms biting one another's ears, or snoring.

The bartender was a good-looking kid in a crisp white shirt with a plastic name tag that said Manuel. Amadeo took over, ordering two margaritas in Spanish. His accent was Mexican enough that the boy immediately started chatting to him animatedly and poured us extra-strong drinks, not that they bother much with measuring in Mexican resorts, the local liquor is cheap enough that they don't have to keep count the way North Americans do. A gringo can buy a liter of tequila for three bucks, the hotels probably pay a third of that.

The drink was excellent. Normally it's not smart to take ice, but I figured that a tourist resort like this one would use purified water. I usually stick to beer in Mexico, even clean my teeth in beer if there's no bottled water available. That way I've stayed clear of trouble. I raised my glass to Manuel. *"Muy bien."*

He showed a wonderful set of pearlies and said *"Gracias."* That's another thing I like about Mexico. They don't lisp their esses there, the way they do in Spain.

A couple of minutes later the two women from the bus arrived. The one who had spoken to me looked good in her swimsuit and was proud of it. I imagined she did sit-ups every day to retain her waistline. The other one was sliding down the hill toward a lifetime membership in Weight Watchers. I stood up when they came in from the sunshine. "Hello, you're all settled in?"

"Yes." She smiled at us both. "It's our first time here, isn't it just marvelous?"

"The nicest place I've been in the whole country. My name is John Locke, this is Greg Amadeo."

Perhaps because there were no other women around, Amadeo made an effort. He stood up for them, and we shook hands all around and learned that their names were Beth, the one I'd met first, and Kelly.

Amadeo ordered them a margarita each, and Manuel, with a Latin male's eye for the main chance, served them a solid double. They weren't his generation, but he thought he would oblige us. Beth said *"Gracias"* to him, Kelly just nodded and took a good slug out of hers. I guessed that Beth was the go-getter, Kelly the passenger, a lot of twosomes of women are like that.

"Are you an agronomist as well?" Beth asked Amadeo.

"Agronomist?" He looked at me, baffled.

"No, Greg is an importer of vegetable extracts," I said. "We work together." Amadeo grinned. I suppose he'd never thought of his trade in that way.

"How interesting," Beth said. She was smiling, too, a nice smile that didn't look practiced. I wondered if her students appreciated her efforts.

"Let me guess, you and Kelly are teachers," I said.

"I am," Beth admitted. "Kelly is a librarian."

"How come you've managed to sneak away, is it the midwinter break already? I thought that came in March."

"It does. But I've been off work for a couple of weeks, had a cold that wouldn't clear up, so my principal told me to take another week and get some sunshine, and here we are."

Amadeo drained his glass and stood up. "Yeah, this'll clear it up. Listen, whyn't you three have another drink, I'm gonna have a swim."

"Good idea. I'll join you. If you'll excuse us, ladies."

"Of course." Beth's smile was only a millimeter less wide, but I could see her mind working. Two inseparable men, what chance did a couple of women stand?

We walked down to the sand and Amadeo said, "Fer Crissakes, you don' have to live in my goddamn pocket."

"No choice, this is business," I said.

We passed a little area of palm trees and a couple of tables under the familiar banana-leaf awnings and moved out onto the hot brightness of the sand. "You swim if you want, I'll stay and watch your gear."

"Have it your own way, but you're missin' a chance to get lucky with that momma back there."

"There's all night untouched ahead of us."

He didn't answer but shucked his shirt and jeans and ran out into the surf. It was gentle, perhaps four feet high, and once he was through the first wave, he swam out, bouncing over the crests of the incoming waves, swimming strongly in a good, disciplined crawl.

I watched him, and then looked around, checking for movement among the boats. Only one was active, the para-sailing boat, pulling its parachute with one of the handlers showing off in the harness, dangling from his knees, a hundred feet up. The boat driver was good. He was leaning just hard enough offshore that the onshore breeze kept his man high over the length of the beach, craning the necks of most of the sunworshipers. Because it was Sunday, many of the people were Mexican. There are no private beaches, and the locals mingle on Sunday, the only day off work most of them get. Some of the boys were looking up wistfully, but the men my age were all married, they didn't have ten American dollars for frivolities like para-sailing and didn't even consider it.

Amadeo swam straight out, past the line of moored fishing boats and out toward the open water, a hundred yards from shore. Then he stopped and lay back in the water. He waved and I nodded at him, and then I saw another boat, one that had appeared to be deserted. It jumped away from its mooring and

42

headed for him. My hand went down to the gun in my pocket, but when the boat neared him, it slowed, and then a man in the back reached over and hauled Amadeo in. He wriggled over the stern and then stood up and waved at me again, straight-armed, with his middle finger sticking up.

The boat speeded up again, out toward the deeper water where the sailboats were moored. I turned and ran along the beach, glancing over my shoulder at the boat with Amadeo in it. Fifty yards from me the para-sailor had come to rest and was standing by the harness while the boat idled out in the surf, fifty yards offshore. I could see Amadeo's boat stopping beside a sailboat, saw him transfer aboard, and then saw the anchor line tighten on the sailboat as the skipper weighed anchor to leave.

"Pronto," I said to the para-sailor, "Quiero coger el velero, por favor." Quick, I want to catch the sailboat.

He looked out at the boat, which was motoring away toward the mouth of the bay, entering the heavier chop of the open sea.

"No es posible." He shrugged. Impossible.

"Sí, es posible, por cincuenta dolares." Fifty bucks should make his mind up. But it didn't.

"Es más grande," he held his hands up, one above the other, the big boat was too high for his small boat to mate up with. I figured he was stalling, but he had a point, if the people on the sailboat didn't want us aboard we'd never make it. I had to leave them no option.

"Sí, es posible, con parachuta." He opened his mouth to speak but I didn't let him, I was putting the harness on. "Por cien dolares, digale a su amigo lo que quiero." I was probably butchering the language, but he got my drift. For a hundred bucks, he would tell his friend what the plan was. He still hesitated and started to explain that it was peligroso, dangerous, but I waved him down. "Yo soy para." I'm a parachutist.

He shrugged, and then I flipped out a hundred-dollar bill. He grabbed it and started yelling and pointing. The driver yelled back, then shrugged and took up the slack. Within ten feet I was airborne, climbing rapidly to the peak of the line. He started to slow then, but I know about parachutes. He was afraid that if he went too fast, I would climb too high, but I furled the lines on the leading edge, cutting the angle of the chute against the wind and losing a little altitude, which I regained as he picked up speed. I could see the original motor-boat racing back toward the town dock, and it suddenly turned and swooped back toward my boat, but my driver was on his toes now, enjoying the challenge, jamming the throttle wide open as I rode the silk carefully out toward the sailboat and then over the top of it.

The driver was very good. He judged his speed perfectly, cutting back, so that I sank toward the sailboat, arcing down toward the stern. Then Amadeo turned from the wheel and picked up a rifle beside him. He raised it, but before he could fire, I drew my clumsy little pistol and put two shots into the stern, luckily missing him but slamming the seats each side of him. It was too much for him, and he dropped the gun and bolted down the companionway into the cabin. I stuck the gun back in my pocket and unsnapped the harness, letting myself fall to the length of my arms below the chute as I sank closer to the boat. It was pitching four feet up and down on the chop, and I had to judge it carefully. If I got it wrong, I would break my legs. Then the boat started to yaw, rudderless now, falling across the wind like a log tossed by the surf. It gave me more space to land, clear of the boom, and I dropped neatly beside it, landing on the seat at the peak of the boat's rise, jumping down to the deck proper as the boat dropped away under me. The rifle was on the seat. I hoped it meant Amadeo was unarmed. I had to stop him, right now, the hard way if necessary.

six

Amadeo had closed the cabin door behind him, maybe expecting me to try to pull it open, giving him a clear swing at me. Fat chance. I was trained better than that. The door had to go. I clenched my pistol in my right fist, then braced myself astride the companionway and swung both feet against the door. It crashed off its rails, and I vaulted over the wreckage and inside. He was at the far end of the short cabin, scrambling to get into the forward compartment. I stuck my pistol straight out, two feet from his face and told him, "Hands on your head."

He did what I said, opening his mouth to explain, but I didn't listen. I took a pace forward on the right side of the table and swung a solid left at his gut. He wasn't braced for it, and the punch collapsed him like a broken paper bag. I stepped over him and tore the forward compartment open. A woman was standing at the far end, her back to the bow of the boat. She was Mexican, pretty, and young, wearing a light summer dress and holding a butcher knife out in front of her as if she knew how to use it.

It was not a time for the Locke charm, not even for the do-it-yourself Locke Spanish. I snapped, "Drop it," and she did, faced down by the snub nose of my pistol. "Get back to the wheel and turn us into the wind," I told her. I backed out of the berth and she followed, but dropped to her knees beside Amadeo.

She looked up and screamed at me in Spanish, but I told her, "He's fine. Get up to the wheel," and shook the gun at her.

She came behind me as I backed up and climbed the companionway to the tiny rear deck, covering her all the way. Then she took the wheel and brought us around into the wind again. I glanced around. The para-sailing boat was on our starboard beam, wallowing in the chop as the driver pulled in the chute. He waved at me, shouting *"Bueno."* I waved back, not letting him see the gun, and grinned. The other boat was cutting toward us, a hundred yards off, pushing a big white bow wave that let me know it was speeding. I picked up the rifle Amadeo had dropped. It was a pathetic thing, a .22 bolt-action with a three-shot magazine, the kind of gun farm kids back home use for plinking at groundhogs. The best his wife had been able to buy, I guessed, shopping in the local hardware store. If this was the best the Mexican mob could do, civilization was safe.

The driver of the boat was standing up, both hands on the wheel, but that didn't mean he was unarmed. I watched and waited as he pulled around us, on the blind side from the para-sail boat. When he got to within twenty yards he let go of the wheel with his left hand and pulled a gun, but before he could raise it, I leveled the rifle at him, and he dropped low and sheered away, just as fast, around our stern and back to the dock. I didn't know how much of a friend he was to Amadeo, but not enough to start exchanging fire for him, not against a rifle. He probably preferred to wait until we came ashore, where he could sneak up on me.

When he was a hundred yards off and maintaining his course back to the dock, I told the woman, "Cut the motor and drop the anchor." Her English must have been good, because she did what I asked without question, and soon we were moored, bobbing gently on the swell.

46

"Back inside, and don't try anything," I said. She glared at me, a lioness with her tail twisted, but went down the companionway and into the cabin.

Amadeo was recovering. His breath had come back, and he was sitting on the deck with his back to the bulkhead, his knees drawn up. His face was deathly pale and he looked at me fearfully, covering his bruised stomach with both hands. I knew how he felt. Being winded like that makes you humble. For almost a minute you're sure you're dead, struggling for air and unable to breathe. But he would recover. On top of that, he was still in his swimsuit and what had looked macho on the beach looked ridiculous here.

I stood over him and spoke softly. "That was a warning, Greggie. Next time you jerk my chain I'll hurt you. You got that?"

He was whipped enough to nod dumbly, and I said, "Good. We understand one another. Now, I'm going to search this thing for weapons. If I find another gun, I'll shoot you in the foot with it. So tell me now, do you have anything else on board?"

The woman answered, spitting out the words. "If we had another gun, you would be dead."

That sounded plausible, so I nodded at her. "Don't expect to get a Christmas card from me this year."

Amadeo looked up at me. "Honestagod, there's nothin' else," he said, then dropped his head back on his chest.

I worked the action on the rifle, flipping out the rounds and catching them, then took out the bolt and put it in my left jacket pocket and laid the useless rifle down. "Okay, next question. Do you have supplies on board?"

"Supplies?" He looked up again, painfully. "Like, you mean food?"

"And drink, good water, or beer."

He spoke to the woman in Spanish, too fast for me to follow, but she shook her head as she answered, so I guessed we were empty.

47

"Is this *bonita señora* your wife?" I asked next, and he nodded.

"Yes. Maria, may I present John Locke."

I nodded to her. "Delighted. I'm your husband's nursemaid. I'm here to see he doesn't get lost this trip."

She listened to me, then turned to rattle at Amadeo in angry Spanish. He was cowed enough to lift both hands from his gut and hold them up. Before he could answer, I told him, "I want everything in English from here on."

"Yeah. Okay." Right that moment he would have learned Urdu if I'd asked him to. He said to Maria, "It's business. I have to go up to Canada for a while. I'll be back in a month, to stay. But first I've got some money hidden, I want to get that out and give you some of it because you'll have to split."

"From my house?"

"Yeah. Some people are mad at me. I don't want them coming after you instead." He was looking straight at her, and I was surprised at the tenderness in his eyes. I wondered if his Canadian wife got the same kind of affection.

Maria said something in Spanish, turning on her heel and then back again, a gesture that would have looked stagy on a WASP, but from her was as natural as breathing. She was nicely built, and her dress floated around her as she moved. It was a lot more attractive to my eyes than the skin-tight blue jeans she might have worn in North America. The women's libbers have made a lot of mistakes, if you ask me, which most of them would fry in hell before doing.

I turned away from them and checked out the cabin. It served as the galley and dining space of the boat. There was a small refrigerator in one corner and a two-burner gas stove mounted on a gimbal so it would stay level at sea. I opened the fridge and found it empty except for a couple of bottles of Coke and a beer. I helped myself to the beer. Now the excitement was over, I was thirsty.

"Where are the rest of the shells for the rifle?" I asked.

Maria lifted the cushion on one of the seats, exposing a flat surface with a finger hole in it. She lifted it and pointed into the locker. There was a flare pistol and a box of flares and a box of .22 bullets. There were three missing, which jibed with the total in the gun. I lifted the flare pistol, too, thankful that Maria hadn't considered it a weapon. Marine flares can burn a hole in you, like a phosphorous grenade. She could have turned me into a Roman candle if she'd been quicker.

I stood for a moment longer, looking at the pair of them, wondering what to do next. For the moment, I was happy to be aboard the boat. It meant I could sleep, out on the deck, while they played Mom and Pop in the forward compartment. In the hotel I would have to handicap Amadeo some way, or sleep with one eye open all night. But we couldn't stay here. Hell, if he didn't go ashore, he couldn't get his cash, and that meant I'd be out ten grand. Besides, we needed food. It would take thought. In the meantime I was feeling magnanimous. Parachute work does that to you, there's an exhilaration about dropping from the sky that doesn't wear off, even if you have to fight on landing. I decided to give them some space.

I went ahead and searched the cabin, quickly but thoroughly, going on through to the forward compartment, flipping the mattress back and opening all the closets. There was nothing on board but some clothes for Maria and a shirt and pants for Amadeo. I tossed them to him and he put them on gratefully.

I considered the evidence, the fact they were running empty probably meant he had a rendezvous arranged close by. There isn't another harbor within a day's sail, but there are a few beach villages. They could have arranged for a boat to come out to meet them and take them ashore, into a car and away. A close call. I'd nearly lost the sonofabitch in the first hour.

I came back into the wardroom and looked at them. He was sitting up on the couch now, still hunched forward as if he was in pain. He wouldn't have been, but I guessed he was embarrassed in front of Maria and was hamming up his reaction so she would feel sympathetic instead of angry at him. His ploy was working; she was sitting with her arm over his shoulder, leaning close to his ear, whispering, probably the Spanish equivalent of "There, there, poor thing."

I picked up the rifle and the .22 shells, and spoke to them. "We can't stay here all night, we'll have to get some food. But for now, it's restful. I'm going out on deck for a while, I'll call out before I come in again. But when I do, we're heading into the harbor, okay?" Amadeo didn't look up, but the back of his neck flushed red. He was humiliated by his failure, and embarrassed by the finger wave he'd given me. Now the laugh was on him, and he wasn't used to that kind of action. He needn't have worried, I've been insulted by experts in my time, sometimes viciously, like when one of my men was shot by a sniper in Belfast, and the street kids gathered around to laugh as they watched him dying. That had hurt, Amadeo's childish little gesture hadn't.

I checked my watch. "It's quarter to two. I'll call you at four and tell you what we're going to do. Play quietly, kiddies, Daddy's going to rest." I smiled at them and went out into the beautiful afternoon sunshine, carrying their entire armament with me.

We were all alone on the water. I checked around for landmarks, and from what I could see, we hadn't drifted since Maria had dropped the anchor. It was holding. We were safe here. I was almost jealous of Amadeo. To be out here with a woman like that was the stuff that dreams are made of. Except that he was down below trying to explain why his life-style had come unstuck and she would have to move out of the casa he'd bought her and hole up in Mexico City for a while.

Ah, well, as the old army saying puts it, if she couldn't take a joke, she shouldn't have joined. I thought about her as I sat and did my best to clean my Colt, using my handkerchief to wipe away the smoke residue from the barrel and to polish the chamber again. Probably the grime wouldn't affect it, not if I was only going to use it for a week, but it had proved its worth once, I owed it a clean. Then I reloaded and put it back in my

50

pocket and slipped off my jacket and lay back on the seat beside the wheel, knees up, staring up into the infinite blue. What a country! They wouldn't get any rain here until May, possibly.

After a while I slept, lightly, as I've been trained to do, waking with a start when the angle of the deck shifted slightly outside the regular rise and fall of the water. I sat up, keeping low in case someone was coming alongside but nobody was, and then Amadeo's head poked out from the cabin.

"Can I talk to you?"

"Sure. Put your hands outside before you step out."

He did, stretching his arms in front of him like a sleepwalker; his hands were empty. "Okay, come on up." I pulled my jacket back on, covering the new glow of the minor sunburn on my forearms.

He came up and sat down opposite to me. "I'm sorry I tried that dumb trick. It was kind of a test, you know."

"And now you're trying snake oil. Come on, Greggie, you can do better than that. I want the truth this time."

The "Greggie" hurt him. It was intended to. I wanted him feeling small. If he hadn't been promised for a court appearance in Toronto when we returned, I would have punched him in the face instead of the gut. That way he would have been sore longer, and every time he looked in a mirror, he would have known he'd been defeated. It's not malice, just behavioral training. I needed him ready to run mazes for me if I asked it.

"Yeah, all right. You're a hell of a lot brighter'n I figured. Like I thought I'd get here an' skip out."

"We knew that. What I need to know now is, where is your money stashed and when are you going to pick it up? The way I see it, we can hop the plane back north the day after. You've seen your wife, you can give her some cash and pay your dues in Canada, then join her back here."

"Look, it's not that easy. I can't get the money for a couple of days," he said.

"It's not in a bank?"

51

"Are you kidding?" His voice had a hint of his old contempt, but he reined it in. "No offense. I mean, I'm talkin' a lotta bread. You don't stick that in a bank."

"I would, if I ever got a lot of the stuff. But anyway, when can you pick it up?"

"It's gonna take a couple of days. First off, I have to see a guy, he's got part of what I need to get it back."

That didn't ring true. "You're pushing me. An operator like you, in your line of work, you wouldn't have anybody else cut in."

"He's not cut in. He's just got part of the control I need to get my cash back."

"Like what, like a key? You've got it in a double-locked place?"

"Yeah." He grabbed my comment so quickly I knew he was lying.

"Sounds like bull-roar to me. You want to get ashore and meet up with the guy who was in the motorboat. Then you plan to back-shoot me and head for the hills."

He pursed his lips in frustration. "I know you're gonna think that, after what happened. But it's not like that, believe me."

"Why do guys always say 'believe me' when they're lying through their teeth? Listen. We'll do this my way. We'll head for shore now and go back to the hotel. Tomorrow we'll make contact with this buddy of yours and you get your money. The day after, we're catching a flight back home."

He narrowed his eyes. "It can't be done that quick. But I promise we'll get it soon's we can, an' we can head back then."

"Okay. Let's go back to port."

I didn't believe him, but he'd been promised the chance to get his cash and see his wife. He'd had his meeting with Maria, now I would go along with him on the other part of the deal. Then I'd haul him back. Keeping him under wraps in Mexico City wouldn't be any harder than trying to watch him here. At least I knew he would be alone once we left Zihuatanejo.

He stuck out his hand. "Thank you. Deal."

52

I waved his hand away. "If you're telling the truth, I don't need the handshake. Call Maria up here, and let's go back to the dock."

He turned and called, and Maria came out instantly. She must have been lurking just out of sight in the wardroom, waiting for the word. "Hoist the anchor. Mr. Locke is taking me back to the hotel."

She went forward and wound up the anchor while he started the motor. I sat in the stern and watched them, wondering what to do about the rifle. The smartest move would be to ditch it, but if I could get it back to the hotel without attracting attention, it might be useful if we had to go out of town on his search for the unholy grail.

When we were under way and steering back to the dock I went below and stripped a bright Mexican blanket off the bed. Folded clumsily, it made a cover for the rifle and I bundled it up and set it beside me on the seat.

Maria took the wheel and steered us back through the moorings until we reached the dock. She didn't speak to me, and her face was stony. Very proper. I was the wicked man who had put the blocks to her beloved.

The dock in town is a long pier with steps down to the water in several places. There were boats tied against all of them, but Maria tucked alongside another boat and we tied up. Then I spoke to her. "I'm going to want this boat tomorrow night, we'll sleep aboard. We'll see you here." I turned to Amadeo. "When will that be? What time will you get to see your contact?"

He shrugged. "I dunno. Could be anytime."

"Right. Then we'll see you here at dusk," I told Maria. "Get canned food and beer enough for three or four days. And no tricks, no weapons. Okay?"

"I will do it," she said. Then she grabbed Amadeo by the hand. *"Vaya con Dios,"* she said, and kissed him.

That threw me. Mexican women aren't demonstrative in public. And the "Go with God" was pushing it if she expected to see him the next evening. Either that or they were rerunning *The Cisco Kid* on local TV.

I picked up the blanket with the rifle inside and followed Amadeo across the other boat and up the steps to the top level. A line of tourists was forming at the cruise ship at the end of the pier. It's an ancient ferryboat with a five-piece band on top. For a couple of thousand pesos you can cruise the bay getting boiled while you listen to mariachi interpretations of the kind of songs that your parents listened to on the car radio while they were trying not to conceive you. By the length of the lineup to get on, it looked like a popular number.

We turned the other way and walked down the pier, through the Sunday crowd of lounging locals with their wives and babies, past the fishing boats for hire, out to the naval barracks where the world's worst bugle band practices at six every morning, and out into the cobbled streets. Amadeo was barefoot, and he was hopping painfully on the hot stones. I was alert, right hand on the gun in my pocket, glancing around constantly. If he figured his jumping bean impersonation would soften me up for an ambush, he was out of luck. In any case, I flagged down the first cab that came by, and we headed back, with me watching every other vehicle that moved.

Cuatro Vientos was out of its afternoon coma now, people were moving around again, heading down to the bar or to the crafts shop on one of the middle levels. Amadeo and I walked around to our room. I opened the door and ushered him inside first. Just a precaution, his old workmates might have been waiting for him with a sawed-off shotgun. Better him than me on first.

They weren't. From the casual way he went inside, I don't think the idea even occurred to him. In any case, he flopped on his bed and rubbed the soles of his bare feet. "I shoulda had Maria bring some shoes," he said with an ingratiating grin.

"Why don't we go back down to the beach and get your stuff, it's still lying on the sand. Then we can grab a couple of beers and come back up here on the balcony." There, good old John Locke, never one to hold a grudge. Just don't try to run away on me again or I'll break your bones.

"Yeah. Makes sense." He stood up and stretched. "There ain't a hell of a lot of company up here, though."

"I figure you've had your quota. Let's go."

He annoyed me. I'm no saint around women, hell, when things are good, I may have a whole circuit going, but I never promise any of them more than a few laughs. If and when I get married, I'll tear up my black book.

We left by the back door and walked along the balcony that overlooks the open-air space behind the building. It's covered in on every floor by the walkway of the floor above and at the top by the wide roof over our story, supported on concrete pillars. Beyond the pillars there is bushy ground cover over the natural slope of the hill, separated from the walkways by about forty feet at our level. That's close enough for a handgun to be useful, a shotgun to be fatal. I would have to watch the slope carefully if we stayed here.

As we reached the end of the walkway, at the main office, there was a sudden commotion as two VW vans arrived together. The hotel visitors all turned and chattered like sparrows when a hawk moves overhead. I shoved Amadeo against the wall and waited, and then saw the reason. The model he had pointed out in the airplane magazine was getting out of the lead van. She was tall, about five-ten, and vital, smiling energetically at all the people around her, crackling like a bowl of Rice Krispies, working for applause, even though the only cameras snapping her were Instamatics. Someone came forward with a paper, and she signed it and smiled as if it was the most fun she'd had all day. Then another woman, about thirty and shorter, wearing blue jeans and a blouse knotted over a bare midriff, got out of the wagon behind her and hustled her through the crowd, polite but firm. "Miss Steen will be in the dining room later," she said. "She's had a long, hard day, she'll see you then."

They whisked through the main office and down the corridor to the left, the internal equivalent of our own walkway, out to one of the best suites in the hotel. I turned to Amadeo. "So, you were right, that was little Miss Face Cream in person."

"Yeah," he said, and his lip curled with contempt. "Y'ask me, that bitch is wired."

seven

I stared at him. "She just looked a little hyper, typical showbiz, I would have thought. What makes you figure she's wired?"

He turned and spat over the railing, "Just say I've seen a lot of it."

"I figured you'd keep the stuff at arm's length. It's for losers, right? Anybody sharp enough to be in the business leaves it alone."

"I've seen a lotta dopers in my time," he said calmly, "an' I'm telling you, that lady's got a big habit."

"Poor bloody woman," I said. I didn't argue with his theory. It fit the predictable pattern. The pressure was on her, the terrible pressure of the calendar, wearing out her beauty day by day as she twinkled her way across the world's magazine covers, waiting to wake up one morning and find she was no longer fashionable. And on top of that, she had the money and the jet set connections that makes coke easy to get and hard to turn down.

"Yeah," Amadeo said easily. "Six months from now she'll be puttin' out for the price of a hit."

He was full of contempt. If it would have improved anything

anywhere, I would have called him down for it. Without drug traders there would be no drug users, and I wondered how he squared his conscience with being in the business. If he hated his customers for fools, how could he do what he did? But then, most lawyers feel the same way about their clients, and it doesn't stop them from cashing their checks. Hell, bodyguards are no better.

We went down to the steps and out onto the beach, past the hotel guests, who were out in the sun now it was declining and bearable on their pale hides. Most of the natives had gone, back to their cars or to the roadway for the slow walk back into town. It was a languid, off-peak time of day, ideal for an ambush if you let your guard down, so I kept my head moving. The hotel is surrounded by native bush, palm trees and cactus, and low withered bushes with dusty leaves, enough cover to hide fifty men. I couldn't see anybody but I didn't want to dawdle on the beach.

The tide was coming in, but it hadn't quite reached Amadeo's clothes. He stooped and put his sandals on and picked up his shirt and pants. "That's better," he said. "Shit, you think your feet are tough until you walk on that hot sand for a while." He was loose again now. He'd lost one round, but he was safely back in his corner with his teeth intact, now it was time to set up the next move. In the meantime, he was acting as if we were a couple of buddies looking for a little action. Maybe he would pick up tempo again when we started closing in on his connection and we got a sniff of the money he was hiding. For now, he was so laid back he belonged in a hammock.

The para-sail boat was doing land-office business, but the attendant put everybody on hold while he ran over and pumped my hand. He rattled at me too fast for my limping Spanish, but Amadeo answered him and told me, "He thinks you're the biggest thing since sliced bread. Any time you want a free ride and they're not busy, he wonders if you'll put on a show for him, drum up some business."

"Muchas gracias, amigo." I told him. "Mañana." The Mexican

tomorrow, meaning some time when hell is a ski resort. He told me that would be fine, *"muy bien,"* and skipped back to some middle-aged daredevil who had just handed his camera to his wife and was fiddling with the parachute harness.

"That was a hell of a stunt you pulled with that parachute," Amadeo said cheerfully as we walked back over the sand. "You a sky diver?"

"Not anymore." I didn't want him knowing my pedigree. He already respected me. If he heard I'd been in the SAS, he would rewrite his scenario for the coming week, giving one of his buddies a clear shot at me with a rifle. As long as he figured I was just lucky, he might go on being sloppy.

The bar was jumping. It looked as if all the younger guests of the hotel were there, couples who had spent the siesta hour up in their rooms were sipping drinks and laughing in the soft afterglow of making love on a warm afternoon. One couple who looked squishy enough to be honeymooners were slow-dancing on the flagstones to the beat of Manuel's radio. You could almost smell the bloody orange blossoms. Beth and Kelly were sitting at a table in the shade. They had glasses in front of them, mineral water by the look of it, and they both had a pinkish glow to their skins from their few hours of sunshine.

Beth got to her feet and came up to me as I reached the bar. "I watched you in that parachute," she said, and put her hand on my arm. "You were fantastic."

"Why, thank you, ma'am. Just showing off, I'm afraid. I had a bet on with Greg. He said it couldn't be done. I knew it could."

She lifted her hand from my arm, out of the corner of my eye I could see Amadeo's lip curling slightly. She was twelve years older than him, maybe seven more than me. To his eyes she was a middle-aged loser. To me she seemed no lonelier or more pathetic than I had looked at times in the past when men outnumbered women and you knew you had to make your moves early. I smiled at her and said, "We're going to duck away from the crowd and have a drink on the balcony. Would you and Kelly care to join us?"

"I'm sure she would. I'll ask her." She went back to the table, and I got to the bar. Manuel looked up and grinned at me. "Hey, amigo, you pretty good." He reached over and shook hands, a quick dap, first a normal shake, then changing the grip to an arm-wrestling stance and shaking again.

I winked at him. "It was a bet with my buddy. No big deal. Now we'd like four *cervezas* for the room and a couple of what the *señoras* over there are drinking."

He was young enough to feel the same way as Amadeo, but too pro to show it. He winked back. "Piñafiel," he said and whipped out two soft drinks from the cooler. I got them, plus four Bohemia beers, paid him, and turned around. Amadeo was talking to the two women, barely able to hold back his amusement. It was embarrassing Beth, who glanced at me to see if I was stringing her along.

"I checked with Manuel, he says you're drinking fine vintage soda pop, so I took the liberty of picking some up," I said, and she relaxed a hairsbreadth. Amadeo took a couple of the beers off me and as he took the necks between the fingers of his right hand, I squeezed them together, pressing carefully on his knuckles. He had enough self-control not to cry out, but his eyes narrowed and he started. "Lead the way," I told him, and he took the hint and went ahead up the steps, with Kelly, panting from the exertion, walking beside him.

I hung back a few steps and spoke to Beth quietly. "Don't pay any attention to him, he's got a big problem."

She brightened. His problem, not hers.

"Yes, he's got a bad substance-abuse problem. His family sent me down here with him so he wouldn't get into trouble. He's run away from a couple of clinics. That's why I'm living in his pocket. It's not my choice."

Her mouth shaped a silent *O*. I winked at her. "Don't mention anything, please. I just wanted to explain."

She squeezed my arm again. "Thank you for telling me. I was beginning to wonder about you two."

"It embarrasses me, too. But his father owns the company,

and I work for them, what can I do?" Not a bad cover story, Locke. Let Amadeo worry about his own conduct while Saint John chats to the women and sips his beer.

He went ahead of us all into the room, and we rounded up the drinking glasses and went through to the front balcony. It was flooded with glorious sunshine now as the sun hung lower in the sky, clear of the overhang above us. There was a hammock and several bamboo chaise longues outside and a small bamboo coffee table. I rechecked the surroundings quickly before sitting down. We were in the last room along the balcony, screened from the hill behind us by the bulk of the hotel. To our right was a space of about a hundred yards before the ground rose up from the beach to our own level. But just above us, a hundred and twenty yards away, the coast road curved into a lookout point where a couple of cars were parked. It would be from there that any attack would come.

Beth was my ally now, and she agreed with me when I told Amadeo, "You sit there, Greg," and placed him against the wall. I took the outermost chair, my back to the ocean, but far enough forward on the balcony that I was out of line of fire of anybody closer than half a mile out. It was safe, and I was placed where I could see anyone who came around the end of the balcony to join us. I had the .38 in my pocket and my jacket was off, lying casually beside my knee, the gun within inches of my hand. The women sat each side of Amadeo, facing into the sun.

It was not the most relaxed soiree I've attended. The women were tentative, they didn't believe in the Easter Bunny any more than I did, but this was the tropics, by God, and if romance was ever going to blossom under the big yellow moon, the way it did in the books in Kelly's library, then tonight was the night. Amadeo and I weren't rich men or movie stars, but if we were straight, we would do. The big question in their minds was, where did we go from here?

At least, that was my reading of the situation. I would have been very happy to whisk Beth away from her roomie and do

61

my best to live up to her expectations, but I had Amadeo to worry about. If I turned my back on him for five minutes he would be gone and I would never catch up with him again. On top of which, I agreed with Cahill's forecast. His old workmates in the Mafia would squash him like a bug once they knew he was turned around.

Picking a time when there were no cars on the lookout point, I excused myself, went into the bedroom and replaced the bolt in Amadeo's little rifle, then I loaded the magazine and slipped it into my pocket. The gun I set in the corner of the built-in closet, out of sight from the room but within a moment's reach if I needed it.

Kelly was talking about the model we had seen. "She's nowhere near as pretty as she looks on television."

"She's a good camera subject," Beth said. "The camera puts about ten pounds on you, and on her it looks better than it would on other people."

"Remind me not to get my picture taken," Kelly said, and we all laughed politely. And then, out of the corner of my eye, I saw a big, low American car slide into the lookout point. I bent my head toward Kelly as if I were listening carefully, but I was watching the car. The rear window slid down smoothly under power controls, and I saw the double glint of binoculars, aimed at us.

Amadeo surprised me. He hadn't shown any fear, but he picked up the vibes of what I was doing. I glanced at him, and he inclined his head sideways minutely toward the vehicle he could not see. I nodded back, a quarter-inch movement of my forehead, smiling at Kelly as I did it. Amadeo forced himself farther back, tighter against the wall, and casually raised his right hand to his cheek, as if he were being thoughtful, masking his face from the binoculars he had not seen but knew existed. His face was drawn and some of the color was seeping out of it, as if he'd just been punched in the stomach again.

I kept the conversation going, watching to see whether the Orphan Annie eyes of the binoculars changed to the lean muzzle of a sniper's rifle, but after another minute the binoculars dropped and the window rolled up. The car made a neat turn and headed back down the hill toward the town, honking at a kid leading a donkey with two water cans on its panniers.

I turned back to the crowd and smiled a big, happy smile that put new heart into Amadeo. He drew in a quick, shuddering breath and said, "How'd you like to be that Debra Steen anyway? Never home, always in the tub or gettin' your hair done or stuck in a mink coat under lights that'd scorch your eyes out?"

"Very gallant, Greg," Kelly said. She was warming to him now, seeing that Beth had singled me out. "And all the time I thought my job was dreary, dispensing secondhand knowledge to undergraduates."

"Fount'f all wisdom," he said and spread his arms, very much the Godfather.

We sat and chatted for about twenty minutes, and then Beth looked at her watch and said, "An hour to dinner. Are you two eating in tonight?"

"At the price they're chargin' who can afford to eat anywhere else?" Amadeo asked, and we all chuckled. He had thrown himself into the role now. Perhaps he was working at turning Beth's interest from me to himself. That was about his speed. He didn't know she had him down as a loser with a hungry nose. All that mattered to him was making a monkey out of me.

The two women thanked us politely for the drink and excused themselves to go and change. Amadeo smiled and ducked into the room, and I walked the pair of them around the corner of the building to the walkway. Beth squeezed my arm, affectionate under the influence of the wonderful sunshine and my fairy story about Amadeo. "We'll be in the dining room at seven," she said, and I tapped her on the cheek with one finger.

"See you there. Thanks for the support." That last wasn't spinach. It was easier to keep a rein on Amadeo while we had company.

I let myself into the front door and found him sitting on his bed, pulling on his second beer as if he'd been dying of thirst. "What'd you see?" he demanded.

"A guy in the back seat of a Lincoln Continental. He stopped and used binoculars, checking us out."

Amadeo put his beer bottle down on the floor and stood up, batting his arms around himself as if he were cold. "Shit," he hissed softly. "I didn't figure they'd send nobody."

"You had to know better than that," I argued. "The horsemen told me they smashed your front door down when they went in. The whole neighborhood must've known you'd been busted."

He turned and frowned at me. "You don' understand. I've been busted before. I've been outa sight before. They don' expect me to punch no fuckin' time clock."

"The other times you must have called a lawyer they deal with. Right?"

He turned and sank down on the bed. "That's it," he said simply. "When they come in an' found the stuff, I was scared. Shit. You got any idea what it's like inside? For eight, ten years? Hell, I'd come out old 'n' queer."

"You'd be thirty-six, which is a year or two shy of your pension, and if you don't kick with the other foot now, you wouldn't then." Easy, Locke, don't sell him on jail. He's about to rip the underbelly out of the organization for Cahill and the boys. I added a happy little postscript to the story. "Of course, you might always run into some guy whose kid OD'd. And then they'd shiv you or pour gasoline on you and set you alight like a big Italian Christmas pudding."

"All right," he snapped. "I made the deal. I ain' gonna back out."

"Tell me one thing. Smart as you are, why did you come to this hotel, if your contacts know you use it?"

"Because the connections I need are all here. Once the reservation was made from Canada, all my people here knew what to do."

"You mean Maria and the guy in the speedboat?"

"Yeah. Yeah. Everybody."

"And the guy in the Continental isn't one of them?"

"No. He's not. He's the Man here, my connection with Canada." He stopped. "I shouldn't be telling you all o' this."

"If I'm going to keep your ass intact, I need to know everything." I pointed my index finger at him as if it were a gun. "I know you're looking to get me wasted and then vanish. But there's more players in the game than you can handle. You want me out of the way, but not half as badly as your people in Canada want to see you holding up a big mound of flowers."

I guess that image got to him. There had been a heavy Mafia funeral in Toronto a few months previously. A realtor with mob connections had been found in the trunk of his car at the airport, and there were flowers enough to fill a cathedral. He looked up at me and I shook my finger at him. "I'm good at what I do, Greg, but if I don't know half the story, I can't do my job. You won't live long enough to get your money. You'll never be able to disappear with Maria."

"Her?" Suddenly his terror evaporated. He laughed in my face. "That dumb bitch. You think I'm takin' her anyplace?" He shook his head and got control of himself. "You guys!" He snorted again. "Cops! Buncha goddamn Dudley Do-rights."

I kept the disgust out of my face. Maria was in love with him, and he treated her this way. He was a twenty-two-karat jerk. I would get him home safely, if possible, but after that I wouldn't care if somebody painted a target on his back. "I need to know your organizational setup," I said.

He wiped his eyes and shook his head again, still grinning. "So, okay, this is more'n I told your buddy in the Mounties. Listen up." I sat down on the bed opposite and he started talking, coolly and calmly, a businessman instructing the new employee.

"Our product starts out in Colombia. Everybody knows 'at. So you need a back door outa there and into Canada. From Canada, some goes over the border into the States, but they mostly use their own pipeline. My job is here. I pay the mules t' bring it this far, then arrange shipment to Canada."

"How's that done?"

He shook his hands carelessly. "Don' matter to you. It's done, 'kay? So the guys I work with here are from Colombia, an' some Mexicans an' a couple Canadians. The way I see it, the Colombians ain' interested if I get turned around. It's always cash 'n' carry. If I don't show up, somebody else will. That leaves the Mexicans an' the Canadians."

Great. We'd narrowed the list to two hundred million people. "So keep it simple. Who owns the Continental?"

"That's Edmundo García. Like I said, he's the Man. He doesn't like me a whole helluva lot because I got my own connections this far. Generally he handles the purchase an' arranges shipment. I got my own mules, so he gets a smaller cut. He was no friend o' mine to start with. He'd be the first in line to blow me away if the guys back home wanted it done."

"And what does he look like? Him and his heavies, all of them, anybody who'd want to take a shot at you?"

"He's little an' very Mexican looking, mestizo, like, you know, mostly Indian blood. He's got a mustache looks like he drew it on with a pencil, an' bad skin. Believe me, this guy sticks out like dog's balls anywhere he goes."

"And who's his hit man?"

"Dark-skinned guy, pretty near black. Always wears a suit so it covers his piece. Carries a .45 under his armpit."

"There's a lot of guys in suits. How will I recognize him?" I needed all the details. These men would kill me if they had to, just to get to Amadeo. I wanted to be able to recognize them. I couldn't wait for him to notice them and point them out to me.

"Well lemme put it this way. His name's César but everybody works with him calls him El Grande. Like this guy is heavy. Not fat exactly, just big through. D'ya ever see a guy like that?"

Plenty of them, and they were mostly bad news. Dark, heavy. Most Mexicans are in better shape than Canadians, he should stand out. "Anything else about him? How tall is he? Any scars? Anything?"

"He's tall for a Mexican, goin' on six foot."

I closed my eyes for a moment and composed a picture. A

big, dark Mexican, almost my height but thick through, that would make him possibly two hundred pounds, two-twenty. And he always wore a suit. Good. I could pick him out instantly anywhere except possibly at a Weight Watcher's ball.

"They know we're here. We have to change hotels, duck under cover," I said.

"We can't, not before tomorrow."

"Why not? If you're counting on meeting a guy here, you can leave him a message."

Amadeo shook his head impatiently. "That's not the way it works. He shows 'n' I ain't here, he's gone. Period. He ain' gonna pick up no goddamn message."

"What time are you seeing him?"

"Tomorrow. Just tomorrow. I told you a'ready. We don't punch time clocks in my business."

"He may not be your first caller. The way I figure it, these other guys will drop by in the night. Maybe El Grande will come alone, with his .45, or maybe they'll shake a can of tarantulas loose on the floor. Depends on how they feel about waking up the rest of the guests."

Amadeo sucked his teeth. "It won't be fancy. They don' fool around. Sawed-off shotgun's their tool."

"Then we have to change rooms. And we can't leave anybody in this one because they'll get blown away instead of you."

"I was thinkin' the same thing. I don't like that walkway out back there. A guy could blast me from the hill, be on the road an' gone before I hit the ground."

"Good thinking. So let's talk to management, try to get a room on the inner wing, the other side of the office."

"They keep that for VIPs," he said.

"A VIP is a guy who can afford the price," I told him. "How much money are you carrying with you?"

He flashed a suspicious look at me. Asking a mobster about money is like asking a priest about his sex life. "Just say I can handle it, all right," he said.

"Yeah, partly all right. But I want my pay. So knock ten grand off your total and give me my cash."

"Look, we gotta deal," he began, but I stuck my finger in his face.

"I've seen the way you deal, Greggie. How much cash are you carrying?"

He pursed his lips and didn't answer for a long moment. Then he took his belt off. It was a money belt, the same as my own, innocent looking from the front but zipped along the inside. He tugged the zip open and laid the belt on the bed. It was lined with green bills, and he pulled out about half of them, each folded. He handed five of them to me without speaking. I opened each in turn, two U.S. thousand-dollar bills folded together.

"Ten of the best. And you've got, what, another ten in there?"

"Twelve," he said sullenly. "How do I know you're gonna do your job, now you've been paid?"

"Because I'm a professional. I don't fool around with my jobs, and I don't back out, even when they get heavy. Thanks for the pay. Now put two of those other thousands in your pocket and we'll go talk to the manager."

"I wanna shower an' change first. You gotta look like money when you're putting up a front," he said.

"Good. Go ahead. Then we move."

I waited while he showered and shaved, using an electric razor that left his chin a natty violet color, and we went out into the dusk and walked quickly to the office.

The man on duty was fairly senior, enough so that a minute of Amadeo's rapid Spanish and a discreet handshake, ending with the manager's hand in his pocket and a very happy smile on his face, scored us a second room. That was the story, our old room was for me, the second was for Señor Amadeo. That way nobody was going to get blasted in error.

We thanked him and went out of the office, turning right instead of left, heading down the corridor toward a middle room.

"Cost me a hundred bucks over the rate." Amadeo complained. "But he's put us in next to the model. Class, eh?"

"Discreet, anyway. You saw the kid on the end of the corridor, he's to keep other people away from her. He'll make a fuss if anybody tries to bully their way in here."

"Good," Amadeo grunted and put the key in the lock. He turned it, and at the same instant, the door next to it exploded open. I spun to face it, crouched, the pistol in my pocket aimed waist high. But it wasn't El Grande who came storming out. It was Debra Steen and she was naked from the waist up.

eight

I let go of my gun and spread my arms as if I were trying to head off a stampeding steer. She yelled and tried to duck under them, but I bent my knees and she gave up, sobbing in frustration, and turned back again into the arms of the woman who had been with her outside.

The other woman ignored us. "Debbie, honey. Come back," she said, almost crooning. Either a lover or a very worried agent was my reading. She turned to us, smiling a formal smile that was almost a snarl. "She's overwrought, too much sun. Thank you. Can you leave us now, please?"

"I know what the problem is," Amadeo said in a gravelly voice. "Don' try bullshitting me, lady. I got the answer to what she needs."

Debra turned and grabbed his arm. "Have you, have you?"

He was beaming, a big, Godfatherly smile. "Sure have, don't you worry none. Just ask us in."

"Come in, come in." She tightened her grip on his arm and tugged him into the room. The other woman tried to head me off, but I said, "I'm his bodyguard."

She scowled, but she let me through, shutting the door behind me and locking it. I checked around in a glance. There

70

were just the four of us present. The room was the same as ours, except for a female clutter on the dressing table and a number of suitcases lying around. Debra was standing in front of Amadeo, who was looking at her breasts, greedily, not speaking.

The other woman picked up a shirt and handed it to Debra, who made no effort to put it on until the other woman started helping her. Then she stood, like a child, letting the woman slip both her arms into the sleeves and then button it.

"You can help me?" she asked at last, her voice trembly.

"Sure. Coke, is it?" Amadeo asked in the same gravelly voice. He was enjoying himself, King Cool, watching the girl the way snakes watch mice.

"What makes you ask a thing like that?" the other woman demanded. "Who are you creeps anyway?"

"This man's name is Amadeo, he's in the business and in a whole lot of trouble," I said. "I'm here to get him back to Canada in one piece."

"Bastards," she hissed. I liked the look of her. She was lean and fit, a weathered, outdoorsy thirty-something-year-old, born beautiful, but careless of it, wearing her body like a suit of clothes. And she was tough. A hell of a combination.

Amadeo shrugged, spreading his hands. "You don't like us, we can take off, leave your pretty friend here in a mess."

"She's already in a goddamn mess, thanks to your dirty business."

"Shut up, Helen." Debra Steen was regaining control of her voice, with an effort. "Shut up," she said again, softly. "I know what I need, better than anybody."

"Then why don't you tell me what you need," Amadeo asked, his voice sweet with reason.

Debra looked at him and bit her lip. "I want a setup."

Amadeo smiled. "There. That didn't hurt, now did it?"

"Have you got any?" Her face was tight.

"Of course," he said easily. I wondered how, and where. I'd checked the room when we took it. There hadn't been any unexplained packages or canisters of talcum powder or foreign objects of any kind in there. And he'd come straight from the care of the Mounties. They would have searched him right down to the skin and beyond. Had he picked up something on his boat? In any case, he was in command of Debra Steen.

"How much?" she asked, then turned to the other woman. "Helen, give him the money."

Helen scowled at her and was about to speak, but Amadeo cut her off. "No need for that," he said. "This one is on the house." He reached into his pants pocket and came out with a small brown envelope made of coarse paper. He opened it and walked over to the dressing table to tip out the contents. He let one small folded piece of foil slide out, keeping the other contents under his thumb. "We don' have to talk about money anyways," he said. "We can work somethin' out between the two of us."

Debra was staring at the foil, but his voice made her gasp softly and flash an anxious look at his smiling, smug face.

I took two steps forward and kneed him in the testicles, and he collapsed, rolling into a ball, clutching himself, unable even to speak. Debra shrieked, and I turned and slapped her face, not hard, just a schoolmarm rebuke. "See what you've got yourself into?" I hissed at her. "Any two-bit slimeball can have you on your knees because of your stupid, goddamn nose. Is that the way you want to live? Is that how you want to die? Standing on some city street obliging guys in cars for the price of a hit?"

She wailed like a baby and turned to Helen, who came forward and put her arms around her shoulders. She stood looking at me, bumping Debra on the back and saying, "Don't cry, baby. Don't cry. You can handle it."

I turned away and looked down at Amadeo. I hadn't put any real force into the knee. He would be in pain for a little while, but in no danger. I prodded him with my toe. "How much more have you got?"

He stared at me, his mouth open, trying to speak. I bent

down and pulled all his pockets inside out. He had nothing else in them except for money and a handkerchief and his cigarettes and matches. I picked up the envelope and took it into the bathroom, standing there whistling softly while I flushed the six packages of foil away, then tearing up the envelope and flushing the pieces down after them.

When I came back into the room, the two women were sitting on the end of one of the beds, their arms around each other's waists. Debra had her head lowered and was sniffling, the other woman was alert, looking around at me as I came back and walked in front of them and crouched to speak to them. "How long have you been using the stuff?"

Helen said, "What's it to you?" But she wasn't angry, she was drained and weary.

"Just answer the question. I can help."

"Since the Los Angeles shoot. When was that, Helen?" Debra raised her head and spoke softly.

"September," Helen said. "That goddamn party at Maxine's."

"And how much are you using?"

Debra shook her head, and her voice was trembly. "Not that much, not really, right, Helen?"

"It's gotten worse, month by month," Helen said. "It used to be just parties, then every day, now it's all day. Don't lie to the man, Debra. I think he can help you."

"Cocaine isn't addictive. Not if you're snorting it," I said, "It's habituating. That means there's no cold turkey, not like heroin. It's just a matter of being tough, of telling yourself no, like an alcoholic. Every day. No. You can do that, Debra."

She raised her face and looked into my eyes, and I sank out of sight in the blue of them, like a diver in the ocean. "I'm not sure," she said.

"Well, I am. You didn't get where you are by letting things stand in your way. I mean, when did you last eat a proper lunch? Haven't there been days when you've just swallowed a couple of tissues instead of eating? Protecting your figure?" I've

73

dated a few models, mostly they are disappointing, but they don't run up your grocery bills.

Helen broke the deadlock for me. "Come on, Debbie, you know that's true. If you can say no to dessert, you can say no to this nonsense. Haven't I told you that, lots of times?"

Debra's head sank again but she answered clearly. "Yes, you have," she said.

I stood up. "Okay, Helen, you know what to do. She's down and she's going to stay down for a while. A drink might be good, or Valium, if you've got some, and some strong coffee. And stick with her. If it was my responsibility, I'd cancel the assignments for a couple of days, say she got too much sun, let her rest but keep her occupied. Play gin rummy, Trivial Pursuit, whatever."

She didn't answer, but she looked at me in a way that sent anticipatory little tingles down my spine. I turned away and grabbed Amadeo by the collar. "On your feet. We're leaving."

He had recovered enough strength to walk, painfully, and he lurched in front of me toward the door. Helen got there before us and put her hand on my arm. There was real strength in her fingers. "What's your name?"

"John Locke."

"Thank you, John. You've done more than anybody has ever done for her."

"Yeah, good. It would be smart to get her into a clinic when you get home. This pep talk is just first aid. In the meantime, we're next door. If you need help, call. But keep telling her about what she nearly had to do this time. The shock could break the habit for her."

Her grip tightened, and suddenly she stood on tiptoe and kissed me on the lips. I patted her on the shoulder. "You're a nice lady," I said and left.

The Mexican kid from the end of the corridor had crept along until he was outside the suite. He looked at us and grinned, the hopeful, longing grin of the sexually underprivileged, dreaming his nightly dreams in his hammock. Maybe he'd caught a glimpse of the promised land when Debra first ran into the corridor. I put my hand in my pocket and pulled out a five-thousand-peso bill. Fifteen bucks, a fortune.

"Un regalo. Diga nada. Sigua trabando." A present, say nothing, keep working. He grinned and nodded, gave me a fervent *"Muchas gracias"* and went back to the end of the hallway.

Our key was still hanging in the lock, and I opened the door and shoved Amadeo through it. He stumbled inside and collapsed on the nearest bed, curling up again, clutching his testicles.

It was already shading into evening, and I drew the drapes and turned the lights on. "Where did you pick up the coke?" I snapped at him. It was time for a change of procedure, I'd decided. I couldn't give him any more rope. I had to take charge.

He just groaned, and I went over and tore his hands away from his groin. "Answer me. Where did you get the stuff?"

"On the boat, where'd you think?" He was whining, a whipped pup, too sick to fight but too proud to be ingratiating.

"Are you using it? Or were you going to try and slip some to me and leave me dying of an overdose while you headed for the hills?" He groaned but didn't answer, and I prodded him in the shoulder with a stiff finger. "Speak up and sit up. If that's the first belt in the nuts you've ever had, you've never played any sport."

Machismo made him roll on one side and sit up, on the edge of the bed, still hunched over. I don't know why that eases the agony of a kick in the equipment, but it's standard posture for a long time afterward.

"No, I don' use it. But it's useful sometimes." He wasn't looking at me, making a big show of crouching, looking at the tiles, but I guessed my hunch had been right. He'd been hoping to get the stuff into me somehow, knock me over so he could put the boots to me, and leave. Nice guy.

75

"Well, it's gone, and if you pick up any more, I'll stick it up your nose until your brains fall out. You got that?"

He didn't answer, but when I tapped his shoulder again, he nodded. "Right. Now rest up while I bring the bags over. Then we're going down to dinner, where you're going to be charming to those nice square ladies from Toronto. Sitting under a warm shower might help."

He groaned and said he couldn't do it, but I told him he was going to, to get used to the idea. Then I went back to our first room. I knew he wasn't in any shape to run away in the time it would take, so I quickly searched his bags. He had nothing in them but his clothes and toilet equipment, including a bottle of expensive cologne. I sniffed it and decided he had more money than taste, then repacked his bags and made up the beds so it looked as if we'd been lying in them. I stuck the rifle back into its blanket and put it under my left arm; then I picked up all three bags in my left hand and went out, leaving the lights off.

There were only a couple of people around, guests waiting for taxis to take them into town for dinner, and they didn't look my way as I came by the front desk and down the corridor to the new room. My brand-new amigo, the kid I'd tipped, reached out to grab a couple of the bags for me, but I grinned and told him, *"De nada, gracias,"* it's nothing, thanks, and let myself into the room.

Amadeo had taken my advice and was sitting on the bathroom floor under a warm shower. I dropped his bags on the bed and then dropped my own and put the rifle under my mattress. I was feeling high with the anticipation of trouble, all my senses working faster than normal, the way they would need to be for the next few days until Amadeo had his cash and we were heading north again. I knew I was in danger, but my system was geared up for it.

After a couple of minutes I called out to Amadeo, "Let's roll, you'll melt if you stay in there any longer." He groaned but got to his feet and turned off the shower and dried himself slowly, moving like an arthritic old man. He dressed again, then lit a cigarette, pulling on it carefully, as if he thought it might explode in his face. But it helped him to straighten out.

"So, okay, let's go sparkle," I said.

He grunted. "I can't eat nothin'."

"Then have a couple of margaritas, they'll take your mind off your sorrows." I put my right hand on the pistol and opened the door with my left. "Out you go, the dining room is on this floor, behind the desk."

He dropped his cigarette and trod on it, then straightened himself up and went out ahead of me. The kid in the corridor bobbed his head and gave us a *"Buenas tardes,"* and I grinned and Amadeo nodded and we went into the dining room.

I found us a table for four against the wall, and the waiter bounced up with the menu. Amadeo looked up at him and ordered a couple of margaritas, and I added, *"Y una cerveza, por favor,"* and he beamed, lots of drinks meant a better tip. He brought the drinks and left us with the menus. I sipped my beer while Amadeo downed his first margarita and reached for the second.

"You reckon the salad would be safe?" I asked him.

"In this place?" He looked at me with a ghost of his familiar scorn in his eyes. "This is a gringo place, they wash everything in bottled water. Why'd you think I'm takin' their ice cubes?"

"Living dangerously? Getting in practice for the next couple of days?"

He shook his head. "It ain't gonna be dangerous. I make my contact, we duck outa here 'n' pick up the cash 'n' leave. Them other guys won' know we're gone. I don' know why I bothered bringin' you along."

"I hope you're right. But if you've got contacts here, it figures they'll have contacts of their own."

"We'll have to be careful, that's all." He picked up the menu and scanned it. "I can handle the seviche an' maybe the chicken."

"Good, that'll put the roses back in your cheeks."

We sat and waited. The room was beginning to fill, and the happy noise level was building. Already the crowd we had arrived with was dividing into cliques. And the court jester had appointed himself. He was an overweight man with a red face and knees to match. Probably a used-car salesman from some suburban lot. Honest Jake or Crazy Casey, free carnations for the ladies, free dirty jokes for the men. He was wearing shorts and a Lacoste shirt, and he stopped at several of the tables to lean over and tell jokes that had everyone loving him. Wait until Wednesday, I thought, when the same wisecracks started recycling and he was reduced to making personal comments on how many margaritas Joe had taken, or how much time Fred and Lois were spending in their room. Then the faces around the tables would start looking like Mount Rushmore. Tonight, though, in the first flush, he was the star.

Beth and Kelly came in, changed and made up for the evening, elegant and casual, the thrown-together look that had taken them every minute of the time we'd been apart. Kelly still looked like a librarian, but Beth turned a number of heads as she steamed across the room like a cruise ship through a yacht basin.

We stood up, Amadeo painfully, making it a bent-kneed gesture rather than a real effort. "Back problem," he said gruffly. Beth looked at me, and her eyes widened microscopically. She knew the real problem. She thought.

Our waiter came back and took drinks orders for the women. He was young, like all the help, and Kelly looked at him frankly. He smiled back, polite and professional, but I could read his rating in his eyes. Seven out of ten for Beth while Kelly would be safe with him anywhere except maybe a desert island, in the second year of being castaway.

The drinks came and we sipped and talked, Amadeo saying very little but being polite. They wanted to know what we were doing the next day. They were planning to get up at first light, before the sun came up over the eastern mountains at around seven, and play tennis. It was all very civilized, and I explained that Greg had been told to take things easy this trip and we were just going to grab some sunshine. "That must be easy for you," Kelly said to him. "You have olive skin."

That pleased him and he opened up to her about his ancestry, and she stared at him happily, transposing him to the cover of some bodice-ripper romance, with herself fifteen years younger and thirty pounds lighter. I watched the pair of them relaxing, spinning themselves a little web of self-hypnosis that they could lie curled up in, like a hammock, had Amadeo not been under my care. But for the moment it took the pressure off me, leaving me free to enjoy the dinner. The seviche was excellent. It's a simple dish, raw fish, marinated in lime juice with a trace of coriander and finely sliced onion. I was enjoying it until I glanced up and saw El Grande standing in the doorway.

I beamed at Kelly, who was talking about Romance languages, and then tapped Amadeo's ankle. "Excuse me, Greg, you remember that old friend of yours, the big guy?" He looked up in alarm, but had enough presence of mind to keep his head turned away from the door.

"Yeah, I know who you mean. Is he here?"

"Unless he's been cloned since you came down here last. He's in the doorway." Both the women looked around at the door, but that didn't make us conspicuous, most of the people in the room were looking up now. El Grande had that effect on people. He had presence, like Orson Welles. He stood there, radiating importance. For a minute or so he stood in silence; then he spoke to one of the waiters in passing. The boy shook his head but pointed to the other waiter, ours. And then there was a lot of nodding and pointing of fingers, and the big man came slowly between the tables toward us.

Amadeo wiped his mouth on his napkin and set down his fork. I did the same and put my right hand in my pocket. The big man had his hands at his sides, empty. It didn't figure that he would make a move on us here, in front of a crowd of witnesses, but as far as he was concerned, this was war, and Amadeo had committed treason. And he had contacts and money. He could probably buy himself immunity if he decided to leave Amadeo facedown in his fish.

He reached us and smiled at the women, a grim alteration of the creases in his face, then started speaking rapid Spanish.

"Hable inglés!" I said curtly. Speak English.

He turned his head and looked at me as if I'd just crawled out of a cheese. *"No hablo."*

"Sure you do," Amadeo said. He stood up. "If you'll excuse us for a moment, please, ladies, I have to talk business with this gentleman."

Beth glanced at me, her eyes wide. I smiled and got up, and Amadeo said, *"Vamos,"* let's go, and the three of us walked out into the lobby.

El Grande headed toward the outdoors, but I called him back. "This is fine, we can talk here," and I steered him down the corridor, past the kid on watch, who was carefully not watching us but was reading a comic book, classic literature at his level in Mexico. When he avoided looking up at us, I guessed he knew who El Grande was and what he did. He wanted no part of our business.

The big man started speaking in Spanish, but Amadeo shook his head. "This man is my friend, we speak English for him to hear."

"Señor García wants to talk to you," the man said.

"I have no business with Señor García this time. I am here with my friend, who wishes to see Mexico. It is very cold in our country, we come only for the sunshine."

"The sun shines in many places," El Grande said. "Yet you come here to our little town. Señor García notices, he wishes to speak with his good friend Señor Amadeo. It is friendship to see him."

"I will come to his house on Tuesday at three o'clock," Amadeo said. I was interested in that snippet. It meant he was planning to pick up his money and vanish tomorrow, Monday. Come Tuesday, there would be nothing more than a faint smell of his Paco Rabanne left in town. He hoped.

"Señor García has business on Tuesday. He wishes to see him this evening, to pay his respects."

"That would be discourteous to my friends, we have arrangements, I will come on Tuesday."

It was degenerating into a verbal shoving match. They would talk until they were both as blue in the face as Amadeo was in the chin. I broke the tie. "Seems to me, Greg, we could break our appointments tomorrow for an important man like Mr. García. If he sent his car for us at three, we could go with him then."

Amadeo looked at me with surprise. He hadn't expected diplomacy, just violence. "That would be good." He nodded. "Thank Señor García and tell him we are tired from our flight, but we will see him tomorrow."

"I will tell him. Now go back to your *putas*," he said.

It was my opportunity. He was the worst weapon the other side had. If I could handicap him now, it might buy us time and safety. I smiled at him. "Only a man as ugly as you are needs to go with whores. Or do you go to the market and buy yourself a little pig, a blind pig?"

He swore and lashed out a swinging right hand that would have broken my jaw. I ducked and used his own momentum to run him into the wall, face first. I brought his hand up behind him, and he had to wrestle back, using brute force to try to free himself. It wasn't enough. I let go and stood back, kicking him hard in the back of the knee so he buckled. Then I stood on his calf and kneed him in the back of the neck, giving it a lot more follow-through than I'd given Amadeo. He sprawled face first on the floor, and I bent over and took his gun and stuffed it into my belt. Amadeo hissed in concern, but I called to the kid I'd tipped earlier. "Take him out to his car." The sentence was beyond my Spanish but he got the drift. He came and knelt solicitously beside the man and touched his shoulder respectfully, speaking softly until he stood up, painfully, and limped out, not looking back.

Amadeo was white. "You shouldn' of done that. He's gonna kill you."

"He wanted to anyway. Now he's going to be slow for a day or two, and we have an extra gun. Let's get the hell out of here."

nine

Amadeo swore through clenched teeth. "We better. García has all kinds of clout. If he wants, he can have the cops put us away forever."

That wasn't going to happen. A guy who sets as much store by machismo as El Grande wouldn't whine to some five-foot-four cop with a rusty pistol. He would square it himself with a sawed-off shotgun. But they had been planning that anyway; we weren't in any new danger. The only thing that had changed was that Amadeo was scared. That might prevent him from trying to duck out of my company. He needed me for real, not just as a sop to the Mounties back home, and he was starting to recognize the fact. Plus there was an extra bonus. I had slowed their hit man down and scored us a worthwhile gun. Not that a .45 pistol is the Peacemaker that Samuel Colt intended—it's not accurate enough—but when it goes bang, the world tends to listen.

"He won't go to the cops. But we should leave anyway, in case he comes back with a shotgun. We'll go back to the boat."

"We can't. We were just borrowing it. The owner will be back on board, an' he's scared of García."

"Then how about Maria? Is this sonofabitch liable to go after her?" She was Amadeo's concern, not mine, but he seemed too dazed to do anything but shake.

He straightened up enough to say, "Naah, she's not in the open, don' worry about her."

"Well, that's good, but we skip, anyway. Come with me."

I took him back to the room and reached into my bag for the survival pack I'd brought along. Nothing fancy, but sensible. It's a little backpack containing a first-aid kit, water-purification tablets, salt pills, a canteen, a compass, and a plastic sheet. With that along we could manage anywhere there was water. I also picked up the rifle and the blanket, and I was ready. "Right. Let's pay our bill and tell the girls we have to go out for the evening. If the heat turns up, they'll question the women for sure."

Amadeo was still scared. The presence of El Grande had lowered his worry threshold considerably. "There's no place to hide safely, not in this town. Once the word gets out that García is looking for us, someone'll finger us."

"Then we won't stay anywhere formal. Let's go." I fastened my jacket so El Grande's .45 didn't show and handed Amadeo the blanket and pack. "Wait by reception. I'll be right there."

He did as I said, standing by the desk while I went into the dining room and apologized. "Greg has family here. One of his little nephews is sick, and he wants to go visit him. I'm sorry, I was really enjoying the meal, but we'll be back later, maybe I can buy you a nightcap."

Kelly was the more disappointed of the two. Amadeo had been her lifeline to romance, and now it was snapped. Beth was more involved. She patted my hand. "I hope so," she said and I squeezed her hand and winked at her. Lying next to her all night would be a major improvement on the prospects I had. I left money for the bill and walked out.

Amadeo was nervous. He grabbed my arm as I reached him. "There's a cab outside now. Let's get it."

"Sure. And lighten up, you look suspicious."

We went out and got into the Volkswagen cab and I asked

the driver to take us to Coconuts, the most famous bar in town. Then I started joshing Amadeo, two good buddies out on the town. "Hell, why'd you buy that blanket in the first place? Your girlfriend's gonna think you're crazy taking that back, you should've bought her a bottle of Kahlúa, that's more her speed."

"I know," he said. "Yeah, I should've. Maybe I can change it, that's why I brought it along."

So far so good. For the rest of the trip I leaned over the front seat to bore the driver with a lot of dumb questions, loose as a goose, not the kind of uptight gringo who kneed folk heroes into dreamland. Nobody would suspect us. Smoke and mirrors all the way.

Coconuts is close to the town beach, and we paid off the cab there among the tourists in their pastel shorts and the Indian vendors, who were doing big business in painted wooden fish and silver jewelry, stamped with the hallmark but made of alpaca, a local metal that costs about one-fiftieth as much. I cut Amadeo's speed back from the nervous pace he was setting to the leisurely stroll of the other tourists. "Are you sure there's no little place that we could slip into?"

"I'm tellin' you. García's got a lotta guys on the payroll. It wouldn't take him an hour to find where we were if they started asking around." He spat disgustedly. "Why'd you have to clobber that guy?"

"It's called a preemptive strike," I told him. I didn't give him the other half of the reason. From this moment on, however reluctantly on his part, we were a team. He was unarmed, the rifle I'd given him had no magazine in it, and his enmity for the organization was out in the open. He needed me. I wouldn't have to watch my back against him, not until we found his money and were heading out of town.

"You know, the best thing we could do, if you want to sleep in a bed instead of under a bush, is to go to Ixtapa and check in there. García may have contacts, but those are big hotels; he couldn't come storming in through a mess of gringos and expect to get away with it like he could in some local hole in the wall."

"All the people's work there live here," Amadeo objected, but I waved him down. "You worry too much. This guy's just a hood, he can't walk on water. Trust me."

"I guess you're right." He shook his head. "But what'm I gonna do about making my contact in the morning?"

"We'll know by then if there's any flak," I said. "García will probably just try to find us himself. He might have gotten mad and called the police right after we had that showdown, but by tomorrow it's going to be different."

"It'd better be," Amadeo said. He sighed suddenly and put one hand on his stomach. "Listen, I can't walk any more. You punched me in the gut, remember, an' then put the knee to me. It hurts to walk."

"Fine. Let's go back into Coconuts and get a drink. Nobody's going to look for us in the brightest spot in town."

"You sure?" Thinking was almost as much of an effort for him as walking.

"Certain. Hide in plain sight. One of the cardinal rules."

We went back into the bar and asked the pretty American girl who served as maître d' to get us a table. Then we sat on the far side of the bar, away from the doors, where nobody could sneak in behind us. He ordered a double margarita, and I had a beer. My consumption for the day was going to be high, but it's the safest way to avoid dehydration in Mexico, and the stuff isn't as alcoholic as Canadian beer anyway. It's more like an American light.

The drinks came, and he took a good glug of his. All around us the crowd was festive. That's another charm of Zihuatanejo. In tourist season it's one big party. I ignored the noise and the interested looks we were getting from a couple of pink gringo ladies with their piña coladas, and talked turkey with Amadeo.

"The way I see it is, we've got to get your money back and leave here. You've been giving me a line of crap about what's going to happen, and I want that finished with. I need to know the truth, otherwise we're likely to get jumped. So no more fairy stories, give me the straight goods."

He took another shaky drink from his margarita and bent his head toward me. "Yeah, well, listen. I got a proposition for you."

I didn't say anything, but he forged ahead anyway.

"I di'n' exactly level with the cops, back home, all right?" He waited a heartbeat, as if he genuinely expected that to be a surprise to me, then went on. "See, when I said I wanted to come back here, I had a plan. I got connections here, an' I figured the best retirement plan I could have was to take over García's operation."

"You mean grease him and take his place?"

"Exactly." A tiny smile came and went on his face, the kind of grimace he would hand out to underlings once the change was made and he was the Main Man for the state of Guerrero. "Canada's out for me. And if I wan'ed to set up in the States, I'd have to come up against the whole organization. An' they wouldn't trust me anyway, after I've sent the Toronto guys away."

Honesty at last! Flooring El Grande was paying off.

"But anyways, I know this end of the business real well. I know the routes that García's been usin' to move the stuff. I can do good here. Only thing's stoppin' me is him."

"If you need me to help, why did you try to run away from me this afternoon?"

He waved his drink, a practiced move of the hand that looked grand but didn't spill a drop. "I di'n' know how good you were. I figured you'd get in the way."

"And you were going to take that itsy-bitsy gun you've got between your knees now and go to war with García? Don't make me laugh."

"That!" he shook his head. "That was Maria's cute idea. What does she know? She knew I was gonna make a run for it from Cuatro Vientos, an' she figured I might be able to use a piece. That was the best she could get."

"And she's the best connection you've got? Listen, Greg, you better get out of the business. Take a new identity from the Mounties and open a pizza parlor in Medicine Hat. Your old buddies won't look for you there."

"They'll look until they find me, in Canada," he said and waved his empty glass at the bartender. "But if I'm the Man down here, they'll do business with me because they've got to."

It didn't sound likely to me. They'd do business, okay, and then pay him off with a couple of shots in the head and do their usual symbolic knifework on his remains. But he thought he knew them, so I played his game.

The bartender gave him a refill and looked at me, but I shook my head. The proposition was a problem for me. If I refused, he would try to run again. He had this dream of being the authority here. If I didn't help, he would try it without me. I had to keep him scared and then get him away.

"What's in it for me?" I asked when he was working on his new drink.

This pleased him. He didn't answer at once. He pulled out his cigarettes and took the usual ritualistic thirty seconds to light up and puff out the first lungful of smoke. "You work for me, say two thousand a week, U.S."

"That's more than I make now, but I don't know that I could live here year-round." Just noise, not refusal, give him something to chew on while he got drunk enough to be manageable.

"You can take vacations. Colombia's nice. So's California."

"I'm not the palm-trees type, Greg, but the money sounds good. Tell you what. Why don't you get your cash back and give me a down payment, in good faith, then I'll know you're serious."

"You already gotta down payment," he said. He was starting to come unraveled. Not surprising. He'd had six or seven ounces of alcohol over the last half hour. He was sober enough to be cunning but drunk enough to believe I couldn't see through it.

"That was for the job in hand. I need some real bread, maybe six months in advance before I trust you." It was just a game I was playing, and as I did it, I was looking around the bar. A couple of corn-fed California girls had sat down across from us and they were weighing us up. Camouflage, just waiting to happen.

I called the bartender over and told him, *"Dele a las señoritas una bebida, por favor, yo pagaré."* Give those ladies a drink, on us, please. He had personally set up more assignations than Cupid, so he grinned and did as I said. It would have been rushing things in frost-bound Toronto, or even in a singles bar in the States, but a whole lot of inhibitions get left at home when girls pack their bikinis for the tropics. They bridled, but they accepted the drinks, piña coladas, naturally, and raised them to us.

Amadeo waved back, but he spoke to me out of the corner of his mouth. "What's this shit? Why're you tryin'a make time?"

"I think we've solved our accommodation problem for the night," I said. "Make like a gigolo, and we could end up in their room."

He looked at me in half-drunken surprise. "Hey, not a bad idea." He raised his glass to the girls. *"Saludas y pesetas, señoritas."* Health and money, ladies. Cool. He must have cut a swath through high school.

They were a couple of secretaries from San Francisco, Joan and Angela. They'd flown in the day before and were staying in Ixtapa. This was their first trip into town. Apparently their flight had been heavy on pairs of guys holding hands, and the action at the hotel was disappointing. We allowed that we were from Toronto and our own flight had been equally heavy with blue-rinsed widows. However, the night was young.

We had dinner together, steering them away from the wine that is universally putrid in Mexico, and making the discovery that Angela had as big a thirst on her as Amadeo. They were very companionable with their margaritas while Joan and I sank another beer and traded highly edited versions of our lives and times. She worked at an advertising agency and wanted to be an account executive. To get there she was taking an adver-

89

tising course on her own time. It sounded like a living hell to me, but it was her daydream, not mine. I told her that I was working for the Canadian government, and she looked wide-eyed and mouthed the word "Drugs?" I nodded gravely and she was impressed.

We went on to another bar afterward and listened to the strolling musicians while Amadeo and his turtledove sipped their way closer to oblivion. Then Joan and I made the group decision. Neither pair of us could really take the other with them. It might prove embarrassing. But on the other hand, neutral territory was just fine.

We poured the others into a cab and went to a spot I'd noticed from our own cab ride into town. It was a cluster of the typical white concrete buildings of the region, surrounded by bush that included the inevitable banana trees. A burro was tethered somewhere fairly close, and it was sawing away at the night with a regular *eeee-awww* like a giant's snoring. The proprietor turned out of his hammock under the electric light at the front and grinned at us knowingly. I played the part, winking when Joan wasn't looking and telling him we wanted a place with two bedrooms. He probably figured we were going to do some kind of round dance, and grinned again and asked me for twice the going rate, ten thousand pesos. I felt tacky, using the women as a cover, but the relationship was just as casual on Joan's part, so I excused myself as being part of a mutual compromise.

He let us into what must have been his prize suite, a ground-floor apartment with two bedrooms, a bathroom, and a kitchen with a rusty refrigerator and a sink that provided only cold water.

I was carrying the blanket with the gun in it and I tossed that onto the bed in one room and turned Amadeo and Angela loose in the other. They made a great show of starting to get undressed, and I left them and came back to Joan, who was sitting on the edge of the bed with her hand on the blanket. She was pretty, dark-haired, and Irish looking, with the wide face and wistfulness of Connemara. Now she was frowning. "There's a gun in there," she said.

"It belongs to Greg. He loves plinking tin cans. We go up in the hills and and shoot sometimes."

"I'll bet," she said. "And you're with the government?"

"That's not an official gun. It's the farm boy's delight, a .22, no harm to anybody."

"I don't think you're telling me the truth," she said.

"I am about this gun. Forget it." I sat down next to her and she looked at me for a long moment; then her eyes closed and we kissed.

I turned off the light, and we undressed quickly and made love, urgently at first but then again, slowly, until she finally fell asleep making little *urrmmm* noises like a child. In the other room the rubbery flapping of Amadeo and his girl as they tried to cancel out all their margaritas had died away, and the apartment rang with their snores. I lay on my back, my arm under Joan's head, staring at the ceiling. In the faint light from the entrance to the compound I could see a tiny lizard hanging upside down near the light fixture, waiting for flies to blunder within his tongue's reach. The burro was still braying, once a minute, like some metronome ticking away the time until morning. And then, as I drifted toward sleep, I heard a faint rustling outside. Someone was moving around, carefully, close to the door.

I slipped my arm out from under Joan's head and covered her with the blanket, then picked up my clothes and went to stand in the blind spot beside the window, dressing silently as I listened to the tiny sounds from outside.

The noise wasn't panicking me. The owner of the place had seemed like the average sensuous male. It might very easily be him, across to eavesdrop at the window to see what excitements the gringos had dreamed up to while away his night. But on the other hand, this was García's town, and he might have been smart enough to track us down here. It needed looking into.

I put the .45 in my waistband and went out through the

kitchen to the front door. I had checked it earlier; it swung freely without squeaking or dragging. I glanced quickly out of the window. There was no sound. The man outside was either being very quiet or he was against one of the bedroom windows, trying to make out what was going on inside. I checked the angle of the light from the entrance. It was parallel to our front wall. That meant the door wouldn't show up like a blacked-out tooth when I opened it. I did so, keeping low, and moved out silently. My shadow flicked over the ground in front of the cabaña, but there was no burst of activity as I made my way around to the left, away from the bedroom windows, and moved into darkness at the back of the building.

The bushes grew right up against the rear wall, and I sank to my knees and crawled under their branches until I reached the back corner of the building and peeked around it. A man was looking into the window of Amadeo's bedroom. I could see only his profile, black against the light spill at the front of the building. He was average size, in shirt sleeves, and bareheaded. And he was carrying a pistol.

I felt around me on the ground and found something loose, an empty can. I straightened up and flicked the can underhanded, out beyond him in front of the building. He pivoted on one foot, his gun trained on the spot, and I bounded up behind him and chopped him on the back of the neck. He stumbled, dropping the gun, but I caught it, and then him, and lowered him to the ground. He was out cold, his eyes open. I knelt on his right hand and waited, his pistol in my hand, checking all around, listening for footsteps. There were none, no sound except for another repetition of the burro's bray. And then he began to blink. I crouched lower and whispered at him, "*Como te llamas?*" What's your name? Using the familiar pronoun to show I was the boss. He groaned and answered, "You can call me Jesus, Mr. Locke." He pronounced his name in the English way.

"And you're my salvation? You'd better spell it out for me, it's been a while since Sunday school."

"Your friend Martin Cahill of the RCMP in Canada asked me to look out for you."

I stood up and stuck out my hand to help him up. No friend of García's would have known Martin's name. He hadn't even told Amadeo, so there couldn't have been a leak that way.

"Sorry about jumping you. I'm a little paranoid. My boy Amadeo has all kinds of enemies and a bunch of friends who don't wish me well."

He shook hands solemnly, then took his hand away and rubbed his neck. "I've been in this business for eight years, and that's the first time anybody's used karate on me. You're pretty good."

I nodded politely. "Let's get out of the light and talk; a lot's been happening."

He indicated the shade to the far side of our apartment. "Here's fine. You're the only customer's Pedro's got tonight."

"I thought he would have been crowded—this is gringo time in Mexico."

"Not since the earthquake. Everybody north of the line is nervous about coming here."

We went into the edge of the bush and squatted down, talking in whispers. "You've made quite an impression on the locals," he said. "Nobody's cleaned El Grande's clock for him in living memory."

"I wanted his gun."

"Yeah, I figured. That .38 I got you isn't the greatest, but it's easy to hide."

"So, what's the word on Amadeo? Do the local boys know he's going to fink? Have they been asked to cancel his stamp?"

"It's not that easy. They know he's finking, but the whole drug business is complicated. The guys here don't have any family connections with Canada. It's all just business. No matter who gets sent to the slammer up there, somebody will always come down here looking for supplies. They don't get involved."

I was growing accustomed to the darkness of our shelter, and I watched his face. He was in his mid-thirties, Mexican looking, a hint of the Indian heritage in his high cheekbones and handsome nose, and he was lean, the leanness of worry. It wasn't easy being the law in a place as wide open for drug business as the state of Guerrero. He blinked frequently, another sign of worry. I figured he didn't need this baby-sitting chore on top of his other concerns.

"They came to the hotel asking for him last night."

"That's because he has a big mouth. The word is out that he's back here to pick up a pile of money. They want it, not him, although they'd kill him to get it, but what they really want is his loot."

"What's going to happen now? Will they take another run at him? Will they kill him or try to snatch him?"

"Snatch him is my guess. It wouldn't take long to have him singing like a canary, he's a gutless bastard."

That meant that the main danger over the next few days was to me. Amadeo would get his, once he'd coughed up the location of his money. Me they would take out to get to him.

"Then there's nothing to stop us going back to the hotel?"

"No, but remember what the plan is. They want him alive, and that could mean knocking you over first."

"Who will they send?"

"Not El Grande. They've got a big organization, they'll send somebody who looks like a tourist, someone to blend in. He'll strike up some kind of contact and try to take you out. That's my best estimate."

"We have to go back, Amadeo has to make a contact of his own, some guff about needing another guy involved. Doesn't sound like the truth, but that's all he's telling me so far."

"Is it your job to see he gets his money?"

I hesitated a moment before answering. How much did this man need to know? I've handled a lot of security work in the SAS and since then, and old habits die hard. In the end, after a ten-second pause, he laughed and reached out to pat me on the arm. "Okay, I don't need to know. But if you're staying in Zihua until next Sunday, keep your eyes open."

"I will. But for now, how safe is this place? You didn't have any trouble finding us."

"I didn't find you, I followed you, from Coconuts. It's on my circuit, and when I saw you there, I tagged along. There's nobody after you. Not so far anyway."

"In that case I'll grab some sleep. Thanks for the advice, and I'm sorry about the thump in the neck."

"Me, too." He laughed and rubbed his neck again. "Get back to that lady, I'll stick around until daylight. Nobody will come after you once it gets bright."

"Thanks, Jesus. I'll tell Martin what you've done."

"Great," he said. "That plus fifty pesos will get me a beer."

"Fifty pesos. You must be buying it wholesale," I said. We stood up and shook hands; then I went back into the apartment and locked the door.

ten

Joan stirred when I went back to bed, but she didn't wake up. Neither did the other two in their room. Their snoring had settled down now. They were working in counterpoint, sounding like the rhythm section in a bad Afro-Cuban band. I lay and listened to them for about four repetitions and then, safe for a few hours, fell asleep.

I was the first awake, at six-thirty, late for me but still ahead of the sunlight. It was day outside, the shadowed gray of morning when the sun is still behind the mountains. Birds were chattering, and the first of the day's vehicles were rolling up the hill outside the front of the complex, carrying the help to another day at Cuatro Vientos. The burro was mercifully silent. I got up and dressed, putting both pistols into the backpack, and walked out to the front of the place, wishing I had my running gear with me so that I could exercise properly. Just down the hill from me there was a tortilla bakery, a corrugated iron shack with a line of locals buying breakfast. Women mostly, and a few preteenage girls, all of them neatly dressed in clothes that were spotlessly clean. That's another of the many charms of Mexico, the people are all proud of their appearance. Outside of the big centers you don't find any bums.

After a few minutes I went back and found Joan washing her face at the kitchen sink. She turned and looked at me, searching for any sign of condescension, now we had spent time together. I bussed her on the cheek, like a returning husband. "Can you hold off until town for breakfast, or would you like some tortillas?"

"Sounds irresistible," she said, pulling a disgusted face.

"What's with the sleeping beauties?" I nodded toward the closed door of the other bedroom. "Are they making up for time lost to John Barleycorn?"

"That's it." She grinned. "Angie would have gone right back to the hotel, but Mr. Macho had something to prove."

"Eighty-proof male ego," I said. "He's a scalp collector, that one."

"And you're not?" She was in her late twenties, and she had told me the night before that she was just getting over the end of a two-year relationship with a copywriter at her agency, she had cause to be suspicious.

"No." I left it at that. What had happened had been both delightful and convenient. But I like women too much to take an ornithologist's pride in adding a new one to my life list.

After five minutes the bedroom door opened and Amadeo came out, rubbing his hands like a bank manager. "Finally made it, did you?" I asked, and he hated me with his eyes.

Angela was a minute or two longer, and she looked as if she would have liked an Alka-Seltzer over easy for breakfast. An early-morning start close to Amadeo's grizzly chin hadn't done her hangover any good. We walked out to the front of the compound and waited for a few minutes until an empty taxi came down the hill from the hotel. We put the women into it, Angela diving into the back seat like a vampire escaping from daylight. Day-old tequila does not sit well in the gringo gut. Joan turned her face up to be kissed, and then I paid the driver and they were gone.

Amadeo grinned as the cab pulled away. "That's quite a broad, that Angela. I'm tellin' you, she's no angel."

97

"Save the bragging for the pool hall back home. I was next door, listening to you not getting it on." I turned away from him and flagged down another cab.

Amadeo was angry. "Now listen," he started.

"Listen yourself. In case nobody ever told you, you're a punk, and only punks brag about women, especially after a bad attack of the droops."

He bristled and looked as if he would like to take a swing at me, but I poked him in the chest with one finger and he turned away and got into the cab, and we rode up the hill in silence. I glanced at the Parthenon as we passed. A man in a brown uniform was standing on the marble lip at the front of the building, an old American M1 carbine under his arm. He looked like some kind of cop, the Mexican military always wear fatigues or combat gear. I wondered why they guarded the place so carefully. Was it furnished with expensive kitsch picked out by the same hand that gilds the angels on all the altars of the country? Or were they keeping it clear of visitors until the owner had been extradited and shot and some new wheel could take possession, someone with enough clout to keep it guarded against that day?

We went back into our room down the corridor, and I let Amadeo go in first. It was an unnecessary precaution. Nobody was there. He took the first shower while I slipped my running shoes on and pattered up and down the steps to the beach eighteen times, close to three thousand steps, until my pulse rate was up and I felt stretched. Then I showered and shaved and changed for the day. The weapons were a problem. I would have preferred to carry the .45, for its public relations value, but it was too big for the pocket of my jacket. I compromised by carrying the .38 and the magazine from the automatic. The gun itself I put in my pack and locked it back into my flight bag. If anybody did get hold of it, it would be useless to them.

Amadeo sat on the end of his bed, watching me and smoking the fifth of the day's ration of cigarettes. He was sulking, more upset about his lack of performance the night before than about

98

the chance of getting wasted by one of García's gofers. I finished my preparations and told him, "Okay. This is your big day. You make your magic contact, and we pick up your cash. No more runarounds. I know you can do it in one day; then we can get you somewhere safe."

"It ain't that easy."

"You've got today, that's all. I didn't come down here to be used for target practice by somebody with a grudge against you. One day and we split."

He blew out a long, thoughtful plume of smoke and looked at me over it. "What if I say it can't be done? An' what about the proposition I mentioned?"

"First my six months' advance, then the proposition. I don't mind waiting if I'm paid." It wasn't true, but that was only fair, he wasn't leveling with me, either.

"See what I can do," he said.

We went along the corridor to breakfast. On the way I reminded him of the cover story about his nephew, in case we met the two Toronto women. They weren't in the restaurant, so we took a table for two overlooking the water. Amadeo ordered fruit for himself, and I had a guanabana shake and huevos rancheros, scrambled eggs with a healthy helping of jalapeña peppers. Mexican food isn't subtle, but it's got real authority.

From our spot on the terrace we watched the beach fill for the day. A few early swimmers were out, including a middle-aged couple who went up and down the length of the beach, exercise swimmers by the look of them, glad to be out of their northern "Y" pool, out in the warmth and buoyancy of the gently heaving ocean. And the peddlers moved in, the Indian women in their crisp gingham dresses with trays of jewelry on their heads and the nimble children with their painted birds and their baskets. Relaxing over a coffee and watching them, I almost felt as if I were on a real vacation.

"So what's the drill for making contact? We stay in the room or what?"

"On the beach," he said, getting up from the table.

"That's conspicuous. If your buddies decide to stand off with a sniper's rifle, they can cancel your check really easy."

"They wouldn't do that." He waved the suggestion aside. "It'd be bad for business, an' the people at the hotel pay them protection money."

"You should have told me that last night, it would have been useful."

"Yeah, well." He yawned elaborately. "It wouldn' of stopped 'em rousting us out, would it? An' anyway, you got laid, so quit bitchin'."

I sighed. "When did you first notice this poetic streak in your nature?"

"Wha'?"

I didn't want to attract attention, so we went back to the room and changed into swim gear, then I rolled my jacket and pants into a neat bundle and stuck them under my arm, the pocket with the gun in it on top. Amadeo looked at me pityingly and took nothing with him. He didn't have to; I was there to do the fighting for him.

"We're just gonna be on the beach fer Crissakes, why d'ya need alla that stuff?"

"The same reason a sailor puts his shoes on first when the alarm goes on ship."

He shook his head. "Don't you never give anybody a straight answer? Wha's that s'posed t' mean?"

"It means he's ready for hot decks, not dancing around in agony while other people are doing their job."

He shook his head again. He didn't understand. But then, security is like jazz, the way Satchmo described it to some writer who asked for a definition—if you gotta ask, you ain' never gonna know.

As we left the room, the door next to us opened, and I turned reflexively, my hand on the gun in my jacket, but it was just Helen, Debra Steen's companion. She looked tired, but she brightened when she saw me. I smiled back. "Hi, Helen, how's everything going?"

"So far so good," she said ambiguously, and then Debra came out to join her. She was made up, so you couldn't tell how she really looked, but she managed a weak smile.

"Good morning, Debra, are you taking the day off?"

"Yes, we're just going for some breakfast, and then we plan to sit in the shade and rest up for the day. It's been a tiring trip so far." It came out like a press release, but the smile she greased it with would have melted the heart of the most cynical reporter. I hoped her client would let her off for the day, fashion people are money conscious to a fault. I figured he or she would be furious when the help went walkabout instead of working. But if the thought had occurred to either of them, they weren't letting it show. I just said, "Good idea. Perhaps we'll see you on the beach." I let them pass and they went by, Helen smiling at me again, both of them ignoring Amadeo.

"The first day's the easiest," he said, turning down the corners of his mouth. The daydream still lived, his buying Debra's favors for a foil package. I let it pass.

"Okay, let's hit the beach. But don't get out in the open, stick under one of the umbrellas, that way they'd have to get close to hit you. Close I can handle." I nodded toward the end of the corridor, and he looked at me expressionlessly and then sauntered ahead.

The hotel was at its busiest now. Guests were heading for the beach or the tennis courts, and chambermaids were moving along the balconies with their carts of replacement commodities for the rooms. Everyone was as bright as the morning sunlight, which was already hot but still bearable. The air was clear, filled with the chatter of birds, grackles and magpie jays and the occasional tiny Inca dove. People were calling out to one another and trying their few words of Spanish on the smiling help. Toronto's snow and Amadeo's troubles were part of another world.

Amadeo let himself down the steps painfully, like an old man. I guessed his hangover was lingering, sending little reminders from the temperance society up his spine every time his foot jarred down, but he nodded and made gracious grunts at people we passed, and soon we were down on the sand, scoring ourselves a couple of chairs in the shade of a palm-thatched umbrella table.

Amadeo groaned and lay back flat in his. I picked an upright chair and sat comfortably, checking around as if I were waiting for someone to join us. We were as safe as we could get. Behind us was the wall of the bar, blank at its closest point. Nobody could take a shot at Amadeo from there. Our only hazard was from anyone who came along the beach and approached us. And if they did, and Jesus was right about their game plan, they would most likely not take Amadeo out. Their target would be me, preferably with a poisoned drink or a needle full of nastiness. That kind of approach would be simpler to handle.

As a bodyguard I do a lot of sitting around, but most of the time it's possible to read. Here it wasn't, so I kept up a surveillance on everything that moved. A few swimmers were running through the gentle surf and kicking out into the deeper water, and the para-sailing boat was back at its usual stand, the helper unfurling the chute while the boat bobbed on the waves at the length of the line from him. And the same pelicans were looking for breakfast, plunging into the waves and coming up with their bills convulsing over their catch. Peaceful.

After about fifteen minutes Helen and Debra came down the steps and out to a table near us. Amadeo looked at them and thought his *Penthouse* thoughts but said nothing. A couple of hotel guests passed, nodded politely, one woman stopping to speak to Debra, who smiled her professional smile, as wide as the beach itself, and then settled back into her chaise longue. And then a man in his thirties came down the steps. He looked like business. His clothes were casual but not casual enough, the kind of careful carelessness that comes with a big price tag from stores on Fifth Avenue, if you don't have the contacts to get them wholesale. I watched him, wondering if he was Amadeo's contact. He looked slick enough, but he ignored us and went straight to the women.

102

"Debra, honey, how are you? You look just fine."

"I'm really not, Gerry," she said nervously, and Helen stood up at once.

"Hi, Gerry, I'm sorry about the delay, but Debra is really under the weather. Another day working in the sunshine, and we're liable to lose her for a week, you wouldn't want that?"

His voice sank but not so far that I couldn't hear the anger or pick out some of the words. It amounted to his not wanting to force anybody, no matter how goddamn temperamental, but it was a pity that some people couldn't be more professional. That's why they had hired her, because she was supposed to be a pro, the best in the business, and you didn't expect pros to jerk you around, costing you per diems for a whole goddamn crew and setting the job back by a day just on a goddamn whim.

Amadeo looked at him and grinned. "He's really pissed at her. I'll bet you a hundred bucks she goes back to work."

I said nothing, feeling for the girl's insecurity and the withdrawal she was going through. You can't walk away from any drug that easily. I wondered what she would do. After about a minute she showed me. She stood up and walked past him, her long body limber in her high-cut swimsuit, moving like the Girl from Ipanema. He walked beside her, still talking, still waving his arms until the surf broke across his loafers. He swore then and made a grab for her arm, but she ignored him and ran into the water, letting the waves break against her thighs and then throwing herself headlong in a clumsy dive and swimming away from him, not stylishly, just clawing at the water, until she was too far to hear him over the crashing of the surf.

"She's not that good a swimmer," I said, and Amadeo nodded. "Pathetic." Then he stood up. "Shit, I wonder if she's tryin' a drown herself."

We walked down to the water's edge, where the man in the casual clothes was just turning back, pointing his finger at Helen, who had come out from under the shelter of the umbrella. He was making threatening noises of some kind, but she was ignoring him, looking out at Debra, who was still splashing away in a straight line from the beach. I was torn. My job was to guard Amadeo, but I couldn't stand there and let a woman drown. I glanced at her and at Helen, looking for some sign of real alarm, and then down the beach ran Beth, dressed in a practical one-piece swimsuit that looked as if she knew what she was doing, and she dived neatly into the water and swam out after Debra, gaining on her with every stroke.

Debra was fifty yards out now and failing, her strokes getting weaker and weaker until she was only patting at the water like a baby in a tub. Her head came up straight, panicky, uncertain now, with the reality of death resting on her tired shoulders, and then she slipped completely under.

Beth was only three strokes from her and she arched in the water and went down, coming back to the surface with one hand in Debra's hair. I heard the faint cry Debra gave and saw her hands reach up to her hair, but Beth had her tight and she began kicking back toward the beach, towing the model at arm's length.

Amadeo surprised me. He ran into the surf and started swimming out toward them, moving cleanly through the water. I ran in after him, and within a few seconds we were side by side out by the women. Debra was sobbing, "Let me go. Let me go," and Beth was ignoring her, concentrating on her one-handed backstroke, tugging Debra back to shallower water. As soon as it was shallow enough, I put my feet down and called out to Beth. "If you're tired, let me take her."

"No need," she puffed. "I've got her."

Amadeo ignored her and reached out toward Debra, but I touched him on the shoulder and he turned to me, his eyes blazing. "I'm tryin'a help."

"What she needs is room. Come on, back up the beach." We paddled gently in behind the women until Beth finally stood up and put her arm around Debra's shoulders and hugged her. Debra was weeping and shaking her head, but Beth talked to her soothingly and urged her back up the sand. The client was still standing there with Helen next to him. He came forward and started speaking at once, but Beth prodded him in the chest with one finger and he threw his hands up explosively. Amadeo and I came out of the water and stood on either side of the women, looking at him.

"So where does it say I have to stand for this kind of garbage? You tryin'a scare me, what? What? Answer, for Christ's sake. You some kind of dummy?"

Amadeo stepped forward and said, "Whyn't you take a hike, Mac, the lady's havin' enough trouble without you mouthin' off at her."

The man swore at him, and Amadeo hit him clumsily on the side of the head. Dumb. If you hit somebody, make sure they stay hit. All he had hurt was the other man's pride, and the next thing, they were wrestling in the water, swinging big handicapped punches at each other.

I turned to the women. "Listen, take Debra inside, I'll pick up the pieces here."

Helen looked at me, stone-faced. "Don't be too quick, will you? It couldn't happen to two nicer guys."

Beth turned to Debra and said, "Come on, you need a cup of coffee and some dry clothes." Then she and Helen both smiled at me and took Debra away up the beach between them, while I stood back and waited for the fighters to tire themselves out. I felt the same as Helen about them, let them bruise one another.

It took about a minute. Amadeo was fighting out of pride, and maybe even guilt, but he was up against a man who had probably never been humiliated before, and they both had a lot to prove. His fancy clothes were soaked and he had a mouse under one eye, but he could have been a Gurkha for all the surrendering he was going to do. I had to wait until they were both gasping.

I hauled him to his feet, then Amadeo. "You two look like a couple of dorks," I informed them cheerfully. "The only way you can come out of this with any dignity left is to go up to the bar like a couple of buddies and have a beer together, laughing all the way, otherwise it's going to be in the papers, and you"—I prodded the client in the back—"are going to find yourself looking down the barrel of a lawsuit from Debra Steen's attorney."

"I'm gonna sue this bastard for every nickel he's got," he seethed, and Amadeo made another lunge at him.

"He's Mexican, you're wasting your money, let him buy you a beer and you come out of this looking good, otherwise the whole garment district is going to be laughing at you over their corned-beef sandwiches and cream sodas."

"Asshole," he said, but he straightened up and wiped his hair out of his eyes and started to laugh although his eyes were cold. "Lemme buy you guys a drink, hemlock, they got any."

He put his arm on Amadeo's shoulder, and Amadeo flinched but then did the same, and they walked back up the beach to the bar. A couple of people looked at them curiously as they passed, but their cover story was working, two big goofs horseplaying in the surf, the client being the better sport, not worrying about his clothes.

There was a different barman on duty, Eduardo, young and eager, and he got Bohemias for Amadeo and me, an *agua mineral* for the client, whose name was Irv, and we sat and yukked it up at the bar for ten minutes before he finally stood up, his drink untouched, and shook hands with Amadeo and sloshed away up the steps.

The barman looked at Amadeo and grinned. "*Loco*," he said, and Amadeo answered him in rapid Spanish that had them both chuckling. Then we went back out to our place on the beach. Amadeo was sitting upright now, full of himself. He glanced at me and grinned, balling up his right fist. "I showed that mother, eh?"

"You sure did," I said. Showed him how not to fight, but then, he already knew that, or he would have punched your head off.

Amadeo squirmed his shoulders back into his seat. "Yeah.

Didn't need no help, jus' cleaned his clock. Like he made me mad, eh, pickin' on that poor bitch."

"Not the act of a gentleman," I said gravely. I could see a beach vendor coming toward us from the town end of the beach, crunching tirelessly over the soft sand, carrying a bundle of baskets. He was heading straight for us, and I checked that both his hands were visible, each clutching the handles of a bundle of his embroidered straw baskets, but there was a look about him that jangled my receptors. I slipped my hand inside the pocket of my jacket and held the gun on him invisibly. When he came close enough, I said *"No quiero, muchas gracias."* I don't want any, thanks, but he ignored me and spoke in rapid Spanish to Amadeo.

Amadeo answered and then turned to me. "This is the guy I've been waiting for. Give him fifty thousand pesos for me, will ya?"

eleven

Half the money I had drawn from Cahill was in pesos, so I peeled off fifty thousand and handed it over. He took it without smiling and handed me his smallest basket. I didn't want it, but it was his cover, so I took it and put my bundle into it. Now I looked like every other gringo on the beach. The only difference was that I had a gun in my basket instead of suntan lotion.

The man grinned an ingratiating grin and moved away from us, up the beach, past the other sunbathers, but I saw that he didn't linger to haggle with any of them but kept walking at the same sand-crunching pace past our hotel and the few small cabañas farther on.

"What happens now?" I asked.

"We need a Jeep. He's gone to get it for us," Amadeo said, and lay back, his eyes closed.

"And you've wasted a day lining up a Jeep? Hell, you could have hired one yourself, yesterday, we could be on our way home by now."

"Yesterday was a total screw-up," he said.

"I don't need any more games from you. Why do you have to

get this guy to find a Jeep? Maria could have got one as easily as she got that boat, easier maybe."

He opened one eye and peered at me. "I told you before, nothin' goes down in this place that García don' hear about. He knew I was comin' back. He knew I needed a Jeep. He must've had some guy sittin' at the rental office checkin' every Jeep goes out."

I didn't answer, and he shut his eyes again, smug and happy. "You gotta understand, I know how things work in this town, you don't."

"What was to stop her coming into town in a Jeep?"

"Mexican women don' drive Jeeps. They'd a seen her an' been on her quicker'n a dog on a dinner," he said disgustedly. "Now whyn't you relax till it's time?"

"Is he bringing the Jeep here?"

"No. Fer Crissakes. He brings it here, they see it, they follow me."

I wasn't satisfied. "What good would that do them? They couldn't follow you in that boat of García's. The first yard off the road would tear his tank out."

Now he sat up again, his mouth pursed in anger. "They got Jeeps an' they got radios. How d'ya think they run the drug business in these mountains here?"

That made sense, but I didn't want glib answers. "All right, so they've got Jeeps. We'll have to be cute when we take off, when will that be?"

"Later. We'll meet up with my *amigo* where it's quiet an' head out. Thing is, they know I've got some bread down there. They jus' wanna know where."

"You sure do things the hard way. If this was my problem, I would have landed somewhere else and rented a Jeep. That way you could have picked up the cash without coming onto García's turf."

He didn't answer, but I could guess why, this was his fall-back plan. His first choice had been to leave me on the beach,

109

red-faced, while he took off in the motorboat. Getting his money was the fallback situation. Once he'd got it, he would revert to his original plan, shake me and head for cover.

"Where are we meeting him, and when?"

"Two o'clock." He looked at his watch and sighed. "That means we got three hours t' kill. Then lunch, then a cab, then we're on our way. Now whyn't you let me grab some z's?"

He lay back again and was asleep within a minute, his mouth hanging open, snoring gently. After a while I moved out slightly into the sunshine and let the brightness soak into me. I'm not a sun worshiper. I've spent too much time in the desert for that, but I prefer being tanned to the fish-belly whiteness you end up with after a winter of overcoats and fur hats, two borders north of Mexico.

The barman came around taking orders. Amadeo was still asleep, so I ordered a Bohemia and a ginger ale and made myself a shandy. Straight beer, in the quantities it takes to keep your fluid levels up in Mexico, would have slowed me, but I couldn't take to a diet of soda water. The shandy was a compromise.

Nothing much happened all morning. The usual round of vendors came and went, but I smiled and waved them away. I had no room in my plans for extra baggage. If all went well, I planned to pick up some Kahlúa for Janet Frobisher and a bottle of vanilla for my mother's cook. I would do it at the airport. The price would be higher there, but Cahill wouldn't count the change from his grand, a couple of hundred pesos extra didn't matter.

Around noon Amadeo woke up and we took a quick dip, me watching for any signs of trouble but feeling fairly secure on the beach, which was crowded now with hotel guests. And after ten vigorous minutes we went back to the bar for a beer and then up to the room to shower and put some clothes on for lunch.

I was in the shower when I heard Amadeo say, "Now what?"

I turned the tap off and listened as another knock came at the door. Draping the towel around me, I hissed at him to get out of sight. Then I took out my gun and held it underneath a second towel and opened the door.

One of the hotel porters was standing there with a package about a foot square, wrapped in decorative paper and tied with a ribbon. "Señor Amadeo?" he asked.

"Sí, es aquí." Yes, he's here.

The boy held the package out, and I waved for him to come inside. He did, unconcernedly, so I knew that whatever was in the package was news to him. I found my cash and dug him out a hundred-peso piece and he thanked me, put the parcel on the bed, and left.

Amadeo came away from the wall, where he'd been making like a coat of paint, and looked at the parcel. "What in hell is that?" he wondered. He reached out to open it, but I knocked his hand away.

"Don't touch it. It could explode."

He laughed scornfully. "A bomb? You gotta be outa your mind."

"Are you expecting anything from anybody?"

"No." He shook his head. "But shit, look at it, it looks fancy. Why'd anybody send me a bomb dressed up like that?"

"The IRA do it all the time. It's a neat way of getting to the guy they're after. They generally use a letter, but they have better explosives than these people. This could be an old-fashioned bundle of dynamite."

He looked at me, and the grin on his face shriveled up. "You serious?"

"Dead serious. Lie on the floor on the other side of that bed, cover your ears and keep your mouth open."

He did it, reluctantly but not sure of himself anymore. I got the rifle from the closet and lay down beside the bed, putting the rifle muzzle six inches from the package. If it was a bomb, it might be triggered by magnetism, by the presence of a knife used to cut the paper. Now I reached up and used the muzzle of my pistol to shove the rifle against the package, keeping my whole body down below the level of the concrete bed base. I was as safe there as I would be in a bunker.

111

Nothing happened, so I shoved the muzzle against the package firmly, jolting it hard. Again nothing. Still staying down out of the line of a possible blast, I used my left hand to manipulate the rifle to turn the package over, bottom up. Then I waited for a further minute and stood up, still suspicious.

Taking a chance, I bent my head close to it and listened for the faint ticking of a watch. I couldn't hear anything, but that didn't mean a lot. Watches are silent these days. I sniffed it but couldn't make out the faint pickle smell of plastic explosive.

At last I went into the bathroom and got my clasp knife out of my pants packet and went back to the package. Amadeo was stirring, peering up over the edge of his bed, "Keep down," I told him and held the parcel firmly against the mattress while I very carefully cut out a square of the bottom of it, using the finely honed tip of my knife blade and trying to avoid any sawing motion.

It took a minute to get through the cardboard inside, and while I was working a fly buzzed persistently around my fingers. When I had the square cut on three sides I hinged it out carefully, and then I understood why the fly was there. The inside of the cardboard was sticky with blood.

Amadeo had come up behind me and was standing at my shoulder, watching in fascination. "What's that?" he asked, knowing the answer, forming his words carefully in his fear.

I didn't answer but went on cutting around the bottom of the box until I was confident that the box was not booby-trapped. When I could see all the way around, I cut the ribbon and lifted out the bottom of the box. Amadeo gagged. "Jesus Christ." he said, and crossed himself. Then he ran to the bathroom and I heard him vomiting as I carried the box into the room after him and upturned it slowly on the tile floor. I lifted it away and looked at the contents. It was the head of the man we had met on the beach.

Amadeo groaned and reeled over to the sink to splash his face with cold water. He was plaster-white.

"It looks as if renting Jeeps is hazardous to your health," I said.

He snarled at me. "What's with you? The guy's dead, you make jokes."

I lifted the head and put it back in the box, jamming a towel in on top of it to keep out the flies that had started to gather. Then I ran the shower until the tile was free of the blood that had smeared it. "Two questions for you. First, how important is it that you get to that cash?"

"I gotta get to it." He backed out of the bathroom, eyes fixed on the box in its pretty blue paper. "I gotta give Maria some money so she can hide an' I can have something to come back to after the court case in T'rannah."

"Second question. How far is it to this hiding place of yours?"

He looked up at me blankly. "Howja mean?"

"How far is it? A hundred miles, fifty, ten, what?"

"Around thirty."

"By road, or as the crow flies?"

He frowned. I could see that he had trouble concentrating. The murder had suddenly explained to him what kind of trouble he was in. He knew that could have been his own head instead of some Indian's. "By road partway, then cross-country." He wasn't thinking any further than he had to.

"How far is it on foot?"

"Over the mountains? You gotta be kidding."

"How far?"

He rested his weight on one hand and then slowly lowered himself onto the bed. "Maybe twenty-five. It's on a track from the road, but if you was to go straight, uphill, downhill, twenty-five."

I stood and thought about that for a while. We had two choices, either we could take a taxi out of town to the beginning of the trail and walk in from there, or else we could walk the whole way. It would be a stretch, especially for Amadeo, who was developing into the kind of guy who would die of exertion pressing the button on his TV remote control. But that way had the advantage of being secure. If we took a cab or hired a car and drove out of town and left it anywhere near a trail, a local would know where we were headed and could be there before us.

"Well, we've got to get rid of this box. If we call the cops in, we'll never get out of jail. The locals will make sure of that," I said. "And we've got to do it fast. By tonight there are going to be vultures hanging overhead." He shuddered but said nothing.

"So the way I see it, if you want to get your cash, we've got to walk in and get it. When we get back out to the highway, we can flag down a truck, maybe, and ride north, out of state. Then we can take a flight back to Canada."

"You've never been up in those hills," he said angrily. "They're steep, an' it's hotter'n a bitch."

"Not as bad as country I've fought over before this. My only question is, can you make it?"

He was shaken enough to be honest. "I'm not sure." He looked up at me, his face still white. "Do you think we could do it?"

"It depends how much you want what's at the other end. How much are we talking about?"

"Half a million bucks." The thought gave him some of his cunning back, and he looked at me closely to see if I was going to keel over with amazement.

"How big are the bills? Hundreds, thousands, what?"

He frowned, thrown. "What difference does that make?'

"I want to know how heavy the load's going to be, that's all."

He nodded slowly, understanding. "Oh, yeah. Well, it's a mix."

"What's it in?"

"A metal briefcase. It don' weigh that much." He made a little hefting motion with his right hand.

"It might not have done while you were lifting it in and out of a Jeep, but if you're carrying it for ten miles, you'll wish you took it out in diamonds instead," I told him. "So what do you think? Do we go for it, or do we run off home without it?"

He lit a cigarette and sat back against the head of the bed thinking. I guessed he was weighing up the chance of getting back into the state of Guerrero after he had testified against his old workmates in Canada. I didn't think they were good. The people here already hated him. The Mafia in Canada would tail him from the courthouse, no matter what kind of tricks the Mounties tried to play. You don't send a bunch of Godfathers down the river for twenty years without making some serious enemies. They would alert the people here, and he might never get his money. On the other hand, he had me with him right now to run interference. He had a chance if he could handle a couple of days' march over tough terrain. I tightened up the screws a little. "You want to tell me how you managed to set aside a half million for yourself?"

Now his face relaxed into its usual expression of casual cunning, like a kid who habitually cheats in school. "I saved it."

"Sure you did. And your employers in Toronto found out, and that's how come you ended up being fingered with a key of cocaine in your house. They set you up, Greg, after you cheated them."

It was a wild guess. It didn't seem logical to me. They would have taken care of him more simply. A bomb in his car and lots of crocodile tears at the funeral would have been more in keeping. But I'd touched a nerve, even if not the right one.

"I brought that back last time," he said.

"Like, off the record, a little sideline for yourself, right?"

"You might say." He drew deeply on his cigarette. His color was returning, and he allowed himself to expand a little. "Like we're talkin' big money here. A guy like you wouldn't understand."

"I understand that you're a dead man walking. And I understand that you've got more chance of getting your money back now then you will have later. These guys here aren't dummies.

If they know the money is within a Jeep ride of here, it won't take them forever to find it."

He lay back with his eyes closed and his right arm lying flat, palm up, clear off the edge of the bed, the cigarette forgotten between his fingers. He was making up his mind.

"What do you think's the best?" He opened his eyes and sat up as he asked it, an unconscious commitment to action.

"I think we go for your money or we leave, right now. The choice is yours, but we do one or the other."

He sniffed, then dragged on his cigarette and blew out the smoke. "I'm not gonna leave that money for García. Let's go."

"Have you got any running shoes with you?"

He stood up and dropped his cigarette, stepping on it casually. "No. But I gotta pair of lace-ups. Topsiders."

"Put them on, over your thickest pair of socks."

I was still wrapped in the towel, so I slapped on some talcum powder and dressed. Amadeo watched me in surprise. "Wha's with the powder?"

"We're going to be sweating before the day's over. It helps."

I tipped out my backpack and rechecked the contents. First I filled my canteen and added a halazone tablet and shook it up. A liter of water would be a start on our needs. Next I reloaded the .45, cocked it, and told Amadeo, "Okay. We're going to need a meal before we start and some beer to take with us. Grab that straw basket and bring the rifle and blanket and we'll go."

He picked up the rifle and checked it. "There's no magazine."

"I've got it. We'll put it in when we're out of town. Now, let's grab a cab into town. And carry that box with you in the basket."

I waited until he had squeezed the parcel into the basket, towel side down; then we walked out through reception and into the sunshine. A taxi was standing in the thin shade of a jacaranda outside the hotel, and we took it back down the hill and into the main street where the market stands. I paid the

116

driver off and we got out. "Okay, we'll take some bread, some canned meat, and some beer. Let's shop."

He ducked ahead of me into the shady old building with its crowd of shoppers, local women with their beautiful bright-eyed children, picking over the produce on all the stalls. The place was rich with the smells of peppers and herbs and fish and the blood from the tough thin slices of beef at the carnicería. Amadeo looked at the meat as it hung over the edge of the counter blackening in the heat, and swallowed. But he didn't weaken. He bought us a bag of rolls and a couple of tins of meat and, at my reminder, a couple of razor-sharp machetes and a pair of big straw hats, the same as the natives were wearing.

"Great souvenirs," I kidded him. "Imagine having this hang-ing over your fireplace?"

He looked at me as if I were out of my tree, and I smiled a big happy smile and told him, "Look amused. We're a couple of dumb, happy gringos on vacation, no sense looking glum."

He smiled weakly. "I'll try to remember that." He bought a bag to carry our purchases, glancing around the whole time, expecting one of García's men to pop up. I watched him, but he didn't react to any of the faces in the crowd.

At the back of the market, close to the little lunch counter, where the locals were eating tortillas loaded with a thick pep-pery stew and drinking the local equivalent of Kool-Aid, we saw a beggar sitting on a step. She was a tiny old lady, almost blind, wearing a crucifix and mumbling over her rosary. She had a flat little basket beside her with a few coins in it. If that was her day's take, she was on a pretty lean diet. Amadeo bent and spoke to her and folded her fingers over a thousand pesos. It wasn't much in our terms, three dollars possibly, but to her it was a fortune.

I watched him wait, head bowed while she blessed him. Then he straightened up and came after me, carrying his two bags.

"Let's grab some lunch," I said, and he shook his head.

"I can' eat, not with this bag next to me." He raised the basket containing his parcel and shook his head.

"Okay, then, we'll get some beer and get going," I said.

I led us out, across the broad, dusty boulevard in front of the market, and picked up ten portly bottles of Superior, *muy fria*—very cold—from one of the dozen or so refreshment stalls. We didn't look out of place here among the lounging local men and bustling women and the few tourists poking around with their cameras around their necks. "Take one now," I told him.

"Didn' we oughta get used to going without?" he asked.

"No. The secret of survival is to drink your fill, every chance you get. When we're up in the hills, we can start water discipline. For now, drink up."

We stood back against the rough brick wall that ran all around a big old hacienda. Nobody paid us any attention, although we both scanned the crowds and the passing cars for familiar faces. As we drank, I asked Amadeo, "Is it any closer if we go to Ixtapa?"

He thought about it, narrowing his eyes. "Yeah. Not a hell of a lot, but maybe a mile."

"A mile counts. Let's go."

We flagged down a cab and left town, driving out on the noncommercial side where the locals live, with no cluster of hotels for tourists. Some of the houses were handsome, but most were simple, brick-built, or corrugated-iron sheeting roofed with banana leaves. Some had a pig tethered outside, feeding on the fruit rinds and stale tortillas from the family table. One or two had fighting cocks tied on strings just out of range of one another, all of them preening and practicing their victory crows.

The taxi climbed the hill that divides Zihuatanejo from Ixtapa, and I studied the terrain we were going to have to cross. Steep hills, dry as the inside of a snuffbox, covered with coarse, irregular growth, low bushes, and a few tall trees. Here and there was a cactus, but mostly scrub.

118

Amadeo looked out the window at the hills and then at me. "It ain' gonna be easy."

"I know. That's why you'll get away with it. They don't know you've got the *cojones* for the job."

"S'long's it's just one way," he said. "We hitch a ride after, right?"

"Right. It's a good payday for a hard day's work," I said.

We pulled into Ixtapa, a well-irrigated garden spot lined with big hotels. It was typical Mexican planning, allowing for the fact that most tourists want a beach and a bar, that's all. So they build a place with all the charm of the row of hotels alongside a northern airport, except for the fact that it has an unswimmable beach with picturesque killer surf and lots of pools with swim-up bars. In the middle of all the hotels they build a tiny shopping plaza with banks and restaurants and souvenir stores. Half the visitors never get farther than this from their hotel. And they go home thinking they've been to Mexico.

We paid off our cab outside the little plaza, then sauntered down the road beside it as if we were out for a stroll.

twelve

The road was only a quarter of a mile long. It ran through the irrigated area where the native scrub had been cleared and thin grass planted among palm trees that would look good on the free postcards in the hotel lobby. On our way we saw a workman riding a mower. He looked at us curiously, and I waved at him.

"That's right. Make sure he sees you," Amadeo said.

"He saw us anyway, now he thinks we're a pair of fun-loving hikers, out for a look at the bush. He'll forget us before he gets back to the end of his row."

Amadeo swore under his breath and changed hands on the bags. The provisions were heavier than his parcel, I noticed. The road stopped abruptly at a concrete curb, but a small trail went on ahead into the brush. It ran the same way as the road, so I followed it, pausing only to clip the magazine back into the little rifle. It wasn't much firepower, but it would be accurate over a longer distance than my pistols.

Once we were out of sight of the road, I stopped and let Amadeo catch up. He did, sweating but, so far, not short of breath. Good, we were still on the level. I slipped off my pack, and he set down his bags gratefully. "Now what?"

"Now I need to know exactly where we're headed. All I know so far is we're looking for a track that runs in from the highway about fifteen miles from town." I took out my map of the region; it was not very accurate, it came from the tourist department's guidebook, and it devoted most of the space to the town of Zihuatanejo, but it was the best I had.

Amadeo lit a cigarette, dropping the match negligently. I stooped and picked it up. "Before you drop another one, break it, that way you know it's out and we won't have a brush fire on our backs. And when you've smoked that butt, grind it all the way out on your shoe before you let go of it."

"Yeah, okay." His eyes widened momentarily. He hadn't thought of any more trouble than he was in already. He came and peered at the map. I looked at the scale and used my fingers as compasses, marking off the radius of fifteen miles from town.

"From what you said, the trail was about this far up the highway. How far in from there is the place we're going?"

He thought for a moment. "Yeah, well, it's fifteen miles, but that's all around the mountains, it's less'n that in a straight line."

I held the radius on my fingers and drew another curve, using the road as the center of the circle. "About there. What am I looking for, a house, what?"

"Used to be a house, it's half fallen down now."

"And how clear is the track, will we find that easier than trying to home in on the house itself?"

He nodded, breathing out smoke. "Yeah. Maybe we should aim to cut the track."

"Okay. That means we're heading north-northeast." I took out my compass from my pack and took a bearing on the most prominent landmark I could see, a bare tree on the side of a mountain about a mile from us. It was ten degrees east of what I wanted, but our track was leading almost directly to it. I would need to make up ten degrees west in the mile after that.

I slipped the compass into my shirt pocket and then took off my jacket and folded it into the top of my pack, then shouldered the pack again. "We're making for that tree. Let me have

121

a machete, and we're on our way. If the path turns off, we'll have to go through the brush. Ready?"

"Yeah." He stooped and rubbed out his cigarette on his shoe sole. "But how about I leave this behind." He pointed to the basket containing the parcel.

"This is too close to the hotels. The vultures will gather, and somebody may come looking. We carry it until we're up in the hills, clear of civilization."

He snorted. "What's this 'we'? You ain' carryin' it."

"He wasn't my *amigo,* and I'm walking point. Carry it until I say." I snapped the words at him. I couldn't afford arguments. Until we were back on the highway with his money, I was in charge.

He grunted and picked up the bags, and I headed on up the path. We were lucky. It ran the way we wanted for another half mile, growing steeper and washed out in places but wide enough for one man to walk easily. Then it swung west, so I left it, checking over my shoulder that Amadeo was with me.

Now the going was rougher. Fortunately the ground was too dry for the brush to be thick, but we had to cut our way around the edge of some of the denser bushes, and we were climbing a forty-five-degree slope. It felt good to be working, but the sweat ran down my face and dripped off my chin onto my shirt. I glanced around at Amadeo and saw that he was in worse shape, his mouth hanging open, gasping with exertion, but he was keeping up, still carrying both bags.

It took us fifty-five minutes to reach the tree, and when we did, he collapsed against the trunk, not even bothering to light a cigarette. I slipped off my pack and crouched beside him. "Five minutes' rest," I said.

He was wearing a T-shirt, and he tugged at the right sleeve with his left hand and used the cloth to wipe his forehead. "I need more'n that," he said, drawing deep breaths.

"We've got a long way to go. And we can rest all night if you're tired. I want to get well away from Ixtapa before we start to kick back."

He glanced at his watch. "You realize it's one-thirty, the hottest time of the day?"

"Yes. I know that most of the locals are resting, but they're not expecting half a million dollars' pay for today's work. You are."

He closed his eyes and said nothing. I wondered what was going through his head. Was he thinking about spending the money? About toppling García and taking over the drug business in Guerrero? Or was he planning ways to take a swing at me with his machete once I'd brought him close to his cash? What was that thing Spike Milligan wrote? *The Small Dreams of a Scorpion?* Amadeo's were probably smaller, and meaner.

I gave him seven minutes while I walked ahead to the peak of the hill and took a bearing on a white rock on the next mountain, about another mile and a half. Then I called him, softly, and he caught up with me, not speaking. "We're heading for that rock. When we get off this hill, you can leave the package behind. Open if it you want, but I guess the vultures will find it anyway."

"I ain' touching that thing." he said sincerely. "All's I'm gonna do is take the towel off it."

"Keep the towel. It's not bloody and it belongs to the hotel, it could lead people to us later."

He pulled a disgusted face, but he nodded. "Guess you're right. Okay, let's go."

It was marginally easier downhill. Not as easy as going down steps, I still had to slash some of the brush, and we had to hang on to bushes in the steep places, but the law of gravity was working with us instead of against us. I glanced up and saw that the vultures were starting to gather. Where there was usually only one in any square mile of sky, there were now four of them, lying flat on the updrafts like scraps of burned paper over a fire. But they were below the level of the hilltops, out of sight of Ixtapa. Unless some driver with keen eyes saw them from the crest as he came in from Zihuatanejo, they were invisible. And that meant we could deposit the parcel.

123

When we reached the bottom, I looked around for a clear spot on the baked ground. "Here," I told Amadeo. "Give me the basket."

He handed it over without speaking, then set down the other bag and wiped his streaming face on his sleeve. His T-shirt was soaked through with perspiration, and he was openmouthed and silent. I took out the parcel, lifting off the towel and turning the box upside down so that the horror inside slipped out onto the ground. Then I burned the wrapping and box, making sure nothing else caught. I glanced at Amadeo's shopping bag. It was sturdy plastic mesh, the universal carrier of the region. But the handles were thin, and I could see they would cut his fingers. "You want this basket for the goodies?" I asked him.

He thought about it and nodded. "Yeah. When we pick up the case, it'll go in there, people won' know what it is."

"Now you're thinking. Stick the bag in here for now."

I gave it to him, and we waited until the paper was all burned. "You want to say something over the remains?"

He nodded and crossed himself. I bowed my head and waited. I'm not religious myself, but I'd never knock it. I've served with a lot of men who were, tougher men than I am.

When he had finished, in silence, he crossed himself and said, "Now let's get the hell out of here."

By the time we reached our second landmark, I was beginning to think he would never complete the march. His shirt and pants were black with sweat and he was pulling in every breath openmouthed, like an old emphysema patient. He fell rather than sat down in the small patch of shade from the side of the rock, letting the basket drop carelessly from his hands.

"Watch that, don't let the beer break." I picked up the bag and took out two bottles. They were warm but still not hot, and I opened them and handed him one. He nodded gratefully and glugged it. That was a mistake. The beer foamed, and he coughed and some of it ran over the side of the bottle.

124

"Take it easy, sip it. Make sure you wet all your mouth with every drop before you swallow."

He looked at me angrily, but he was too tired to argue. I noticed he didn't bother with a cigarette. "We'll break for half an hour. If you can sleep, go ahead and do it."

He grunted and lay flat, closing his eyes, but he wasn't sleeping. He said, "You tired?"

"Not yet, it takes more than this." I thought back to training marches in the army. We had carried heavier packs, heavier weapons, and we covered the ground at twice the speed. Train hard, fight easy. That had been the motive that forced us on. By comparison, this was a nature hike.

I went around the rock and tried to pick out a landmark ahead, but the brush was too thick, so I climbed a little higher, to the top of the rock, and from there I could see a col, a dip between two hilltops right on our course. That was a break, less climbing.

Amadeo was feeling better by the time I rejoined him. He had opened his eyes and was staring up at the sky like a little boy in one of those old storybooks that were read to you as a kid. He turned his head to look at me as I came back down the last few yards and sat beside him. "Look at that sky," he said. "Not a goddamn cloud anywhere, an' hot." He snorted out a quick, disgusted little breath. "Can y' imagine being born here, poor?"

There was nothing to say, so I let him wander on. "My mother was. Her father died, just worn out, when she was twelve. Then a tourist, Jewish woman from Montreal, Mrs. Gold, she took a shine to her and got her mother's permission to take her to Canada. Sent her to school with her own kids."

He rolled onto one elbow and reached for his cigarettes. I was glad to see that, it meant he had recovered his strength. He lit up, breaking the match afterward, and went on. "She died, the year my mother turned eighteen. One of the other kids in the family was a lawyer, he cut her out of the will real fast, so

125

she went workin' in a bakery. Hard work, like back here. An' then she met my father. Now she's, what, fifty, got a big house with a garden, grows everything, really." He drew on his cigarette and blew out a luxurious cloud of smoke. "That Mrs. Gold, she was some kinda saint."

"There's more good people than bad in the world. It's just that they're not as organized as the opposition." There! The biggest part of everything I'd ever learned about life, and it whistled over his head like an outgoing artillery shell.

He said, "I just wish I could've met that lady."

She'd have been real proud of you, I thought, a full-fledged Mafia princeling, pushing crack to any kid with ten bucks. Ah, well, it was a dirty job, but someone would have turned up to do it. Don't blame Mrs. Gold's generosity.

We started out again, moving slowly down the side of the hill toward my landmark. It was after four by now, and the worst of the heat was over. It was warm, the way pale northerners dream of its being when they're sliding home through the slush of a February rush hour. We made good time to the col, rested there for ten minutes, and pushed on, in the shadow of the mountain to the west, making another six miles before nightfall.

By then we had reached the top of a steep scarp. I knew we would have to get off it before dark, it was too hazardous to rest here, but Amadeo was beat. He dropped his bag lightly on the ground and lay down next to it, breathing heavily.

"Take care of that bag. It's got all our rations in it," I said.

"Yeah, I was gonna say, how's about eating now? I ain' had a thing since that fruit for breakfast." Without waiting for an answer, he reached for the bag, sitting up quickly, so that a flurry of loose dirt slipped away from under him, washed around the bag like an incoming tide and gently carried it over the cliff. He swore, and then we stood and listened to the rush of falling earth and the music of breaking glass as our entire supply of fluids was lost to us.

He turned to me, his face pale in the gloom. "Now what?"

126

"Now we prove how much you inherited from your mother's side of the family."

"Wha's that s'posed t' mean? Haven't you got any food in your pack?"

"Never carry it, there's always something to eat."

"Yeah, like what?"

"You'll see. Come on, lets's get off this cliff face. Follow me, I'll steer by the stars."

I turned away, fixing my course by the polestar, then relating it back to Arcturus, which was high enough to be visible when we got down below the mountaintops. It was rough and ready, and I would have to adjust my course every time I got a glimpse of the polestar, but it would do.

Amadeo scrambled behind me, edging nervously away from the cliff edge. "What about the food, we can get that?"

"We don't have a flashlight, we'd waste hours looking for it, and in that time we can be another six or eight miles on."

"But what about water?" His mouth was dry, I could tell from the choked sound of his voice. It was over an hour since we had stopped for a beer, our third since starting.

"You won't dry up and blow away, keep walking, we can cover more ground while it's cool."

He swore at me in an angry hiss, but I could hear him lurching on behind me as I slashed into the brush and kept on down the hill.

By the time the last light of day had gone, a quarter-moon had risen, and our night vision had built up to the point where we were easily able to move. I kept us at it for an hour, ignoring Amadeo's complaints. Then I stopped and sat down against a tall tree, satisfied we were still on course. Amadeo caught up to me and collapsed. "If I don' get a drink, I'm gonna die," he said hoarsely.

I checked my watch. It was nine forty-seven. "We'll have a mouthful at midnight, that's only a couple of hours. By that time, we'll be halfway if we keep up this pace."

"Bastard," he hissed. "Why in hell I let you talk me into this I'll never know."

"Greed," I told him. He was still fresh enough to work without reward. By noon the next day he would be exhausted, even after a few hours' sleep. That's when I would start using the carrot. For now he needed lots of stick to keep him mobile. But he needed a little help, so I opened my pack and felt inside the breast pocket of my jacket. There's a spare button in there, and I pulled it out and gave it to him. "Suck this button, it'll keep your mouth moist."

He didn't argue. He accepted the button and slipped it into his mouth. I could hear him clicking it against his teeth. "Don' do a thing," he said at last.

"It helps, believe me. A pebble is good, but the rock around here is all jagged, you'd never find a suitable stone, and it's probably coated with Montezuma's revenge anyway." I was healthily, glowingly tired, and I sat back gratefully against the tree. "Five minutes," I said.

After our rest we marched again, glad of the coolness, alert to the tiny rustlings in the undergrowth, birds mostly and a few local rodents with a metabolism that let them produce their own water from the food they ate. In the morning I would catch something for breakfast, I thought; for now, on toward the leading star.

At ten to twelve he stopped me, calling out from forty yards back. "Wait up. Hey. Wait up." He sounded pathetic, his words each separated by a breath, and I knew he was at the end of his rope, so I stopped and whistled softly so he could track me, now he could no longer hear my machete on the brush. He caught up and sat on the ground, swinging his machete around him, using the flat of the blade to make sure there was nothing to prevent his lying down. Then he stretched out. "This is it," he said after a minute's silence. "I'm beat. We gotta stop."

"Okay, it's pretty near midnight. Why don't you sleep for an hour or two, here's the blanket." I pulled it out of my pack and he took it gratefully, not saying anything. He was too tired even to think about being thirsty. I didn't remind him; it would be worse in daylight, and we would need the water I brought with me.

I lowered myself gently to the ground and stretched gratefully. Two hours should be enough, I thought. By that time it would be as cool as it got. Walking would be better than shivering, and I knew that Amadeo would wake up cold. I set my mental alarm for two and slipped off into a deep sleep.

It was three minutes to the hour when I woke. Amadeo was snoring. The moon was beginning to slide down toward the hill peaks to the west of us, but there was plenty of light. I stood up and scouted around, keeping within earshot of Amadeo's regular snores. I was lucky, there were two agave cactus plants next to one another. And both had developed the central spike.

I went back and woke Amadeo. "Time for a drink," I told him.

He sat up. "Yeah, good." He held out his hand, but I said, "Follow me," and he did, mumbling, over to the cactus plants.

I slashed the leaves away from one side of each one and then cut the central stem. "What now?" he asked.

"Now put your mouth on the cut part. There's a couple of quarts of sap in there that you can drink safely."

He did as I said, then swore. "This tastes like hell."

I was preparing the other one for myself. "Just pretend it's been distilled and you're drinking tequila," I said.

We stayed there for twenty minutes, picking up about half a pint of cheesy-tasting sap that did nothing for our thirst but at least put some fluid into our systems. Then I slashed open the two spikes and handed one of them to him. "Rub this on your arms and face, it'll freshen you up."

He was too defeated to argue. We stood there, washing our hands and faces, like kids on a watermelon binge, sucking at the pulp as we worked. "There. Now you're ready to go," I said.

"I am like hell," he snarled, but I turned away and let him follow as I walked on, over the rising ground toward the pointer of the Big Dipper.

By four-thirty the moon was gone, and I stopped again. It

was cool now, perhaps as low as fifty degrees, and I put my jacket on when we stopped, and wrapped the hotel towel around my shoulders. Amadeo had the blanket and he wrapped himself up in it, and we lay down again and slept until dawn, the true dawn, before the sun had climbed high enough to clear the mountains.

Amadeo was stiff and tired. It was time for a little of the carrot I had planned. "We've come most of the way, and we're still on track. I figure we'll reach your place by noon," I said.

"There's no water there," he said feebly. "No food, nothing."

"Don't worry, there's half a million bucks, that'll buy you an ocean of beer and all the *pollo con arroz* you can put away."

"Beer, yeah. Chicken and rice, no. I want a big steak with four fried eggs on it. And lots of fried onions."

"No pasta?" I kidded. "No spaghetti marinara?"

"Steak," he said doggedly, as if I could come up with one if he fixed his mind on it.

"First we walk. Let's get started."

The stars had washed out of the sky by now, and I used the compass to lead us north-northeast over a dry arroyo and on over the hills. We stopped twice more to suck on slashed cactus. Amadeo was weaker now. If this had been a training march with a vehicle trailing us to pick him up and ship him out of the SAS selection course and back to his regular army unit, he would have given up, but there was nothing anywhere but dry country and the endlessly circling vultures overhead, and he knew what they were waiting for.

By ten-thirty I figured we were three miles south of the track. Two more hard hours would put us there, with perhaps an hour's easy walking after that. I called a halt and took out my canteen. It has a small cup-lid and I filled it and gave it to him. He took it like a sacrament, sipping slowly, rolling the water around his mouth and swallowing gratefully. He tipped the cup upside down on his mouth and tapped the bottom with his fingers, then handed it back to me. "Nothin' ever tasted better," he said.

130

"You can have another one next stop," I promised, and took my ration. Then I recorked the canteen, very firmly, and screwed the top back on. We rested for another five minutes, Amadeo sprawled flat on the ground. He was a mess, his chino pants torn from the brush we'd passed through, his T-shirt soaked through and black with fresh sweat. His lips were beginning to peel, and he touched them tenderly.

"If we see another cactus, we'll stop, okay?" he asked with his eyes closed.

"For sure. Never pass up a chance to drink."

He rolled up onto one elbow and looked at me. "You're a tough sonofabitch, ain'cha?"

"Trained is all," I said. "You could be the same if you worked at it, there's no trick, you're not born hard, you harden yourself."

He sat all the way up and hugged his knees. "I'm tryin'a think. I don' know anybody could've come all this way an' still look like he could do it again."

"The trick is to be ready to fight when we get there."

"You think we'll have to? Hell, no way I could."

"You could, and would, for your half million."

He thought about it silently, then nodded. "Yeah, I guess I would."

thirteen

We got up and marched on, over the highest mountain we had come to all the way. Amadeo flopped down on the crest and looked around. "Yeah, I remember this hill. The locals call it El Padre."

"And we're on course?"

"Yeah, you can see this from the track, if we keep on the way we're goin', I figure we'll cross the track about a mile east of the shack."

"Good, then let's have another drink and go on."

"What I need is food, my guts are hurtin', that's how hungry I am." He snarled it, angry that the world hadn't laid any breakfast on for him. I doubt if he had ever missed a meal before. I was hungry, too, but I'm used to it. Meals are a bonus in a soldier's routine on active service. Twenty-four hours without is a discomfort, that's all. I could have kept on for a day or so more without folding, but his resistance was dwindling. It was time to find food.

He took the water, and as he drank, I saw an iguana flit along the ground, a big one, eighteen inches long, weighing about two pounds. I flung my machete. It didn't snake out and cut the lizard's head off like it would have done in a movie, it spun

132

in the air and hit the iguana butt-first, not killing it but slowing it down, so I had a second to catch it by the tail and bang its head on a rock. "Breakfast," I said.

Amadeo looked at me in horror. "You kidding?"

I took out my clasp knife and gutted the lizard, stripping the bile from the liver and tossing it aside. "Want this?" I offered the liver to Amadeo, but he shuddered and shook his head. I gulped it down, and he turned and spat thinly onto the dry ground.

"Jesus Christ, now I seen everything."

"The meat's like chicken," I said, and quickly stripped off the scaly hide.

"I know that, the Indians sell 'em in the market, but shit, we got no place to cook it. We can't light a fire."

"No need. Cut it real thin and it goes down easy. Want some?"

He shook his head. "Okay, then you can have one more cup of water, I'll be getting some juice out of the meat."

He turned his head away while I ate, cutting the meat into slivers and swallowing it without too much chewing. I won't say it's tasty, but if you can handle sushi, you can manage.

The flies had already found the entrails, and the vultures were clustering again before I finished. I glanced up at them as I shut my knife and put it away. "We could do without those birds, they're a giveaway."

"We'll leave 'em behind when we move on." He was getting stronger again, proximity to his money pumping up his sense of importance. He stood up. "If you've finished makin' like a vulture, let's go."

Now he led, walking more quickly than he had all night, slashing at the brush impatiently until I caught up with him and spoke softly. "Listen, keep it quiet. If there's anyone up ahead, they'll hear you. We don't want that."

He nodded and moved more quietly, flanking the bushes wherever possible, cutting silently when he had to. I followed, cranking a round up the spout of the rifle and adding another

133

to the magazine. If García knew we needed a Jeep, he would have made an assessment of where we were going. He wouldn't need to know exactly, he could set men on each of the tracks within range of the town and wait for us. They would wait for weeks if necessary for a couple of dollars a day each, peanuts to a dope wholesaler.

At last Amadeo gave a triumphant little gasp. "Made it," he whispered.

I came up with him and looked. We had reached a track, formerly a road wide enough to accommodate a Jeep, now brushed in on both sides but still a highway in comparison to the route we had taken through the night.

"How far to your hiding place?"

He stopped and looked back at the mountain, locating himself. "A mile, maybe more."

"Okay, we'll walk the track part of the way. I'll go first. You keep on looking around and behind you, check there's nobody following us."

"You think they might?"

"If García wants your money badly enough, he'll have men on every Jeep track there is. Keep your eyes open."

I handed him my machete and slipped the safety off my rifle, then moved on cautiously, scanning every bush, every rock for signs of life. The trail twisted around obstacles, so there was never more than fifty yards' view ahead of me, but I watched the slopes on both sides, everywhere they might have posted a lookout.

Insects chirred in the heat, and a few birds clattered in the bushes, pecking at them, but there was nothing to indicate that anyone else was ahead of us, and I moved quietly on for almost a mile before stopping and signaling Amadeo to catch up.

He came up and crouched beside me, his face glistening with sweat but not streaming, not today; he was dehydrating. "How much farther now?" I asked him.

"Quarter mile should do it."

"Okay. It's time to get off the track. Try not to use your

134

machete. We'll work our way out a hundred yards, up the slope to the left here and stop when we can see the place. You go ahead."

He nodded without speaking and forced his way into the brush, swearing softly as it tore at him. He had given me my machete back, and I used it to move branches aside, not slashing them.

That last quarter mile took us almost an hour, but at last he stopped beside a big bare rock face and pointed down to his right. I caught up and looked. The skeleton of a shack was standing there with a roughly cleared patch of ground around it and a well sitting out in the yard.

"It's there," he said hoarsely.

"Right. You go ahead and pick up your money, and check that well, see if there's any water in it. I'll watch from closer in, but I'll keep under cover until we know it's clear."

He nodded and set off, moving faster than I would have done, slipping once and sending a small torrent of soil down the slope. I sighed. That was all the warning a Mexican would need, our caution had been wasted.

He made it to the edge of the clearing and went on into the yard, not stopping to look around. I followed and crouched at the edge, keeping out of sight and silent, waiting for someone to challenge him. The sun was directly overhead, resting its weight on us like molten brass, shrinking Amadeo's shadow to a puddle around his feet as he walked boldly up to the house and glanced inside. Then he turned and stood with his back to the doorway and paced out twenty steps from it, then turned and paced another ten away from me, almost out of my line of sight. He crouched there and began to hack at the soil with his machete, chopping and prying, the blade chinking on the hard ground.

He dug for five minutes, then lifted his machete triumphantly in his right hand and began to dig more carefully, scraping around what he had found. I backed away from my hiding place and moved down to my right, where I could hide again but with a good view of what he was doing. I saw him set the machete down and reach into the hole, coming up with an aluminum briefcase, which he set on the ground and unlocked.

I was watching everything around us, seeing nothing but the abandoned banana trees and the brush. But I felt uneasy. There was someone here. I could sense it.

I watched Amadeo toss his machete aside and open the briefcase, brushing impatiently at the lock, then snapping it open with his thumb and flipping up the lid. He knelt there, looking into it like a child with a beautiful storybook. And then a rifle cracked, and a bullet ricocheted off the hard ground in front of him and skipped up over my head.

It had come from the hillside, an area I had scanned fifty times without seeing anything. I held my fire, waiting for the man to shoot again, but Amadeo bolted down the trail as if it led to safety and not an ambush, as I was sure it did.

I swore but waited. He would stay on the trail and I would find him, but if I came out now, I would be dead. And then, after a thirty-second wait, I saw a movement high up in the rocks opposite and recognized a straw hat among the boulders. It was two hundred yards out, beyond the calibrated range of Amadeo's little rifle, out where I would have to guess at the bullet drop, aiming high and hoping for a hit. Besides, the hat might be a decoy, a test to check if Amadeo was alone.

After another minute a man stood up, and then another, and they ran across the slope, which was almost bare on that side on the trail, the remnants of burned-off fields that had grown corn for a year or two and been abandoned when the lateritic soil baked itself hard. They ran parallel to the trail, and when I was sure they had not seen me, I slipped out of cover and ran softly down the trail after Amadeo.

He had cleared the first hundred and fifty yards, but then I slowed. This was the dangerous part. We had turned off the trail a quarter mile from the shack. The ambush must have been waiting after that, somewhere close to where I was now. I pushed into the brush on the opposite side of the track from where the men had been and made the best time I could, listening for sounds of activity.

I found them, around the next corner. I could hear Amadeo blustering in Spanish, and then the sound of a slap. It was still beyond me, and I came closer to the trail, hoping he would keep his mouth shut about my being there. If they thought he was alone, I had a chance to get him back. If they expected me, we were both dead men.

I crept down through the edges of a bush, glancing around behind me but seeing nobody. The voices were louder now, two other men and Amadeo, his voice pleading, theirs curt and contemptuous.

The .45 was in my belt, ready, cocked. I took out the little .38 and stuffed it into my right sock. I was as ready as I could be.

I inched out onto the trail and rounded the corner of a tree and saw him kneeling on the ground, his hands on his head, pleading in Spanish. The two men were standing over him, one of them holding the briefcase, the other leveling a pistol at Amadeo's face. I saw his thumb move, pulling back the hammer, and I shot him through the right ear.

He fell on top of Amadeo, and the other man froze in alarm, his own pistol pointing vaguely toward me. I shot him in the chest, twice, and he fell, clawing at his heart. Amadeo got to his feet and grabbed the briefcase, then came pounding toward me shouting, "Thank you. Thank you."

I put an urgent finger to my lips and he shut up, but kept running. I grabbed him and he started to speak, but I dragged him off the trail and into the bush beside the trail, "There's two more of them. Shut up," I hissed.

He was almost blubbering with relief, but he sank down to the ground and lay there while I waited, listening to every sound. If the other men were good, they would come quietly, I had to expect an attack. While I waited, I refilled the three-shot magazine. Amadeo watched me, licking his dry lips. "Give me a gun," he whispered, but I shook my head. Guns are for experts. In his hands they would be a liability.

It took three long minutes before the other men emerged onto the trail. Only one of them had a rifle. It was old, all the blue worn from the barrel, and I doubted if it was accurate, or he would have killed Amadeo with his first shot. But he held it at the ready position, across the body, the butt raised to his armpit, braced to swing up the muzzle and sight a shot, not just blaze away. He stood, looking around alertly while the other one checked the two dead men. I waited. This was Amadeo's fight. If they attacked us, I would shoot, but I wasn't about to murder them just to clear us a path to the highway.

Amadeo whispered, almost soundlessly. "Plug the guy with the gun," and I shook my head. "They tried to kill me, fer Crissakes. Waste 'em."

I shook my head again and he hissed, "What in hell are you waiting for?"

This time he was too loud. Maybe it was on purpose. I didn't have time to discuss it. The rifleman turned suspiciously and moved along the trail toward us, his finger on his trigger. I could see the rifle was an old bolt-action Remington, probably a 306, a hunter's gun. That meant he was a hunter, which meant he would be good at this range.

Behind him the other man had gathered up both pistols and was moving toward us, checking all around him as he came. He didn't worry me. He was still forty yards away, and pistols are chancy. I was wrestling with the choice of shooting the man with the rifle while I had the drop on him or warning him first. As a soldier, I would have fired. As a bodyguard for a dope-smuggler, I was faced with ethical problems. Then Amadeo shifted his position and the sun caught the corner of his brief-case, and the hunter fired, drilling a shot right through the sparkle.

I fired in the same instant, hitting him in the forehead, so his sombrero flew up and away as he toppled, dropping the gun.

The man behind him fired wildly, blazing from both hands. I took aim and shot him through the right arm, above the elbow. He screamed and dropped his guns, grabbing his shattered arm. Amadeo came off the ground in a run, grabbing the fallen rifle and pumping shot after shot at the wounded man, hitting all around him until I sprang out of cover and clobbered him with the butt of my own rifle. He fell, sobbing with frustration. "Lemme get him."

"Leave him alone." I bent and picked up the rifle and cranked out the last couple of rounds, catching them and slipping them into my pocket. "Let's see to him. He's hurt."

I advanced on the injured man, who was lying in the dust of the trail, writhing with pain. The pistols lay beside him and I picked them up, slipped out the magazine from the automatic and then threw it and the revolver away, high into the bushes where it would take an hour to find them.

Amadeo caught up with me, clutching the back of his neck, swearing in Spanish. His foot swung back to kick the man on the ground, but I shoved him off balance and he fell, spitting, helplessly angry.

I stooped to the wounded man and took his hand away from the blood that was seeping through his fingers. He fell suddenly still, staring at me out of frightened eyes, like a steer in a slaughterhouse.

I dumped my pack and took out the first-aid kit, pulling out the bottle of Dettol and a gauze pad. His shirt sleeve was torn by the bullet, and I ripped it away, exposing the wound. The bullet was still inside, flattened against the broken bone that deformed the back of his tricep. I slapped on the Dettol, holding him as he squirmed against the pain, then put the gauze pad over it and wrapped a bandage around it. Blood seeped out into the dressing but it didn't escape, just stained the bandage and stopped. Then I took out the triangular bandage and put it over his head, tucking it around his arm and making a sling. He stared at me, baffled.

"*Tienes agua?*" Do you have water? I asked him.

He nodded and pointed up behind me into the hillside. He spoke then in a rush of Spanish that Amadeo interpreted for me.

"They've got a can of it, back on the hill where he was waiting."

"Good, let's get it. We all need water. Tell him to take us there."

Amadeo spoke to him, hissing savagely, and the man got to his feet and walked back along the trail, stopping to look down at the dead men. "Ask him if there's anybody else. Tell him if there is and they jump us, I shoot him first, then them," I instructed.

Amadeo told him, and he shook his head and spoke rapidly. I made out the word "*todos*," everybody. "He says this is all of them."

"Good." I reloaded the .22, and when I got to the hunter's gun, I threw that up into the bushes. Our prisoner looked after it, licking his lips, wanting to speak but afraid. I knew he would be out here again as soon as he could, finding all three guns. For now he was grateful to be alive. He would try nothing.

His water supply was in a jerrican. There was most of two gallons left. I let him drink first, knowing the local water wouldn't harm him, while I drank what was left in my canteen, very little. Amadeo stood looking on, swallowing noisily as we drank. I took out another purification tablet and shook it up with a canteen of water and handed it to Amadeo. "Drink all of it."

He did, gulping it down like a university student at his first beer-drinking boat race. He didn't lower the canteen even once until it was empty. Then I filled it again and did the same. It was the temperature of bathwater and tasted of gasoline, but it went down like champagne. Afterward I filled the canteen a third time and purified it, then put it back into my pack. We were set to travel.

"I think we should walk to the road and wait for nightfall," I said.

Amadeo asked, "What about him?"

140

"We'll take him with us for the first couple of miles, that way he can't find the guns and backshoot us."

"We should've wasted him," he said angrily.

"Ask him how he knew where to wait for us."

He spoke to the man, who answered almost before he had finished.

"What's he saying?"

"He says that García sent men out to all the trails where you would need a Jeep. This one he sent four men to because the guy who used to live here was a cousin of my contact on the beach. He figured it was the best spot to look."

"That means he could be coming out here himself to check on them. How did they get here, were they dropped off?"

He asked again, and the man nodded as he answered. Amadeo said, "Yeah, they came out yesterday, after we left the hotel. They had a man watching the place. When we left, García shipped them out here. The Jeep's coming back for them tonight. I guess they figured we'd be here by then if we were coming."

"Don't guess, ask him."

He spoke again, and after a long exchange Amadeo said. "Yeah. They figured we would come by cab to the trail and walk in. His buddies were waiting for us on the trail." His face dropped. "Shit, it's a wonder we didn't walk right into 'em." He looked at me with new respect. "You knew they'd be waitin', didn't you?"

"Fortune favors the prepared mind." Louis Pasteur said it first, and it was the motto of Alexander Fleming, the guy who discovered penicillin, and I believe it implicitly, but it skipped over Amadeo's head like the ricochet in the clearing.

"Let's go," he said.

"First we pull these corpses off the trail. The vultures will be on them in an hour, but the skeletons will hang around forever. We don't want García to tip off the cops if he finds them."

Amadeo swore, but he saw the sense of it. We all three of us carried the bodies through the bushes where they wouldn't be obvious from the track. I made our prisoner help, just to keep an eye on him. It also made him extra respectful.

Amadeo didn't pray this time. As soon as we were finished, he set off down the trail faster than he had walked since I met him. The wounded man came next, stumbling with pain and shock, but carrying the can of water and keeping up. When we had covered a couple of miles, I told him, *"Alto,"* and he stopped.

"Quédate aquí." Stay here, I told him, and he nodded and sank gratefully to his knees.

Amadeo came back down the trail, blazing with anger. "What's with him? Let's go."

"He can stay here—we'll travel faster without him."

"An' what about when García comes out to pick him up? He'll spill his guts, an' García will have the police lookin' for us."

I had an answer for that one, I'd been making my plan ever since we set out. "Give me a thousand bucks," I told Amadeo.

He tightened his grip on the briefcase. "For this scum? You think that'll work? He'll take my money an' screw us. Kill the bastard. You should've done it right off."

"Give me a thousand-dollar-bill before I get impatient," I said, and he knelt and opened his briefcase, keeping the contents out of the prisoner's sight, glaring at me as he did so.

He handed me the bill. "Hiring you was the biggest mistake I ever made. You're a goddamn wimp."

"Yeah, that's why you're dead on the trail back there with the vultures pecking your eyes out," I said. It was time for more stick and less carrot. He was getting uppity, now he had his money.

The prisoner was watching the bill like a kid at his first magic show. I tore it in half, jaggedly, and handed him one piece. He glanced at my face, convinced now that I was the neighborhood conjurer. Then he took the bill, carefully, as if it might burn him.

"Now tell him he gets the other half on Sunday morning. If

142

he keeps his mouth shut until then," I told Amadeo, smiling at the prisoner as if he were my favorite nephew.

"You think that's gonna stop him talking?" Amadeo was spluttering with rage, but I just turned and smiled at him, and he rattled at the prisoner. I could make out the word *domingo,* Sunday. That was fine.

The prisoner nodded, bobbing his head excitedly. For a whole grand he would have let me take his arm off. It was a year's pay for the kind of sleaze work he was doing for García. Hell, he could buy a farm and work himself to death an honest man.

Amadeo paused for a moment to shake his finger at the guy and hiss a last warning, then he turned and stomped off down the trail, his half-million bucks pulling down his left arm as he carried it inside the beach basket he had picked up again at the shack. Except for the tears in his pants, he looked like every other gringo tourist. I winked at the Mexican, who smiled ingratiatingly, showing a mouthful of good white teeth. Then I started after Amadeo.

He soon slackened speed. I caught up with him, and he started snarling again about how hungry he was. He also demanded water, but I didn't give him any. What we had was insurance. If we ran into another ambush, we might have to take to the hills again, and a quart of water would be worth more than all the paper he had in his basket. That was one of the things he swore about.

"That sonofabitch put a bullet through about fifty grand. It's torn all up, hell of a mess."

"It could have been your head," I reminded him, still watching the trail ahead. I didn't expect any more trouble. Our prisoner would have told us. He wanted to collect the other half of his hush money. And besides, even García would run out of help if he struck a couple of ambushes on every trail.

We stopped for half an hour in the shade of one of those huge gray-barked trees that look like monster beeches. It had no leaves, but the trunk was six feet through, and there was a block of shade to the north side of it. Amadeo even loosened up to the point where he lit up a cigarette, breaking the match carefully and burying it in the dust of the trail.

"Can you get in touch with Maria? Or will we have to keep our date with her on the boat?" I asked him. Color me true-blue. I'd been hired to help him find his cash, pay his wife, and leave. So far we'd done the first part.

"We'll have to meet her. She's got the boat for three days this time. I told her to keep looking for us, every night at dusk. We see her, we can head home back to TO."

He tried to make his voice businesslike. Carry out the mission, then home. But I didn't believe him. Half a million bucks isn't big money in drug-dealing terms, but it does buy you a couple of kilos of coke and the use of somebody's light airplane. Starting from here, Amadeo could be big-time within six months if he didn't still have the embarrassing business of squealing on his Canadian buddies to go through. I knew he was planning to dump me and take off. I wondered how he would do it. He'd tried running away, and that hadn't worked. I figured that this time he would try to kill me. My assignment was entering its most dangerous phase.

fourteen

We reached the highway at five o'clock. We had drunk nothing since our quart of water at midday, and Amadeo was clicking my button between his teeth again. He hadn't spoken to me in a couple of hours, but when he heard the rush of cars passing on the highway, he turned and said, "Nearly there. Now what?"

"First, we make sure there's not a Jeepful of García's gunnies waiting for us. Then we hitch back into town and get in touch with Maria."

"Who in hell's gonna stop for us? Look at us," he said impatiently.

"Some good-natured gringo. Which is why I want you to stay back in the bush while I do the thumbing. I look safer to pick up than you."

"What're you sayin'?"

"With that hat and a day's worth of whiskers, you look like a bandido. You step out, and most guys would automatically put their foot down on the gas."

He swore but didn't argue, and when we could see the highway and be sure there was no welcoming party from García waiting for us, I tossed the rifle into the bushes. It had been a

145

lifesaver, but it would be hard to disguise. Then I divided our water between us. Amadeo drank his share and sank down, hugging his money to his chest, and I walked out onto the shoulder of the road. It's my experience that people don't mind picking up bona fide travelers, so I put my pack at my feet, fixed a big dumb grin on my face, and stuck my thumb out. A couple of cars passed, locals who didn't figure a gringo was worth saving from the late-afternoon heat. Then a big van with Arizona plates pulled up in a squeak of dry brakes, and the door swung open.

I bounded over, stretching my grin even wider. "Thanks a million. We're going to Zihua, and my buddy hurt his ankle, do you mind taking him as well?"

The driver was a lean man in his sixties, wearing steel-rimmed glasses and a baseball cap with "Wilson Feeds" on the front. He nodded. "He American?"

"Canadian. He's a nice guy. Thanks, just be a minute."

I left my bag on the seat of the van and trotted over to Amadeo. "You've got a bad ankle, limp over to the van, all right?"

He nodded and straightened up, favoring his right leg and resting his right arm on my shoulder. In fact, he was so convincing that the driver of the van said, "Hell, that looks sore. Want some ice on it?"

"Just to get the weight off it is fine, thank you," he said. "I'm gonna get a whole glassful of ice with my first margarita when we get into town."

We climbed between the front seats and sat down on the bench behind the passenger seat. I dropped my pack beside him and sat up next to the driver. "We had this crazy idea of going bird-watching. Seemed good at the time. Then Greg twisted his ankle," I embroidered.

The old guy looked at me shrewdly, then flicked his gaze ahead again to the road leading downhill in front of us. "See many?"

"Nothing unusual. Some warblers and doves, vultures, of

146

course, grackles. But once Gimpy here started hurting we both lost interest."

"Could've seen a manakin. That's the long-tailed, of course," he said. "You a real birder?"

I shook my head. "Naah. Just got bored with beach life. I mean, how long can you sit on a beach looking at rosy-breasted pushovers? Especially when they're all teamed up already."

He laughed at that one, the dry creaky laugh of a man who doesn't use it very much. "Rosy-breasted pushovers. Haven't heard that one in a coon's age."

"You a birder?" I just wanted him launched on a monologue, it would make the journey simpler.

"A hobbyist," he said, with the quiet pride of a man who knew every bird that ever flew. "I generally come down here in the winter. It's best along the tidal flats, all kinds of action there."

From that he went on to talk about his life list and his disappointment at never having seen a nightingale. "Oh, I heard plenny of 'em, in Britain, waiting for D day. Then in Normandy. They sing at night, you know. Most beautiful song ever you heard."

"I take it you were in Berkeley Square," I said, grinning to show I was only kidding.

"Not a damn sound there, except for German bombs dropping. Mind, it was a hell of a town for women. Even though there was thousands of us, hundreds of thousands, every GI seemed to end up with a girl." He sighed. "I married mine. Lost her last fall. Cancer. Just when we were set to do some serious traveling."

"I'm sorry," I said. Everybody has a story, it's a pity that so many of them have downbeat endings.

He was immediately embarrassed at showing his grief, and he chatted about birds all the way down. It took only twenty minutes instead of the twenty-four hours we had spent walking the same distance. When we reached the town monument, he

147

grinned. "Second year that thing's been broken. Any luck at all, they'll take it down." He spat out of the window and went on. "I'm turning here, heading for a place with a wall around it where the van'll be safe. El Paraíso. You know it?"

"Yeah," Amadeo said. "We took a couple broads there last night." Classy or not?

"Should've left one of them for me," he said. "Anyways, y'all mind getting out here? You can get a cab."

"That's fine, thanks. Can we buy you a beer first?"

He shook his head. "Naah. It's been a long day. Came all the way down from Puerto Vallarta without stopping. I'm due for supper."

We thanked him again, and he nodded without speaking as we got out, then drove away without looking back.

"Old goat's likely lookin' to get laid." Amadeo grinned. He had a child's inability to keep anything in mind. His own problems were forgotten now. The dead men on the trail were history. He was amused at the passing scene.

"He's probably had a bad couple of years, watching his wife die," I said. "I hope he finds himself a nice bird-watching widow."

Amadeo sneered. "Miss Lonely-fuckin'-hearts."

I checked my watch. Five-thirty. Dusk was an hour and a half away, and García was still looking for us. "I don't think it's smart to go back to the hotel. It's a sure bet that García's watching it. Let's duck in somewhere for a meal and a beer, then head down to the boat."

He nodded. "Makes sense."

We started walking, drawing odd glances from the locals who were used to seeing gringos in smart new summer wear, shaved up and ready for romance. We looked like a couple of apprentice forty-niners.

I kept up a constant watch for anyone trailing us. Amadeo didn't. He stumped along as if he didn't have a fortune in his hands and a vengeful drug boss looking for him. Ego, I guess. You drop it very quickly in enemy territory, but he didn't know the rules. I hoped that García wouldn't demonstrate them for him.

148

We came into the center of town, and I stopped and bought us a couple of fresh T-shirts. It didn't compensate for the lack of shaves and showers, but at least we were clean enough to go into a decent restaurant without questions.

We chose a good place, not Coconuts, but upscale enough that the waiter took one look at us and stuck us in a corner behind a potted plant. He wrinkled his nose, too. Mexicans are scrupulously clean, and we sure didn't match that description. Amadeo figured the water would be safe, and he drank a couple of jugs of it. I didn't. Montezuma's Revenge was the last thing I needed while I was watching both our backs. Cramps are more debilitating than most wounds. I ordered a couple of cervezas with Piñafiels and mixed some shandies. They both went down well, and I ordered another with our meal, *huachinango*. The fish was excellent, bigger and better than anything I'd seen at the hotel.

As we were sitting there, a group of musicians came in, looking apologetic about their costumes, flamboyant national dress. But that wasn't the reason I watched them as they circled the tables, asking all couples if they had requests. I was interested only in the lead guitarist. It was my contact, Jesús, staying under cover.

I was glad to see him. I knew he wouldn't be able to cover me through the next couple of days, but this was a lonely job, and I wanted somebody to know where I'd gone, in case Cahill had to send somebody in to find me.

Jesús had chosen a good cover, I thought. He would be free most of the day and all night. And when he worked, he was circulating through all of the bars in town, keeping an eye on comings and goings. And it gave him a legitimate source of income, so he would never look suspicious to the Garcías of the world, who probably knew the business of everybody in town.

While they were keening some Neapolitan love song for a couple of honeymooners with a poorly developed sense of geography, I borrowed a pen from Amadeo and scribbled the word "boat" on the corner of a thousand-peso bill. Amadeo was too busy with his fish to ask questions, but when I wrapped it up and beckoned to the group, he spluttered, "What's with you? They're playin' for couples, fer Crissakes. You gay or what?"

"A lifelong music lover," I said. The group came over, and I passed the bill to Jesus and told him " 'Guantanemero,' *por favor, amigo.*"

He frowned at me and said, "I am sorry, *señor.* I do not know this song. I have a writing with our songs."

His accent was thick today, part of his camouflage, I supposed, and I took the hint from his eyes and looked at the list he showed me. He held his thumb at the bottom of it, and written in pencil I read: "García is looking for you. Hide."

I looked up at him. "You sure you don't know 'Guantanemero'? It goes like this," and I hummed the refrain. He allowed himself an oily grin. "Oh, *sí.* We know this one. How you write it?"

"Here." I wrote the word on his list, adding "30-foot catboat, *Juanita.* Maria."

He read it and beamed again. *"Muchas gracias, señor."* Then he tuned a string, and they all warbled into the song.

I sat and watched them and listened until they had finished, then applauded politely. Amadeo grimly concentrated on his dinner. When they had gone, he hissed at me, "I feel like a goddamn fairy, sittin' here with you serenadin' me."

"Roll with it. You just learned how to charm some sunstruck tourist lady. Could be useful when you take up your new career as a gigolo." He just swore and went on eating.

By the time we finished dinner, it was dropping dark. The streets weren't well lit, so we were inconspicuous in the gloom as we walked down to the waterfront. We came out opposite the outdoor basketball court, where two teams of girls were playing, to the delight of the silent crowd of mainly young local men sitting on the stone surrounds. It's a very formal country, and the men don't see a lot of native skin, On *turistas,* yes, but not their own women. Those flashing fifteen-year-old thighs were enough to start a sexual revolution.

We walked north on the beach for another hundred yards, past the back of the coast guard barracks, and then ducked out to the street and onto the pier. The music boat was just docking, winding up its gig with a bravura version of "We'll Meet Again," with all the trumpets competing for lead. Vera Lynn would have spun in her groove. A slow tide of revelers was coming against us down the length of the pier, middle-aged couples, some of them holding hands under the spell of the music and margaritas. A few locals were standing around, glancing at everyone who passed. They could have been boat owners looking for custom, or equally, García's foot soldiers, looking for us. Amadeo strolled, seeming casual but glancing around for Maria. In that environment, close to the boats, our day-old whiskers and torn clothes didn't seem out of place. We might have been fishermen or yachtsmen in from a carefree cruise.

"She ain' here," Amadeo said at last.

"Can you recognize the boat? Maybe she's just standing off, waiting for you to come aboard under your own steam."

He gazed out over the harbor, shading his eyes from the town lights. "Looks like there. That's the right kind of boat, an' that's one o' the permanent places to tie up."

He pointed out to a catboat, with its characteristic single mast and aluminum curved boom, like a closed bracket. In the dim light it looked right to me.

"So let's grab a dinghy and go aboard. We can't hang around here trying to second-guess Maria." I was anxious to get him out on the water, where his range of possible tricks would be diminished and where intruders couldn't creep up on us.

"Right." He turned away, and I followed as he went to the first set of steps that led down to the water. There was a small boat there, a rough old wooden craft with a good outboard. The owner was a middle-aged guy, sitting in the stern. Amadeo spoke to him briefly, then said, "He'll take us out, come on."

I checked around. Nobody was paying us any attention, so I stepped down and sat just forward of the boat owner, where I could jump him if he pulled a weapon, before he had time to use it.

He cast us off and started the motor. He had it tuned well and it caught first pop, and we chugged out between the other moored boats, many of them with parties of gringos aboard, laughing and drinking and listening to music. Relax, Locke. This is a vacation paradise, remember.

The boat we were making for was out past the others, about three hundred yards from the pier, perhaps twice that from the town beach. Our boatman asked Amadeo a question, and he nodded and pointed to the port side. The boatman nodded back and slowed the motor, curving in so he came up to the port side from the stern. Amadeo gave him some cash and then, as we approached, stood up to jump aboard. I thought he might have bribed the boatman to take me off before I could follow him so I got up behind him and was one second after him onto the deck of the *Juanita,* dropping my pack beside the basket he had set down and drawing El Grande's pistol from my belt.

There were no lights aboard, and we stood for a moment on the deck, adjusting our eyes to the shadow of the companion-way down to the accommodation. Amadeo said, "I hope that dumb bitch ain' up on shore somewhere, waitin'."

Around me I could hear the faint overlapping beat of the music from the other boats and an occasional squeal from the basketball players on the waterfront. There were no sounds aboard but our own breathing. But I still didn't relax. Amadeo moved to the head of the companionway and called, "Maria?" softly. We had swung slightly as the other boat sheered away, so that the moonlight was splashing down the steps and I could see that the doorway was still broken, the way I left it. And then, back from it, about one pace in, I made out the shape of a crouching figure, with a pistol pointed at Amadeo.

I shoved him sprawling as a bullet flew through the space his chest had been occupying a second before. Then I fired into the center of the muzzle flash that still glowed in my after-vision, the sound of the .45 filling the whole bay. There was the clatter of a falling gun and a rushing thud as the figure collapsed backward out of out sight.

Amadeo scrambled to his feet. "Jesus Christ."

"Keep down. There may be another one."

He dropped flat and whispered from there. "What're we gonna do?"

I held one finger to my lips and picked up my pack and tiptoed to the bow. The boat was heavy enough that my movement didn't register below decks. I stopped beside the forward ventilator, a plastic hatch, hinged upward from below. I knew it served the forward cabin where I had confronted Maria my first time aboard. I felt into the side pocket of the pack and came up with my map of the district. Not much, but it would have to do. I turned away from the hatch, concealing the flare as I struck a match, and lit one corner of the map, which I had formed into a torch. Then I shoved it through the hatch and listened as it fell.

Bingo! A woman screamed and a man swore. I pounded back along the deck and vaulted into the cabin, half stumbling over the body of the man I'd shot but hitting the inner cabin door with the full weight of my straight leg, sending it crashing inward. I was fast, but not fast enough. The man inside had Maria by the hair, and his gun was jammed against her head. He had a revolver, and the hammer was back. All it would take was two pounds' pressure on the trigger and she was gone.

The paper flare on the bed was burning down and as I leveled my gun at the man's face, I recognized him. El Grande. Then, as the last of the paper burned and the flare died away, the lights clicked on, and I flicked a glance back to see Amadeo at the cabin door with a grin on his face and the dead man's pistol in his hands, pointed at me.

I dropped to one knee, but he didn't flinch. "Don' try nothin'. You can't kill me, or I won' be able to sing my song, will I?"

He was right, but I didn't drop my gun. "I'll kneecap you," I said. "You can still testify from a wheelchair." He was holding a

153

revolver. The hammer was down, and I had a second to fire before he could cock it, even on double action. But he wasn't trying to. He spoke rapidly in Spanish, and the other man said something short. Then Amadeo said, "If you look up, you'll see that the *señor* has his gun on you. That's two of us. Either way you're dead if you don' do like I say."

The Mexicans invented the standoff and that's what we had here. I could get one of them. The other would get me. From four feet away neither one of them would miss. Amadeo said, "Put the gun down nice 'n' easy an' you live. Try anythin' an' you're dead meat."

Slowly I laid the gun on the deck and stood up. If they got sloppy now, I would win. Under the old rules there would be two corpses in the cabin. Mine and one other, possibly the woman's. This way I was still alive, and given any kind of break, I could think of something brilliant and noninjurious to my health.

El Grande said something and Amadeo translated. "Lie down on the floor, your hands behind you."

I did it, still watching for the chance at a leg sweep if one of them took his eyes off me for a moment. But they didn't. All that happened was that El Grande let go of Maria and shoved her. She chattered at him fearfully and Amadeo chimed in. Then she stepped past me into the cabin and came back with a piece of rope. Both the guns were still pointed at me. El Grande directed her as she tied my hands behind my back, kneeling on the base of my spine as she did it. She pulled the ropes as tight as she could but not as tight as the men would have got them.

Then El Grande told her something else, too fast for my meager Spanish to understand, and she left the cabin. A moment later I felt the motor start up, then the rustle of the anchor cable coming in. Now I knew what they had in mind. They were going to take me out to sea and drop me overboard, probably after I'd taken a bad beating, or worse. Not nice.

El Grande lit a cigar and dropped the lighted match on my hands. I shucked it off, and he laughed. Then he said something else to Amadeo, who left, heading up to the deck. I had a chance now, not much of one but a chance, if El Grande tried to kick me. But he didn't. He sat down on the bunk, his gun loosely pointed at me, and enjoyed his cigar for about five minutes. I didn't try anything. I lay there like a bundle of laundry and waited for him to make his first mistake.

After a while longer Amadeo came back into the cabin. Neither one of them said anything, but they lifted me up, levering my arms up so I couldn't struggle, and steered me through the door and out to the companionway at the back. Then Amadeo said, "We don' wanna get blood on the deck in there. Out here we can wash it off with a pail o' water."

"I like tidy guests," I said. They still had me too tightly for me to do anything, but if they were taking me to the foredeck, we would have to walk in single file. Unless one of them walked ahead of me, I could make my move then.

They didn't think it through. El Grande got impatient and put his pistol in his pocket so he could grab my arms and force me forward, levering my arms up behind my back. As I stepped up onto the walkway around the little deck, I could see that Amadeo still had his own pistol pointed at me.

"Don't do it, Greg. We can get clean away. You can keep your money," I said, but he ignored me. El Grande pushed me on until I was forward of the raised roof of the main cabin, then shoved me down. I rolled as I fell and came up on my feet. He had his mouth open to swear, and I kicked him, putting all my strength in it, up under the chin, snapping his jaw and probably his neck. He fell backward in a rush, like a sack of potatoes coming untied, and from six feet away Amadeo fired, but the other man had knocked him off balance as he fell, and he missed me by a foot. I didn't wait for him to take another shot. I dived overboard and pulled myself down into the dark water, as deep as I could.

fifteen

Amadeo's yell of surprise was cut off as if a door had slammed, and I was in a void, hearing only the shrilling of the inboard motor and the rush of air escaping from my clothes as I sank. Being down under the water like that, in total darkness, is as close to a phobia as I've got. Agility and speed mean nothing there. You don't know which way is up. You just have to hold your breath and wait for your body to bob vertical as your feet draw you down and the air in your lungs lifts your chest. Then you can kick, knowing you're going to come out in the air on top instead of down on the seabed. I had grabbed a big gulp of air as I jumped, enough for maybe a minute under water, but it seemed like an hour before my body drifted upright. Then I kicked hard. The motor noise had receded a little so I guessed the boat had pulled ahead of me. If it hadn't and I came up into the propeller, it was game, set, and match to Amadeo.

I broke the surface, facing the mountains, rounded and fuzzy with trees, lit by the low moon. They looked a hell of a long way away. Behind me I heard the low purr of the motor and Amadeo's voice as he swore at Maria. It was difficult to turn with my arms behind me, but I kicked around and saw the running lights of the boat, only fifty feet from me. I concentrated on overbreathing as the boat turned to port and came around in a curve that would take it between me and the shore. I could see someone standing on the pulpit that jutted out from the bow of the boat. Amadeo, I expected, armed with both the pistols on board, looking to tie up all the loose ends with a bullet in my head. I took a last deep breath and let myself sink, making sure to stay vertical, hoping he didn't have a floodlight on board. The water is vividly clear this far out from the roiling of the beach.

I was less panicky this time, working on priorities. I couldn't swim ashore in shoes, with my arms behind me and a gun in my right sock. But I didn't want to lose shoes or gun. I had to get my arms in front of me. On land that wouldn't have been a problem. I skip a lot of rope in winter when the roads are too icy to run, doing it boxer fashion, in three-minute rounds, with the last thirty seconds spent jumping my knees up to my chest. All I had to do was retract my legs that high and pass my arms under my buttocks. Like I say, easy on shore, if you're limber. But in the dark water it meant sacrificing my buoyancy, letting myself slide deeper and deeper. And if my wrists locked under my upraised feet I couldn't swim. I would never come up again.

It took me no longer than the entire pre-Cambrian era. For centuries, it seemed, the note of the motor grew fainter as I sank and struggled. Then my ears started to pain me as I passed the equal pressure zone and I had to gamble, exhaling slowly to lower the pressure in my system while I heaved the rope on my wrists over the heels of my Nikes. And then suddenly it was clear. I clawed my tied arms upward and kicked like a madman, pushing up with the last of my strength until I popped through the skin of the sea into the moonlight and the blessed air.

The boat had passed in front of me and was circling back. Amadeo was calling out instructions to Maria, who was at the helm, but he didn't sound as if he'd heard me surfacing, there was frustration in his voice. I trod water and watched the boat

157

as I sucked in air and bit at the knots on my wrists. They were on the undersides of my hands, the top when I had been lying with my hands behind me, and I had to screw my neck around like a bird to get at them, but I was just able to reach, and I worked at loosening them with my teeth.

It took me five long minutes, while the boat circled twice more, forcing me to sink out of sight again as it approached me, bow on. I was tiring, but finally I pulled the last knot loose and unwound the rope. I reached down then and pulled off my running shoes and socks, keeping the gun inside the right one. Then, as I struggled out of my jacket, I saw the boat sheer away and head southwest. He was free. And if Maria had done what she'd promised, they had enough provisions on board to sail all the way to Colombia if they chose. He could start all over in the drug business.

I swore, then concentrated on saving myself. I wrapped shoes and gun into my jacket, which I zipped up and tied with the sleeves and the rope that had tied my hands. Then I made a check of direction to the closest land, related it to a star behind me, and started backstroking slowly toward the shore.

Swimming is hypnotic. Themes come into your mind and stay there as if you were in a trance. I found myself oblivious of where I was, listening to the long-ago chant of the Royal Marine sergeant who had given me and my fellow SAS recruits our distance-swimming lessons. He had gone ahead of us in a power boat, ostentatiously taking it easy while he harangued us nonstop as we swam across the coldest bloody loch in the whole of Scotland. And when we reached the shore, proud of ourselves, he had formed us into two ranks and doubled us eleven miles in our wet clothes and boots before he let us stop for a breath. Tonight I could remember every word he had bellowed from the boat. They hadn't been clever, only infuriating, giving extra strength to every stroke we took. "What a bunch of pansies. Christ! A Marine could swim this piddling little pond with an anchor under his arm. Call yourself swimmers? Bunch of bloody ponces, the lot of you." Then in an aside to his companion, "Yes, please, Corporal, I will have another cup of tea."

That last sentence became my mantra. I couldn't get it out of my mind. I stroked on "yes" and "will" and "tea," lifting my weary arms back and kicking each time I said them. I had the sleeve of my jacket between my teeth, the weight of shoes and gun resting on my chest, as I sucked in air on every stroke, ignoring the lead that was creeping into my arms and legs, concentrating on the words and on the star behind me until suddenly I heard the rushing fall of surf, and I knew I could make it.

I was lucky. There are only a few places in and around Zihuatanejo Bay where the rocks reach right down to the shore, and only one coral reef, at La Playa Las Gatas, Cat Beach, and I missed all of them, coming ashore on a narrow sand beach on the headland at the south end of the bay. The full force of the open ocean spends itself in the surf out there and the six-foot wave spun me head over heels as I came out of the water, knocking me down with the force of a concrete wall falling on me.

I stumbled out of the water and collapsed on the sand just above the waterline. Slowly my strength came back. The air was warm, still in the high seventies, so I didn't chill, but I was as close to exhaustion as I've ever been. The long march over the mountains had been a strain, and now the fight and the long swim had spent any nickels and dimes of vigor I had left in my bank. I was flattened, but I was angry at myself, playing back my last moment on the boat. Could I have taken Amadeo? Could I have hopped over El Grande's body and kicked him senseless? And if I had, would Maria not have picked up his gun and shot me? Who could tell? I'd given the assignment everything I had short of my life, and I had lost Amadeo. I didn't relish breaking the news to Cahill, even though he had told me to bail out if things got too hairy.

I must have dozed, but I woke with a start when the incoming tide slapped itself over my bare feet, and I started up and

159

ran back a couple of paces, reacting automatically. I found I was stiff but after a half minute of stretching I was back to almost normal, and I put my shoes and wet socks on, tucking the .38 into my waistband, then pulling on my damp jacket and walking along the narrow beach around the edge of the bay toward Las Gatas.

In a couple of places the tide was up to the cliffs, and I had to leave the beach and scramble over jagged rocks. I was tired and I slipped a couple of times, skinning my hands and knees, making a fresh tear in my jeans. After twenty minutes I came to the row of outdoor bars along the beach. There's nothing much to them. Bamboo and palm-thatched open bars with concrete-block buildings at the back, where the owners live and store their precious supplies of beer and liquor. By day they do a lively trade with tourists who come across from the town pier on local ferries. Now, at nine o'clock, it was dark except for a couple of candles and the glow of a fire as one of the women cooked a late supper for her family.

I debated whether to stop. Mexico is an odd country. The people are largely honest, despite what you hear, but there isn't much love for gringos, and a lone norteamericano in an isolated place like this might seem a gift from a benevolent heaven. But my thirst won. I had swallowed some seawater as I swam, and my mouth and throat were parched. I needed a nice safe hygienic beer. And anyway, the only way to get by without being seen was to walk up around the settlement, over the rocks behind it, and I couldn't face that challenge, tired as I was.

I came up to the first place with a candle burning and called out cheerfully. "Hola, amigos. Tienen ustedes cerveza, por favor?" Hi, friends, do you have any beer, please? Not the smartest choice of question. They would think I was borracho—drunk— God's gift to the felon. But the lights of Cuatro Vientos were a long, hard mile away over soft sand that sucked at my feet. I needed that drink.

A woman came out and said in an angry tone, "No hay.

160

Cerrado." But then a man's voice spoke, and she backed into the bar and a fat man came out, grinning to let his *amigos* know this was his sucker for the skinning.

"Yes. We 'ave beer," he said. "Is five hun'ed pesos." Five times the daylight rate.

"*Es demasiado.*" Too dear. I shook my head and walked on, but he followed me, carrying the bottle by the neck. I wondered when he would make his move. His anger in smiling all day at tourists who didn't even try to speak his language was eating him up. He would make me pay for it.

"*Cien pesos,*" I said over my shoulder. A hundred was plenty. He looked as if he would move on me no matter how much I paid. I just wanted to get the beer and walk on. We were out in the open now, in the center of the beach, and I saw that he had the beer in one hand and a machete in the other, his right. He changed the nature of the transaction, keeping it simple for me. "*Dinero,*" he said. Money. And he waved his machete to show me how he intended to collect.

"Look, it's been a long, hard evening. Now, why don't you sell me the beer, and I'll let it go at that," I told him, but if he understood one word of it, he didn't let it show. He raised his machete and waved it at me, about a foot from my face.

"*Dinero,*" he repeated.

I backed off a pace. "*No tengo dinero,*" I said, and pulled the little .38. "*Tengo pistola.*"

He dropped the machete as if it had been struck by lightning. I held my hand out to the beer. "*Una cerveza, cien pesos. Sí?*"

He managed to croak out "*Sí, muy bien, señor.*" Yes, very good, sir. I nodded politely and took the beer out of his hand. It was frosty to the touch. He glanced down at his machete, lying a yard away, but he made no move toward it. I put the bottle under my arm and pulled out my change. There was a hundred-peso piece among it, and I handed it to him. Then I raised the beer bottle toward all the darkened bars and called out, "*Buenas noches, amigos,*" and waited until he backed away

161

before turning my back on him and crunching on over the sand.

At the end of the beach the rocks come down to the water, and tired as I was, I couldn't find the path in the darkness, so I lay and rested for a while, not sleeping, I didn't trust the guy with the machete, but I gathered my strength and built up my night vision until I was able to find the track and head on down to the corner of the hotel beach. From there it was sand all the way, and I took my shoes off and walked on the firm wet surface of the water's edge, passing the row of modest little Mexican hotels, listening to the musical ripple of the language and laughter and guitars as Mexican tourists enjoyed the same atmosphere the guests at Cuatro Vientos were paying fifteen times as much for.

At last I reached the hotel, and I stopped and thought about my next move. Jesús had said García was waiting for us. I wondered if that really meant me as well as Amadeo, or just the turncoat himself. Probably I was just an inconvenience, a fly he would swat as he grabbed the man he really wanted. But if I went in alone, he would jump me and have me tortured until I told him where Amadeo was. It was still a risk I couldn't afford to run. But I needed dry clothes and a shower and a night's sleep before I was fit for anything.

I sat and put my shoes and socks on, tucking the pistol into my sock again, trying to form a plan. At last I made one. It was time to call any markers I had out. I marched up the steps into the forecourt where the bar stood. And fortune smiled. Beth and Kelly were sitting at one of the tables. It was dimly lit where they were, a cheerful Mexican nod in the direction of romance, while saving big bucks on the power bill, ideal for honeymooners or for bodyguards on the lam. I went up to the women and spoke softly. "Hello, ladies. May I join you, please?"

They looked up, surprised, and Beth said, "John! What happened? You look a wreck."

"What you see is what you get," I said, trying to make it sound flippant. "How are you two?"

162

"Fine," Beth said. She was craning close to look at my growth of beard and the flush of new sunburn that even my sombrero hadn't been able to keep off. "Where did you and your friend get to yesterday?"

"He got away on me," I said. This woman was too bright for any more games. I was going to have to level with her, at least part of the way, if I was going to get help. And I needed it badly.

She had a drink in front of her. Just mineral water by the look of it. She picked it up and sipped carefully, not disbelieving me but not ready to invest any more concern unless I started telling the truth.

"I need help," I said, and she looked at me over the top of her glass, her lips pursed over the straw she was using. "I don't have any right to ask for it, but there's nobody else I can ask."

Kelly spoke first. The librarian. She lived among romance, tiered shelves of the stuff. "What kind of trouble are you in?"

"Personally, none. But Amadeo is in a whole lot of it, and I'm his bodyguard. I'm down here on assignment from a government agency to take care of him while he does some personal things. Then I have to take him home."

Beth lowered her glass. "You've told us a number of different things, you know," she said softly.

"Security. But he's broken it now. He's picked a fight with the biggest drug boss in Mexico. We went undercover yesterday, but he got away from me, and I hear that the drug boss is watching our room." There, as much as they had to know if they were going to help me.

Beth said. "This all sounds a little fanciful, you know." She was cool, maybe bruised a little from the way I had dipped into and out of her life, without fulfilling the implicit promise there was between us.

I held out my arm toward her. "Feel that jacket."

She did and said, "You got it wet."

"I got wet all over. I was thrown off a boat out past the mouth of the harbor. That's how fanciful it all is. Right now I need some dry clothes, a razor, and a night's sleep, but I think

163

my room is being watched by somebody working for the drug business."

Kelly spoke first. "You were thrown off a boat? What for?"

"They were trying to kill me, but I can swim a lot better than they thought, that's all." I looked from one to the other of them, they were still skeptical, the defense mechanisms of single women who have been lied to by a lot of men. Was I trying to tell them a story that would open their bedroom door to me? And if so, was it worth it?

I said, "Look, this is nothing to do with either of you. I'm sorry to have taken up your time. And I'm sorry I've had to spin you some fairy stories along the way, trying to cover up for Amadeo."

They looked at one another, two good friends who had seen a lot of liars come and go and had sat over drinks, like this, or maybe morning coffee, picking up the pieces. Then Beth said, "You say you need help."

"I do. I need someone to get my clothes and toilet gear from our room, and I would like, but can live without, a shower and a night's sleep somewhere safe. Once I've showered, I can get a room somewhere without attracting attention to myself."

"Do you have your key?" She held out her hand.

"I do. Would you do it for me?"

"Why not?" Beth stood up, smiling. "This seems to be my week for doing good deeds."

"It is," I said. "But please, take a bellboy with you. Don't go in there alone, in case somebody's waiting inside. If there is and he wants to know where I am, tell him. It's my battle, not yours."

"The key," she said.

I gave it to her and sat back while she walked away, tall and willowy and courageous. I felt humble. I hadn't done anything that entitled me to this kind of support.

Kelly pumped me about Amadeo while we waited, and I filled her in, partway. He was a Canadian drug dealer, period. She tried to get more out of me, but I told her that the rest of the story was classified. She would read about it in the papers if I could get him back to Canada. That satisfied her, and she sat and nibbled at her coco-loco, the rum-gin-coconut-milk cocktail they serve up in a green coconut. It looked as if she was the drinker of the twosome. Beth was probably the one who had the romantic adventures.

Beth came back five minutes later, carrying my clothes rolled neatly around my toilet equipment bag. She handed the bundle to me and said, "You can shower in our room if you want."

"Thank you very much, Beth. I owe you one."

I stood up and she nodded at Kelly. "I'll be right back, Kell."

Kelly waved one finger, and we left. Manuel was on the bar and he noticed me but did not change expression. I wondered if he was García's lookout man. "Was there anyone around the room?" I asked, and Beth shook her head.

"Nobody. I think perhaps you're being a little paranoid."

"I hope so. A few days of safety will cure that."

Their room was on the second level, and she led me to it, almost proudly, as another couple came the other way along the balcony, young and wrapped up in one another.

"I'll wait here while you clean up," she said. "That way your paranoia can take a small breather."

"No need, if you trust me not to use all your hair conditioner," I tried, but she wasn't easy to entertain.

"You sound like Kelly did after we watched *Psycho* on the late movie one night. Company outside the bathroom door will keep you from panicking."

Their place was the same as the other rooms. The same pair of double beds, the same built-in furniture. I went into the bathroom and stuck the clothes in the washbasin, taking out my toilet gear. The shower was marvelous. My skin was gritty with salt, and under the hot water I could smell yesterday's dried sweat coming back to life. I stayed there for five minutes, then shaved luxuriously and dried myself, using unscented talcum powder to complete the process, and dressed again in clean dry clothes. When I was ready, I took another few minutes to rinse all the salt water off the pistol and each of the rounds, then dried everything carefully with toilet paper and put the gun back into my sock and went out of the door.

Beth was sitting in the room's single armchair. "That's an improvement," she said. "What are you going to do now?"

"Find a place to sleep. I have to go after Amadeo, but there's not much chance of finding him tonight, and I'm in no shape to tackle any more trouble for a few hours."

"You can stay here," she said.

I shook my head. "I can't impose any further. Besides, it might be dangerous for you."

She looked down at her knees, her fingers picking at the material of her dress. "How much less dangerous would it be if you went away and someone came looking for you here?"

I sat down on the bed. It felt like a cloud after the bare ground of the night before. "But what about Kelly? I can't inconvenience the pair of you like that."

"Kelly likes to sleep in the hammock on the veranda," she said. The invitation hung in the air like the frail first strand of a new spider web.

I sat for a moment, thinking it all through. I was fit for nothing at the moment. And all I could do was search out Jesús and ask for help in finding the boat. Chances were he was gone from downtown now, or would be by the time I could hit all the bars. And if García did come looking for me in this room, it would be better for the women if I was here.

"Thank you," I said at last. "I owe you."

She smiled quickly. "We'll see," she said ambiguously. "Now, shall we go down and have a nightcap while Kelly uses the room?"

"Of course." There was a strength to this woman that reminded me of Janet Frobisher. I wondered what her story was. Single still, at her age? Possible. But it was more likely she was an ex or a widow, looking for a new direction in her life. I wasn't it, and she probably knew that, but in the meantime I was a lame dog to be helped over a stile, the way she had helped Debra Steen the day before.

We went back down to the bar, and I ordered drinks while she spoke to Kelly, who got up when I reached the table and said, "Hi, roomie," and winked. Then she got up and walked up the steps, nodding at the barman, who beamed at her widely enough that I knew she did a lot of business here.

I'd bought *agua mineral* for both of us, and we sat and sipped politely and waited. It was a strange experience. She was cool and had made no moves, but I wondered whether she would really use the other bed. The tension became hard to bear, and we chatted about trivialities. Where did we both live in Toronto? She had an apartment not unlike my own, only in Cabbagetown, the former slum now being reclaimed by the white painters and turned into an artistic enclave close to the city center. She asked me about my job, and I told her some of my previous clients. She was interested in Dee Sade and said, surprisingly, that she had a couple of the group's records. I asked her about her own career, and she brushed it aside with "It's a living," so I asked how the model had settled down and she told me, flicking a keen glance to see whether I was one with the rest of the world who idolized her beauty. I laid that one to rest. "I have a feeling she's like most models, narcissistic and very insecure."

"Beauty can be a penance," she said, then laughed. "Which leaves me grateful for being the way I am."

There was nothing graceful to say there, so I just looked at her and shook my head silently. Then she set down her glass. "Come on, Kelly will be through by now."

We went into her room the front way so as not to disturb Kelly, and when we were inside, she said, "You go first," and pushed me toward the bathroom. I cleaned my teeth and came out and undressed, putting the .38 under the pillow and climbing gratefully into bed. Beth came out of the bathroom a minute later, naked. She put out the light and got into bed beside me.

"This is fantastic," I said. "I wouldn't want anybody telling lies about us," and she laughed.

sixteen

I didn't get as much sleep as I needed, but as much as I wanted. Beth was a surprise, an eager lover, an enjoyer who made sweet moan, like La Belle Dame Sans Merci. And then suddenly I was asleep.

I woke at first light and started upright. Beth was sitting on the edge of the other bed, wearing a robe, smoking a cigarette, and looking at me.

I rubbed my face. "Good morning."

"Good morning," she said and smiled. In the early light she looked older than I had thought, forty-five perhaps, although her body had been lean and handsome and firm. She stubbed her cigarette into the ashtray she was holding.

Foolishly I said, "I didn't know you smoked."

"Not often," she said and stretched. "Not often enough. I'm sure you've heard it said that the best three things in the world are a whiskey before and a cigarette after."

I laughed. "Yes. I heard that once."

She crossed the space and sat down on the edge of the bed. "Still tired?"

"Not anymore." I could have used another couple of hours' sleep but not now, not in daylight.

"You went to sleep on me," she said. "Am I that boring?"

I reached over and slipped my hand under her robe. "Not very gentlemanly, was it? I'm sorry."

"Prove it," she said and giggled.

Half an hour later she lay and drowsed while I showered and shaved, trying to make a plan while I frowned at myself in the mirror. All I could do was try to chase Amadeo down. It was no use calling Cahill. That would just make his February morning in Toronto even more dreary. He couldn't help me from that range. I would try to reach Jesús and work with him at this end.

I went back into the bedroom, where Beth stretched luxuriously and hoisted herself onto one elbow, letting the single sheet slip down from her small breasts. "Going?"

"I have to." I sat on the edge of the bed. "Thank you, for everything."

She sat up and cupped my face in her hands, and we kissed. "Ships that pass in the night," she said softly. "Take care of yourself, sailor."

I winked at her. "*Hasta luego,* Beth. The good Lord willin', I'll be on the flight on Sunday with Amadeo beside me. And I live a three-dollar cab ride from your door."

"Maybe I should buy a whole carton of cigarettes," she said, and we kissed again, and I felt under the pillow for my gun.

She jerked herself away from me as I pulled it out. "Was that there all night?"

" 'Fraid so. One of the tools of my trade," I said.

Her mouth was tight and she frowned, showing tiny little vertical lines around her lips. "Use it in good health," she said.

I winked and left, going out the back door, onto the veranda where Kelly was lying facedown in the hammock, one arm trailing down to the tiles. I glanced around, then walked out to the end of the veranda and dropped down, over the end onto the next veranda and then again, down to ground level at the base of the slope that led back up onto the road. I could hear Spanish voices as the workmen began to gather for the construction that was going on at one side of the hotel, laughter and chatter that would be the same in any language, no anger, no alarm. Good. I hadn't been noticed. To the north of the hotel there is a rocky headland that makes it impossible to walk to town along the beach, so instead I clambered up through the brush to the side of the road, coming out directly under the Parthenon. The same bored guard, or a clone, was standing at the front with the same ancient rifle, waiting to catch the first rays of the sun when it came into view over the mountains behind us. The road was deserted.

There are a couple of restaurants halfway down the hill, not fancy, used mostly by the locals. I stopped in at one of them and sat in a corner and ordered huevos rancheros and tostadas with black coffee. It came quickly, in generous portions, and I was ready to tackle the world. A couple of workmen's buses had passed as I ate, carrying the help to the hotel, and then the taxis started to flow. I didn't know what to do next, except stay out of sight and look for Jesús, so I lingered over my coffee and then went out onto the road again and headed down toward town. I was hoping that if anyone was looking for me, they were concentrating on the hotel, although it still didn't make sense that they hadn't followed Beth the night before and surprised me with her. Perhaps García had given up on me and was looking for Amadeo. News travels fast in a small community like Zihua. Maybe someone had seen us take the boat the night before and García had called off the search in town.

The thought of the boat gave me a focus. I would start at the waterfront. If *Juanita* was back at her mooring, I would get out there and look her over. With luck Amadeo would be on board, and I could take over where I had left off, without the menace of El Grande to worry about.

As the sun came over the mountain, I walked down the hill toward town, almost cheerful. And then I saw the sleek shape of García's Continental sliding up the hill toward me.

He was a hundred and fifty yards off when I saw him, and I was at the gateway of El Paraíso. I turned and ducked inside the gate and glanced around. The row of cabañas stood silent, deserted probably. But there, on one side, stood the van that had picked me up the day before. My best bet. I ran to it and hid on the far side, waiting to see if the car turned in after me. As I stood there, I heard a dry little cough and glanced up to see the driver from the day before sitting at his breakfast.

"You still gonna tell me you're birdin'?" he asked dryly.

"I'm hiding. Can you let me in? I'll explain later."

"Sure." He opened the side door of the van, just before the car pulled into the gateway, gunning over the dry ground in a spurt of gravel. I sank to the floor.

"Thanks," I said. "Those guys are looking for me."

"Stay outa sight," he said. He moved his breakfast aside and put the table down, then lowered the bunk bed from the far wall. It almost filled the van and I crouched at the end of it, in the storage space that would only be exposed if anyone opened the rear door. I was out of sight of him and of whoever was in the car, so I drew the pistol and waited, one hand on the door lock, ready to flip it open and roll out, shooting, if I had to.

There was a knock on the front door, and the driver said, "Howdy, *buenos días, señor.*"

A man's voice asked him if he had seen a man come in, and he lied cheerfully. "Nope. Just this second got outa bed. Haven't seen anybody before you."

The voice got more insistent. "I would like to look in your bus."

"No can do, *amigo.* My wife, *mi esposa,* she's asleep."

The man hissed something in Spanish, but after a moment he went and I heard him calling to another man, then a crashing in the bush and a rattling of doors as one of them checked behind the cabins while the other one tried all the doors.

The van driver came back and sat on the edge of the bed. "They're goin' all over this place," he said. "What in the Sam Hill is goin' on?"

"They work for a guy called García. He's the drug boss in town, tied in to the Mafia in Toronto."

He looked at me, his eyes narrow behind his no-nonsense glasses. "That the line of work you're in?"

"No. I'm a bodyguard, working with the Mounties, watching that guy you saw me with yesterday."

"That greaser? Where's he at?"

"He got away on me last night. We were due to meet his wife on board a boat. He had money for her, then I was to take him back to Toronto to testify. Only instead of her, we found some of García's men. I stopped one of them, but they dumped me overboard, and I had to swim ashore."

He didn't say anything when I'd finished. Instead, he turned and looked out the window. When he turned back he said, "They've gone. You can come out now."

"Thanks." I straightened up, and he swung the bed up into the wall again.

"They didn't take your piece when they had you?" he asked dryly.

"Not this one. I had it in my sock," I said, and he looked at me again without speaking. I got the impression he knew what he was doing. He acted professionally, not out of simple curiosity.

"How about you cut the bullshit an' tell me what's really goin' on," he said at last.

So I did, starting in Toronto and bringing him right up to date. He had put the table up again, and he ate his breakfast, cereal with fruit sliced into it, and we both drank coffee while I talked.

"You mean that guy had half a million bucks with him yesterday? An' you killed three guys?"

"Yes. I'm not proud of it. But if I'd kept hold of him, he was going to testify and tear the guts out of the drug organization in Toronto. That's why I did it."

He sniffed and picked up his cup. "Where'd a guy your age learn to use guns good enough to take out three guys?"

"I was in the British army for ten years, the SAS most of the time." I was wondering where these questions were going. Was

172

he just curious, making coffee-klatch conversation before turning me loose?

He looked at me over the rim of his coffee cup, then said, "What weapon did you carry?"

I blinked in surprise. "You mean in the SAS? A Heckler and Koch HK33E, 5.56 millimeter, why?"

He grinned. "What rate of fire?"

I told him and he grinned again. "And what did you use to clean the badge on your beret?"

"It's cloth. As an officer, I wore metal collar dogs on my dress uniform, but the badge on the beret isn't metal." I realized he was testing me. My story sounded preposterous, but he was prepared to believe me unless he found I was lying about my background. And that's what he was probing. Good for him.

He finished his coffee and set down the cup. "Either you're legit or you been doing your homework. Not many guys know about the SAS, beyond the name."

"I did my research the hard way."

"Yeah. I believe you did." He stretched, like a runner warming up. "Okay, then," he said, I guess we better go see if we can find him." He stuck out his hand. "Calvin Thurlbeck. Up until last month when I turned sixty, I was police chief in Flagstaff."

I shook his hand. He had a good grip. "Thanks, Calvin. If I don't get Amadeo back, a lot of people are going to be hurt. Kids mostly."

He stood up and stuck the cups and dish in the little sink. "I know. Crack. It was just starting to come in before I quit. Not in town, of course, we're too square for it. But I was at a chief's conference an' I heard all about it."

He washed and wiped the dishes and put them away. "I guess our best bet is check out that boat. I'll drive downtown. You stay low, we don't want them bastards knowing you're aboard."

I sat on the floor and he picked up his feed-store cap and got behind the wheel of the van. He drove carefully, keeping to the

173

limit, humming to himself at first, then switching on the radio. There was mariachi music, followed by news. My Spanish wasn't up to it, but he listened carefully, then glanced back over his shoulder. "Sounds like your count's up to four. They found a guy in the bay this morning, washed up. His jaw an' neck were broken."

My huevos rancheros churned in my stomach. I knew I'd connected hard, but not that hard. I wondered if Amadeo had finished the job. "That's why they were looking for me. He was their top muscle," I said, then added, "You quite sure you want to be a part of this?"

"I already am," he said. "You hand in your badge when you retire but not your conscience. I been doin' this kind o' work too long." He paused and added, "Anyway, I'm sick o' lookin' at birds. That was Fay's hobby. I'm just a natural-born cop."

He drove to the dock and parked beside the naval monument. "Stay here. I'll check," he said, and got out. I took the .38 out of my sock and stuck it into my waistband, under cover of my jacket, which was stiff and tacky from yesterday's salt water.

He had parked in the sun, leaving the windows up, and within a couple of minutes the inside was like an oven. I shucked my jacket and sat thinking cool thoughts and waiting. He was back within five, and when he opened the door, he frowned and stood for a minute, letting the heated air pour out before getting into the seat. "No sign of the boat," he said.

"I didn't expect it, not really. I was thinking maybe I should charter something fast and go looking for him. We told his wife to lay in food and drink enough for days. He could head right down to Colombia the way he's provisioned."

Thurlbeck backed up and turned his van. "This guy a good sailor, would you say?" he asked over his shoulder.

"Sailor?" I realized what he was getting at and brightened. "No mention of it in the briefing they gave me in Toronto. And all I've seen them do is motor."

He eased back out onto the cobbled street, waving at the cop on the corner. "Well, if he's a sailor, he could make Colombia okay, but if he's just motoring, he won't be that far. Likely gone into one of the bays lower down the coast. He's gonna need fuel, diesel, likely."

I slapped my hands together. "Then he'll have to stop in some town farther down the coast. Great, we can chase him down."

Thurlbeck cleared his throat. "It's fifty miles to the next town. He wouldn't motor all that way. My guess is he'd put into the next bay down the coast. There's no town, but the locals have a truck, they'd go get him gasoline if he paid them."

"Where would that be? La Playa Blanca?"

Thurlbeck glanced back at me over his shoulder. "Yeah. You know the area pretty good."

"I know that place, I was there once." La Playa Blanca, the white beach, a small bay with an island covered with birds and guano. A group of locals lived on the beach in typical back-country houses, fishing the brackish lagoons and catering to the very few gringos who got that far, bird-watchers mostly. They were remote enough that none of them spoke English at all. I had spent a day there once with my family as a kid, when my mother was going through her short-lived bird-watching phase.

Thurlbeck turned left down a side street past the church with its open front. "Just be a minute, sit tight," he said.

He got out, leaving the door ajar. I wondered if he was religious, looking for peace before setting out to tackle Amadeo, but he was back within moments carrying a big brown paper bag.

"*Dulces*," he explained. "Candies. Terrible garbage, y'ask me, but this stall by the church does land-office business, the local kids love 'em."

"Who're they for?"

He slammed the door and drove off, picking up speed down the quiet street and turning right at the end, heading back up through town toward the highway he had driven the day before. "The *niños* up at Playa Blanca. Fay always made a helluva fuss of 'em. They're living on fish an' hope, they never

175

see treats." He cleared his throat. "She was big on kids. We had three of our own, got five grandchildren now. Just give me the chance, an' I'll bring out the photographs."

I said nothing, and he glanced back at me and laughed. "Got you worried, huh? Young buck like you. Likely makin' out with everything that moves."

I didn't answer, and he shook his head and laughed. "You need to be married to know what it's all about. Living it up is good. I did a lot of that." He paused and added, "A helluva lot, in France and Germany. Then I got back to Britain, and Fay was waiting, so we got married and that was it. Forty good years."

Abruptly he realized where his thoughts were leading him, so he shut up and turned on the radio. I sat and listened to the mariachi beat while he drove north, then turned off on a small side road, not much bigger than the trail Amadeo and I had walked the previous day. He had to slow down to about ten miles an hour, and still we bumped and heaved over rocks. I called out. "Okay if I come up front?"

"Sure. Just lay low again if we see any strange cars in there. I'll know, watch me."

It was more comfortable in front, and I looked around at the barren fields that had been slashed and burned. Now they were fenced in with two strands of barbed wire between the odd-shaped posts that are the only thing available in Mexico, where they can't grow conveniently straight cedars like we do at home. And then we came out into a coconut grove with piles of yellow husks under all the trees and splashes of white insect repellent around the boles, and at the end of it saw a cluster of rough shanties and a small area covered over with thinly laid thatch.

"That's the bar area. You can rent a *hamaca* an' kick back, or you can swim and fish and drink beer. Nice place," he said. He looked all around. "Their old truck's gone, no other cars. Good."

We pulled up under the shade and a crowd of kids ran up, the tiny bright-eyed Mexican children that fill you with their energy just by watching them. An elderly woman came out from behind the low brick barbecue that was burning with a row of good-sized fish on it. She smiled a toothless smile and held out both arms. Thurlbeck got out of the car and embraced her, chatting rapidly in Spanish. Then he turned back to the van as I got out. "*Mi amigo,* Juan," he said, and the old lady smiled and shook hands.

I said, "*Buenos días, señora, cómo está usted?*" Good day, how are you? My whole store of Spanish courtesies spent in one sentence.

"*Muy bien, gracias, señor.*" She smiled again. The kids had all clustered around her, and Thurlbeck reached into the car and came up with his bag of goodies. They started chattering instantly, and he handed the bag to the woman, who thanked him and started handing out the sticky candies to the kids, who jigged from foot to foot waiting their turns.

"Makes me feel like Santy Claus," he said cheerfully. He grinned, a big happy copper out of uniform. I wondered what I'd done to deserve his help. Fate only favors fools and drunks, I thought. Maybe I'm more of a fool than I'd figured.

He talked to the woman for a couple of minutes more. She asked him about his wife, I made out the word "*esposa,*" and he broke the news. She wept briefly, and he patted her on the shoulder and spoke to her, and she went over to their cooler and pulled out a Tecate beer and a soda. He handed the beer to me and then said, "There's a pair of good glasses behind my seat, go get 'em, see if the boat's around."

I got the glasses and walked out almost to the edge of the clearing. There was no need to go all the way. Out in the bay, between us and the white rock, a sailboat was rocking at anchor. A catboat. I focused the glasses and checked the stern. Bingo. *Juanita.*

Thurlbeck looked up over the old woman's head as I came

back, and I nodded. He grinned and then started speaking rapid Spanish to her. She answered, and he beamed and then asked her another question and she left.

"She's gone to find us a boat an' one o' her grandsons to take us out there. Looks like your boy got in at first light, lay at anchor for a while, then came ashore and asked to be driven to the gas station."

"How far is it? And how long ago?"

"It's back at the edge of town. First one you come to the other way is twenty miles."

"You think he'd risk going back to town?"

"I'd doubt it." His accent made the *ou* sound a soft coo. "Last thing he needs is people on his trail. My guess is he'd go farther on, away from trouble."

"Did you ask the *señora* if he was carrying a straw bag, like yesterday?"

"She said he was. A beach basket like *los Indios* sell on the beach at Zihua."

I frowned. "Then maybe he's not coming back. He could just take the truck and make a run for it."

Thurlbeck pondered that one. "Could be you're right. The best thing we can do is check the boat, talk to his lady. That's why I asked Consuela to get us a boat."

"Makes sense. If she wasn't expecting him back, she'd be long gone. She's a capable woman, handles the boat just fine on her own."

Consuela came back through the trees and chattered to Thurlbeck, who thanked her. "Boat's coming out to the edge of the lagoon. Let's get over there."

We waited at the water's edge, and a young man came down the lagoon in a broad old flat-bottomed rowboat. He grinned when he saw Thurlbeck and pulled up to us. We got in and Thurlbeck shook his hand. "Luis? *Sí?*" he asked, and the young guy grinned and nodded. Then I was introduced as Juan and shook hands, and the boatman shoved his oar into the sand and pushed us away from the beach.

The boat ducked and dipped as we rounded the corner of the lagoon and moved into the bay, rolling on the incoming tide that was curling up onto the beach. I sat back in the stern, keeping low, as much behind the rower as I could. If Maria had any fuel left, she could start up and motor away before we could row two hundred yards. And I kept my glasses on the boat, staring at the ports on our side, checking for anxious faces looking out. Nothing. Maybe they had spent the night making up for lost loving and Maria was still sleeping. Maybe.

She didn't come up on deck as we approached the boat, but I kept my hand inside my jacket, resting on the handle of the Colt as the boatman pulled up to the stern and Thurlbeck reached up and grabbed the steel line that served as a rail. "You first, an' keep your eyes open," he said.

I stood up and stepped past the boatman, who had shipped his oars and was also holding the rail. It was a longish heave up to the deck but I sprang and pulled myself up and over the rail in one move and down onto the rear deck. Still nobody moved, and I stood for a moment, staring down into what I could see of the cabin, drawing the .38. Then I vaulted down the steps and inside. And I saw why Maria hadn't been looking out for us.

seventeen

She'd been beaten, pistol-whipped by the look of it. Both eyes were swollen closed, and her fine black hair was matted with blood, but she was alive. Just. I knelt and found the pulse in her throat. It was faint but regular.

"In here," I shouted, and Thurlbeck pattered down the steps and joined me.

I guess cops are used to violence; he didn't gasp or swear or do anything unproductive, the way most people would in the same circumstances. He just stooped down and looked at her injuries. "She alive?" was all he asked.

"Yes, the pulse is still in business."

"Takes a lickin' and keeps on tickin'," he said. "We better get her to a hospital, pronto."

I lifted her head, gently, checking that her neck was uninjured. It seemed to be, so I picked her up in my arms and carried her out onto the deck.

"This is gonna be tricky," Thurlbeck said. "I'll get in the boat an' you lower her over the rail. Be easier if you keep her vertical."

"Right." I lowered Maria to the bench beside the wheel and then put my arms around her chest, one hand behind her head, and stood her up as if we were going to dance. She wasn't heavy, but her body was lifelessly limp, and it was difficult to step up onto the bench, then to the deck, then over the rail.

Luis stared at her in horror and almost lost his grip of the yacht rail, but Thurlbeck spoke to him comfortingly, and he swallowed hard and hung on while I lowered Maria into Thurlbeck's arms, then vaulted down beside him and helped him lower her to the flat bottom of the boat.

Thurlbeck said, "This is getting complex. We gotta take her to the hospital, but that bastard could get away on us while we're gone."

"I can fix that." I pulled myself back aboard and dropped down to the cabin. The boat was a Nonsuch, and I knew where the fuel filter was located, behind a panel under the cabin steps. I removed them and unscrewed the nut that held the filter in place. A gout of diesel fuel ran out into the bilge, then stopped. I took the glass bowl of the filter with me. Amadeo was stranded without it. I climbed over the gap where the steps had been and jumped into the boat. Luis pulled on the oars like an Olympic hopeful, and we hurtled toward the beach like a landing craft. As soon as we hit the sand, he jumped out and towed us up as high as the incoming wave would carry us; then he hovered at my elbow as I cradled Maria again and Thurlbeck jogged ahead to his van. He drove it closer to the beach, as far as the edge of the trees, where the footing was still firm. Then he opened the side door and lowered the bed. I put her on it, smoothing down the hem of her dress that had flopped up, uncovering her brown thighs.

Thurlbeck spoke to Luis, who nodded grimly and turned away to talk to the old woman. "I've warned them about your good buddy," Thurlbeck told me. "They have a gun some-where, an old shotgun, they'll keep it handy in case they need it, but I've told them to go along with him, not to argue, he's a mean bastard." He reversed the van and spun around. "Keep her as comfortable as you can, I'm gonna get us out as fast as I dare."

"If you see their truck coming back with Amadeo in it, just pull over and let him go," I said, then sat on the edge of the bed, ready to make sure Maria didn't bounce around when we hit the rough part of the track.

"He ain't coming back." Thurlbeck shook his head without looking around. "He'll likely hijack the truck, or buy it, maybe, if he's feeling generous, and he's gone. We're too late."

Maria groaned as if she was taking her cue from Thurlbeck's gloom. "She comin' 'round?" he asked, not turning his head.

"Could be. That's the first sign of life we've had out of her."

"I hope the hell she does," he said. "We could be in a mess of trouble, two gringos bringing in a pistol-whipped girl. They're liable to think we did it."

"I thought of that, but we couldn't leave her aboard to die."

"I know," Thurlbeck said. "Should maybe have brought Consuela along. She could tell them about Amadeo, keep the local yokels from snappin' at our ass."

He slowed to pick his way over a deeply rutted spot in the trail, then said, "Maybe the best thing is I go in there. I still got accreditation from Flagstaff. It's bullshit, they gave me my badge to keep when I retired. That and a new set of birding glasses. But it makes me look legit. Meanwhile, you take the van an' head up the highway to the gas station."

I looked at him and shook my head silently at my good fortune. I've worked with a lot of nationalities in my time, but the casual generosity of ordinary Americans is something that never fails to stagger me. Here the guy was willing to lend me his home while he dealt with a bunch of suspicious coppers in a strange country. "If you don't mind. I'll head up there and find out which way he's gone. I appreciate the offer."

"Yeah, well, just don't leave me hanging by my thumbs. I live here," he said and gave a short gruff laugh.

Maria groaned again and opened her eyes, then stirred, mov-

182

ing her hand up to her face. "She's waking up now," I said. "You want me to drive while you talk to her? She won't be talking English if she speaks."

"No. I know the way to the hospital. You tell her '*Vamos al hospital*,' that should hold her."

Maria was struggling to focus, and she turned her head and concentrated her eyes on me. I noted that her pupils were both the same size. That was a good sign; it indicated that she didn't have a concussion. Then when she recognized me, she gave a little scream and covered her face with her hands.

My Spanish isn't up to more than ordering a few beers or giving the courtesies. I couldn't tell her I wasn't the bogeyman and I hadn't come back from a watery grave, so I just repeated Thurlbeck's words over and over as if I were talking to a child, "*Vamos al hospital*," until she started to believe me and lowered her hands and stared at me.

"*Lo creia muerto*," she said. I thought you were dead.

"I'm a good swimmer." I grinned at her to show it was all good, clean fun and made swimming motions. She shook her head and rattled out a quick sentence that included the word "*manos*."

"I untied the knots with my teeth," I said, and mimicked the action I had made so frantically the night before. I was starting to feel like a Limey tourist on his first trip overseas. Speak clearly and loudly, and the poor benighted heathens will understand. After a while she remembered that she spoke English, and she started asking questions just as I was about to ask her some.

"Why did you come back?"

"I want to take your husband back to Canada. He must speak in court about the drug business."

She said nothing, closing her eyes slowly as if the action hurt her. After a moment I probed, keeping my voice soft. "Did he do this to you?"

Still she didn't answer, and then she nodded her head, very gently, once. "I wanted to go with him, but he told me I was to

183

stay with the boat, he would come back. But I did not believe."

"Did he give you some money?" I wanted to know. If he had, then a second part of this caper was over, all I had to do was find her sleazebag husband and take him home.

"No. I asked him for money, to get back to my *familia*. And he called me a greedy *puta* and he beat me."

Thurlbeck's voice came back from the front seat. "I'm gonna have a hard time not going up alongside his goddamn head when we get ahold of him."

"You'll have to take your turn," I said. I reached out and squeezed Maria's hand. "We will find him and make him pay you money. Do you know where he would go?"

She shut her eyes again and said, "No. He tells me nothing."

We were reaching the edge of town, and Thurlbeck spoke up. "You know, the best thing we might do is get the police after him. Just tell them he did this, plus he's carrying a bunch of money, and they'll find him like a shot."

"Two things wrong with that plan. First, they're likely to shoot him and disappear with that cash. I think that would be pretty tempting for a lot of people, not just some underpaid Mexican copper."

"Yeah, could be right at that," Thurlbeck agreed. "And on the other hand, if we find the right cop, some dedicated true-blue Boy Scout, he's gonna want to slap Amadeo in jail right here, and you'll never get your evidence."

"Exactly. We've got to keep them out of it and go it alone," I said. "At least, we've got to try."

Maria tried to sit up. I shook my head and put one hand gently on her shoulder, but she persisted, pushing my hand away. Then she spoke rapidly to Thurlbeck. He listened and said "*Bueno*," and she lay back again.

I looked at her but her eyes were closed again. Then Thurlbeck translated for me. "She doesn't want to go to the hospital. She knows a doctor in one of the little clinics in town, a Dr. Juarez on Calle de la Concepción. I'll take her there, it'll cut the risk of trouble with the police."

"Anything for a quiet life." I sat and watched her as Thurlbeck drove fast down the highway and into town. Her eyelids flickered painfully once or twice, but she didn't speak again. My guess was she had spent all her strength in talking and now realized how rough she was feeling.

He pulled up at the clinic, making a U-turn in the narrow street so the side door of the van was against the clinic door. He got out and opened it. I touched Maria on the shoulder. "We're here now. Can you walk?"

She sat up, very slowly, and I put my arm around her shoulders and helped her up, easing her off the bed and down the step onto the hot sidewalk. There was an old woman sitting in a cane chair on the stoop of the clinic, but no other passersby close enough to see what kind of shape Maria was in. Thurlbeck went ahead, and I heard him speaking Spanish to the old woman, who pointed inside. I helped Maria after him into the dimness of a tiny ward with a couple of empty hospital beds and a strong smell of old-fashioned antiseptics.

I put her on one of the beds, helping her up so she could lie flat, which she did, groaning softly and putting one hand over her eyes. Thurlbeck had found the doctor, a heavyset guy in his fifties wearing a white coat with a bloodstain on the left sleeve. He brought him over, and he was all business, moving Maria's hand to look at her injuries, speaking soothingly to her as she opened her eyes.

Thurlbeck turned to me. "I'll wait here, all day if I have to. You do what you can to find this prick."

"Right." I took the keys and went out to the van, slamming the side door and driving back up the street onto the main cross street and out to the highway. I watched the oncoming traffic as I drove, checking every pickup that passed. There were a number of them, but I didn't see Amadeo in any of them, just ordinary working stiffs moving into Zihuatanejo with produce for the market.

The gas station was a dusty little place with a couple of pumps, one for regular gas, one for diesel. I pulled the van alongside the gas pump and got out. A kid of about fourteen came up, wearing a Red Sox baseball cap, a souvenir from some gringo who'd stopped by. He spoke the rough, aggressive English of the standard salesman, the kind they advertise for in Canadian papers as "self-starters." "Hello. Jou want to fill-er-up?"

"Yeah, please."

I let him start the gasoline pumping, then pulled out a five-hundred-peso bill and folded it, tapping it against my left thumb while he watched. "You been here all day?"

He nodded. "*Sí.* Since six hours."

"Did you serve a man in a pickup, a gringo, like me, only dark?" The word made him narrow his eyes, so I simplified. I stroked my hair. *"Negro."*

He didn't say anything, but his expression changed.

"Yeah, the man I want to see, he speaks Spanish like a norteamericano."

Now he nodded. "*Sí.* A norteamericano was here."

"What did his truck look like?" I wanted facts, not some fiction concocted to earn the five hundred.

"Was ol', a pickup, not norteamericano, was Guerrero."

"Bueno." I grinned to let him know my grip on the bill was loosening. "What did he buy?"

"He buy gas, like you."

"Did he have a gas can with him, in the truck?"

"*Sí.* He have a can, but he no fill it."

"Was he alone?"

"*Sí.*" He finished filling the van, fastened the cap, then hung the nozzle up.

"And what did he do then?"

The kid shoved his cap back, then looked at me. "This guy is your frien'?"

"No. But I want to see him. Which way did he go?" I didn't have any doubt that he had headed up the highway, northwest toward Puerto Vallarta along the coast road, or maybe to the highway that led into the mountains and eventually Mexico City and anonymity.

186

The kid said, "He say can he use the phone. So *mi padre* say *sí*. An' then he turn aroun' an' drive back."

"*Bueno. Muchas gracias, amigo. Para usted.*" I handed him the bill and pulled out two thousand to pay for the gas. He fumbled for change, but I waved him off. "*De nada.*"

He grinned. "This guy, he cheap bastar'. I wash the window, he don' teep."

That pleased me. It meant the boy was telling the truth. If Amadeo had bribed him, he would have said nothing, or lied, but he wouldn't have made up a story. I tugged the brim of his cap and grinned back at him. "Boston, *bueno.* Toronto Blue Jays *muy bueno*," I said and he made a disgusted little fan's gesture and laughed.

I swung the van around and started back down the highway. This time I drove more slowly, thinking. Who would Amadeo have called? And why was he heading back to Zihua? Maybe he was planning to carry through on his dream of canceling García and setting up shop as the Man for the state of Guerrero. With El Grande in the morgue and a .45 on his hip, he might feel equal to the attempt. And maybe his phone call had been to some contact or other, someone who could help him set up the assassination. Bad news for García, potentially better for me.

Something else was niggling at me as I drove, and then I remembered, the boy had said Amadeo was alone. Knowing what kind of man he was, that probably meant he had gotten rid of the guy from the beach who had offered to drive him to the gas station. The questions were: How? And where? The thought made me even more observant as I drove, and as I came over a ridge about midway between the gas station and the turnoff to La Playa Blanca, I saw something that made me ease up on the gas. Vultures were gathering over an arroyo that ran under a bridge about a quarter mile down the road.

I pulled in and stopped on the shoulder, just short of the bridge, then ran down the embankment and through the brush

187

to the arroyo, a scarred, dry riverbed about six feet deep. A heavy bird flapped away as I ducked under the corner of the bridge, then another, and I saw what they were eating.

Amadeo had shot him in the back and he was sprawled facedown on the hard-baked ground at the other end of the bridge, not quite under it. I checked the body but he was beyond help, so I just noted what he was wearing, white cotton short-sleeved shirt and light blue summer pants and a pair of flip-flops, not even a hat.

I didn't touch him. It was time to leave. Somebody would notice the vultures soon, and then they would come down to look, checking if it was an animal with a skin worth taking, and the hunt would be on. I had to get away. A gringo carrying a gun would be the prime suspect. You couldn't expect some unsophisticated local cop to bother checking the ballistics of the bullet in the dead man's back. I ran back and jumped into the van, hoping nobody had noticed it while it was parked. If they had, Thurlbeck would be a suspect when the investigation started.

It took me only twelve minutes to reach the clinic. Thurlbeck was sitting in a chair opposite the old lady, gossiping in Spanish. He looked like the kind of retiree you see in insurance company advertisements. When I arrived, he excused himself and the old lady smiled at the courtesy.

He stepped down to the passenger side of the van. "What did you find?"

"He's back in town. He killed the guy from the beach. I found the body in the riverbed. It's my guess he wants to have a meeting with García, maybe to try to ice him and take over, maybe to set up a purchase."

Thurlbeck sucked his teeth and looked at me without speaking, and I remembered he was a cop. Maybe he thought I'd killed the other guy. I just looked back at him and waited.

Finally he spoke. "I talked to Maria while the doc patched her up. She tells the same story you did about last night." Then he grinned. "An' you brought the van back like a good fellah.

188

So I believe you. The only thing is, this is getting sticky. Somebody's going to find that body, an' when they do the foo yung will be in the fan."

I'd already followed that line of reasoning, and I nodded. "They'll want to talk to us, as witnesses, but it's Amadeo they'll be looking for."

He nodded. "Yeah, but that won't do you any good. They won't want to let him go back to Canada to testify and get away free. They'll want to throw his ass in jail."

"You're right. Which means we have to get him out of the country before they know who they're looking for."

Thurlbeck sniffed and nodded. "Any luck at all, we'll have the rest of the day before they find the body, then identify it, then start asking at Playa Blanca and then start looking for Amadeo."

"And when they do, they'll start asking at the hotels, and they'll soon want to talk to us, for being interested in him at La Playa Blanca." The thought did not thrill me. I've heard a little about the way these policemen conduct their investigations. I didn't want them asking me any questions, especially if they had the idea that Amadeo and I were a couple of kindred spirits. It's not that I don't like beer, but I prefer to drink it rather than inhale the stuff while hanging upside down.

Thurlbeck was making like a policeman, thinking logically. "If the kid at the gas station was telling the truth, then the first thing we do is make a search for the truck."

"Did you get a description from the lady at the beach?"

He grinned. "You're talking to a pro-fessional," he drawled. "We are looking for a '58 Chevy, red color, box-bodied—you know how I mean, with the wheels outside the box. Guerrero license number 4763."

"So let's make a sweep." I turned to the van. "If it was me driving a truck like that, I'd dump it close to the market among all the farmers' trucks, where it won't stick out."

He walked around to the driver's side and got in. I opened my door and got in beside him. He shoved his cap back on his head and wound the window down. "Market'd be a good place to start," he said.

He drove slowly up the street and turned left at the top, the four-lane main road through town. It was in poor repair, with potholes every few yards, but there was a boulevard down the center with dried-out grass and a few dusty trees. On the north side of it lay the three blocks of the market, a thrown-together affair with a few buildings and a cluster of permanent stalls with canvas covers joining them all up, so the whole thing looked like a circus tent. There were elderly trucks all down the curb next to the stalls, farm trucks mostly, with empty produce baskets in the backs of them.

We drove in silence, checking everything we passed. Then Thurlbeck said, "If you see him, on foot, I mean, tell me. I'll go another thirty yards an' drop you off. No sense me goin' up against a .45. I'll be better off telling the police what happened if he sees you first."

"Makes sense." I took my eyes off the scene long enough to take my gun out of my sock, check the load with a glance, and then slip it into my waistband. "Going past him is sensible. I don't want to get into any shooting matches. He's not that great with a gun, he'll likely kill some poor bastard and the crowd will jump him, and some farmer will cancel his check with a machete."

Thurlbeck humphed in what might have been amusement. "You know what I'm thinking?" he said. "I'm thinking our best bet is to find García and talk to him."

I frowned. The last I'd seen of García's men, they were trying to round me up for a nice quiet drowning, if I'd been lucky.

Thurlbeck glanced at my face and nodded. "Yeah, I know what you're thinkin'. The only thing is, we know García's a rounder. If we promise him the money that your buddy's carrying, he won't care what happens to the guy. Hell, for half a million bucks he'd give you his sister."

I straightened my back and took a deep breath. "This is

going to be even less fun than getting your pants pressed while you wait."

He didn't laugh. "I know. But if we don't find the truck, or if we find it but don't find him, we'll need help rounding him up."

All that was true, but I'd killed García's bodyguard. It was better than even money that García was feeling miffed. He might be tempted to let Amadeo go, but take out his anger on me.

Thurlbeck wasn't considering that one. "I'd like to see the little bastard get his. But not here. If he can do some good by testifying before your courts, let him do it. He won't live long after that, believe me. They can give him a new name, but the only place it'll ever appear is on his headstone. Those guys don't fool around."

"I just don't want to lose him, that's all," I said as we reached the end of the short stretch of four-lane and Thurlbeck turned north, around the back of the market.

"Nor me," he said. Then he touched me on the arm at the same moment I saw what he had. The red pickup was sitting on a patch of waste ground beside the market, in the thin shade of a jacaranda, but Amadeo was nowhere in sight.

eighteen

Thurlbeck drove around the corner without slowing down, then stopped to let me off. "I guess you know how to stake a place out," he said.

"Yeah. I've done it before."

"Good. I'll get rid of the van and come back. You won't see me unless you're good, so don't panic. I'll be close by."

I raised one finger and nodded. He winked and drove away, and I moved to the inside of the sidewalk, against the back wall of one of the buildings that made up the market.

Amadeo had parked his truck well. There was no place to watch it from complete cover. If this had been nighttime, I could have swung up unnoticed onto the roof of any of the buildings that overlooked the waste ground. But in daylight that was impossible, so I kept going, away from the truck, until I reached the first entrance to the market and could duck inside.

It was jammed with stalls, so close together that any North American fire department would have closed it down instantly, but the cheerful, casual Mexicans hadn't bothered. All the space between the stalls was packed with shoppers, mostly women carrying sturdy nylon-mesh shopping bags and buying their groceries quietly, without the haggling that gringos expect to be part of every exchange. I squeezed through, stopping only to pick up a liter of orange juice in a heavy glass bottle. It would keep me going in the heat, and the bottle itself could be a distraction if I had to move in on Amadeo without using my gun.

It must have been a minute before I reached an opening in the market that gave me a view of the truck. It was still there, and the first stall inside was a refreshment booth with a low counter and a few stools. I took a stool at the end of the row and ordered a Piñafiel and sat nursing it and trying to look invisible. It was difficult. I'm a head taller than most of the locals, and fair hair stands out like a red hunting hat against all of those bobbing blacktops. And as I sat there, I weighed up the situation. Finding the truck didn't mean we would find Amadeo. He might have abandoned it now and be on his way to a confrontation with García.

That reading didn't sit well with me. If all he had wanted was a ride to town, he wouldn't have killed the guy from La Playa Blanca. It figured that he had changed his mind while he drove up to the gas station. After his call from there, he must have decided that he could get back in the drug business here. It meant that he had murdered the truck's owner for nothing. I wondered if he'd glanced sideways as he drove back over the arroyo as he came back to town. Would he have grinned and said, "Sorry about that"?

The other alternative was that he intended to drive over the border, south possibly, into Guatemala, just a couple of days' travel. Probably by then the police would be looking for him and the truck, but liaison between the various levels of law enforcement agencies in Mexico is ragged. And with half a million bucks in a plain gray wrapper he had enough money to buy his way past anybody short of Saint Peter.

For the moment, though, it was worth watching the truck, if only I could find a way to look less conspicuous, so Amadeo wouldn't notice me if he passed. It wasn't easy. Most of the stall's patrons were market workers. The place was too grungy to appeal to tourists, and those who passed the place glanced at me as if they figured I must be conducting some kind of medical experiment with myself as guinea pig. And then an old Mexican sat down next to me and smiled. I smiled back and said, *"Buenos días, señor."*

He murmured the same thing and then lifted his shopping bag up on the counter. In it he had a cloth chessboard and a cigar box filled with his men, an old Spanish-style set carved from onyx.

He flopped out the board on the countertop and indicated the men with another smile. I nodded and said, *"Sí, con mucho gusto."* Yes, I'd like to. Then the waiter came up. He was young but hard-nosed, the way people get when they're born and bred on the margins of survival. He spoke sharply to the old man, but I gave him a big grin and said, *"Desayuno para mi amigo, por favor."*

The old man thanked me and ordered his breakfast and started setting out the men. I watched him and kept one eye on the truck. It made a perfect cover. I was still in plain sight, but I was not a lollygagging tourist anymore, I was a chess player giving the local hustler a game on his home turf, perfect reason to be sitting in this place, and given the curiosity of people anywhere, we would soon be surrounded by spectators. Amadeo wouldn't notice me if he passed this way.

The old man drew white and opened pawn to queen four. I responded with the king's Indian defense, Fischer's favorite, knight to king's bishop three, and we soon had a good game going. I play a fair game of chess, if I do say so. I learned from a fellow officer in Ulster. It was unsafe to leave the barracks between patrols, and we spent weeks at a time cooped up when we weren't taking care of business on the street. It added a lot to my general knowledge. I learned chess from a champion, and heard all the old songs of the forties and fifties from another officer who had every record ever cut before rock became the rage. Neither kind of information is worth money, but it's all part of the general education I should have gotten in college but didn't.

The old man's breakfast came, and I paid the waiter and sat back, pretending to study the board while the old man ate. He looked underfed, but he ate with perfect manners. Then he turned to the board, and soon we had a crowd of loungers around us. It got harder to watch the truck without being obvious. But I managed it, and managed to beat the old man, too. It was tactics that did it. He was a cautious player, and once I realized that, I became a little more dashing until I was two pawns up on him and then played a careful game of attrition. The crowd got noisy then, and I glanced at the old man and saw that I'd hurt him. He was Zihuatanejo's answer to Bobby Fischer, and I'd humbled him, which had not been my intention. So I did what any gentleman would have done, played him twice more and let him win, once by allowing him to fork my king and queen with his knight and once by letting him pin a rook to my king with a bishop. He was quietly jubilant and honor was satisfied. And there was still no sign of Amadeo.

I was set to play another game, but the old man shook his head and pointed to my watch. I wondered what kind of schedule he was on but realized that he had seen through my giveaways and didn't want to press his luck by going another game. So I quietly slipped him a thousand-peso bill *"para mi maestro,"* for my teacher, and he made a modest little gesture but kept the bill gratefully, then bowed and left.

The crowd melted away, and I was starting to stand out like ears on a frog, so I nodded to the waiter, left a little change, and moved away into the market. There were other openings that overlooked the parked truck. I would have to watch from one of them. Maybe I'd be lucky and find somewhere else inconspicuous.

The aisles were still crowded, and I made my way through them, ducking under the canvas awnings, hung about five foot eight from the ground, plenty of room for the average Mexican, even in his sombrero, but a pain for a six-footer. I didn't linger but moved toward the next spot, the only building in town that had collapsed during the earthquake of the previous fall. It looked like a bombed-out building in Ulster, except that it wasn't blackened with smoke and nobody had spray-painted "Long live the Provos" on the wall.

I reached it and stood beside the shattered wall, staring out at the truck, then turning to glance at the crowd. My hopes of finding Amadeo were fading now. He might be off striking a bargain with García and getting ready to bring in a new shipment of cocaine from Colombia. Once his business contacts were made, he would be free to hire a car and he would leave the truck and take off. Besides which, if somebody found the body in the arroyo, the police would be looking for the truck, and there were enough of them in town to turn it up quickly. And then, as I wondered what to do next, I glanced around again and saw Jesús coming toward me.

I flicked my head at him and he came over. There were a couple of other people close by, just shoppers, incurious about me, but he played his role carefully. *"Buenos días, señor,"* he said. Then, in his accented English, "I learn the song you tell me."

"I was going to come to Coconuts again tonight and have you play for me," I said noisily. Then the shoppers walked by into the white-hot sunlight, and I said quickly, "Amadeo got away. He stole that truck and killed the driver. I think he's gone to see García."

"No," he said quietly. "No, he's gone right by García, he's in touch with one of García's runners, a guy who brings in coke. I saw them talking in town. I've been looking for you."

"Is he still there?"

He shook his head. "I doubt it. This was earlier, maybe an hour ago. They were standing on the street outside the restaurant the other guy owns. He's an American, married to a girl from Zihua. She's his front, her and the restaurant. It's called El Huachinango. His name is Blackburn."

"Any idea where my man would have gone?" A dumb question, but maybe he did know. He was on top of what happened in town. He would know any safe houses the drug dealer might have set up.

"No. He's still in town, I guess. This runner, he would

probably take a down payment from Amadeo, then deliver a shipment, maybe tonight, maybe tomorrow. You can expect Amadeo to stay under cover until then."

I thought about that one. It was surprising to learn that a drug shipment could be arranged so quickly. It probably meant that the runner had a stash somewhere nearby and would get it out if the price was high enough. Interesting, but the sixty-four-dollar question was, what did that mean about Amadeo? Would he find his own cover until the coke was delivered? Or would he put himself in the hands of the runner? It seemed to me that the best thing to do was to go calling at El Huachinango and ask a few pointed questions, at the point of my *pistola,* if necessary.

Jesús was becoming nervous. I guessed I was wearing out his credibility as a troubador. Guitar pickers don't mingle with *turistas* through the day, they're off in their *hamacas* resting up for the requests and the big tips later in the evening. He spilled over with his concern. "I must go. People will see me with you and talk."

"Okay, thanks for the help. How can I reach you again if I have to?"

"I will be in the restaurants, starting at dusk. Usually I get to Coconuts around nine o'clock."

"Thanks." More people were passing us, glancing at us in the small-town way that means they are storing everything up in their memory. "But you really should learn 'Malagueña.' It goes like this," I said, and hummed the melody, loudly enough and far enough off-key that even the passersby grinned at me.

"*Sí, señor.* I weel practice har' an' play for your *señora* thees evenin'," he said.

"Good. It's worth five bucks," I said and clapped him on the back, hard enough to make him stagger. He smiled and left. And I turned to glance at the truck, baking quietly in the heat. When I looked back, he was gone.

There didn't seem to be any more point in watching the truck. If Jesús was right, Amadeo was back in the drug business for real. That meant he would rapidly start making the necessary payoffs to divert the police away from himself. And if their investigation of the murder of the man from La Playa Blanca brought them to his door, he would get real neighborly and point them in my direction.

I had to outrun the coppers and get my hands on Amadeo before the police found the body in the riverbed. My first move was to join up with Thurlbeck. I did it by walking out to the truck and standing beside it, putting one hand on my head in the "come to me" sign you use when you're on patrol. Thurlbeck immediately stepped into sight from a doorway on the other side of the street, and I nodded minutely and walked away to the place where he had dropped me off. He walked up behind me and touched my elbow, so that I fell into stride with him, walking on past the back of the market.

"What happened?"

"Amadeo's in town, talking business to one of García's runners. My contact tells me this guy runs a restaurant. I thought we'd start by going down there and talking to him. See if he'll let us know where our lad is hiding."

"Okay. I'll immobilize the truck." He turned away and I waited while he walked back and lifted the truck hood and took out the rotor arm from the ignition. He came back to me, grinning. "That should hold him."

We found his van and drove back through town, going up and down the streets until we found El Huachinango. It was a simple little place, not likely to appeal to tourists. It had waist-high walls all around it, with a metal grille above them, and was thatched with banana leaves supported on tree trunks placed wherever necessary in the floor space. Now, nearly noon, it was deserted except for a couple of waiters playing backgammon. One of them got up when we came in and came over to us, smiling.

I smiled back and ordered a Tecate. Thurlbeck shook his head. *"Agua mineral, por favor,"* he said, and the boy went to get our orders.

"Not big on beer?" I asked him as we sat.

"Used to be real big on it, but I haven't had a drop since 1951, June twelfth."

I nodded and told him, "The owner is an American, name of Blackburn. You want to ask for him, the kids don't seem to have much English."

"Sure thing." He waited until the boy was pouring our drinks, then he asked him in Spanish if Señor Blackburn, his friend, was in.

The boy spoke rapidly, and Thurlbeck smiled and looked politely upset at the answer and made some comment. The boy left and we sipped our drinks. "Seems the *señor* was called away. He'll be back later, my *amigo* thinks. And he's always here for dinner, to talk to the tourists who come in."

"What say we just sit and wait for him?"

Thurlbeck inclined his head, "I think so; it's coming up on siesta time, no sense dashing around in the heat." He grinned. "This beats birding all to hell," he said happily.

"Good." I took another glug at my Tecate; it's a good crisp beer, not unlike a German brew, one of my favorites. Thurlbeck watched me. He seemed charged up with enthusiasm, like a kid who can't help talking but won't mention the thing that's really on his mind.

"Beer is the only thing I miss," he said at last. "It wasn't my tipple. I was a sour-mash man. But when it's hot and I smell that beer, I can remember the way it all used to taste." He glanced at his glass gloomily, then raised it and sipped again.

"You used to hammer it?"

"Yeah. I was a two-fisted drinker for about five years, after I got back from Europe. Started over there. We were in some tough fighting up near Caen, right after D day. Lost a lot of good buddies and had some near misses myself. I started drinking every chance I got."

I looked at his lined face, trying to imagine it forty years younger, flushed with fear and liquor. He met my eyes and sniffed.

199

"Calvados, that was my tipple in Normandy. Then Cognac as we got farther east. Then when the war was over, the pressure came off and I cooled it." His glass had left a damp ring on the tabletop, and he smudged it away with his fingertip. "Then one day I was in a shootout at a bank in town. My partner was killed. I dropped the guy who did it, and the manager poured me a stiff drink, and suddenly I was back on." He set down his glass and shook his head. "Kept at it until I came home one morning and found my wife and kids gone, moved out. I went to see her, and she said I had to choose. Her or the booze. No contest."

"You're a tough sonofabitch," I said. "That wouldn't have done it for most drinkers."

"Thought the world of that woman," he said. "Her parents were killed in the blitz. She didn't have anywhere to go after I brought her home. But it didn't stop her moving out. She said she would save up and take the kids back to Britain. So I quit."

He glanced around at the blackboard. "You wanna eat lunch? We won't get another chance. And I operate better on a full gut."

"Done. Why don't you order?"

"Okay. How about some nachos? They're not real heavy, and the peppers'll light up your life."

"Sounds good."

He ordered and we ate, hoping that Blackburn would return. But he didn't, so we ordered another drink and did some more talking.

Thurlbeck cleared his throat, the way a doctor would before he tells you to get your affairs in order. "I've been thinking. We've got some information that García would like to hear. About one of his guys talking to Amadeo."

"The best news he'd like to hear is that he'd got his hands on me. I've embarrassed the guy, shot some of his heavies, and kicked the head off his bodyguard. He'd like to peg me out on an anthill someplace and sit around while I groaned."

Thurlbeck waved that one aside. "You're forgetting. He's in

the drug business. This isn't like one of the Mafia families. Those guys out at the farm, they were peons, he can replace them with a snap of his fingers."

"What about El Grande? That guy was a landmark around here. Knocking him over was like blowing up city hall. People notice things like that."

Still Thurlbeck shook his head. "And you're forgetting that Amadeo has half a million bucks with him. I know these guys, I've dealt with every kind of slimebag you can think of over the last thirty-five years. For that kind of bread they'd talk to anybody."

I sucked my teeth, it felt luxurious, knowing they were all there. I didn't think they would be once García got his hands on me. "No dice. You saw the way his people were after me this morning. He wants my ass. If he got his half mil, it would just make finding me a little sweeter, that's all."

Thurlbeck looked at me steadily. I looked back at him, seeing him as he must have looked forty years ago, a lean young GI with his M1 and his mission, to hand Hitler his head. He looked tough. "What was the motto of this outfit you belonged to?" he asked quietly.

"The SAS? Who dares wins. Why?"

He grinned and sipped his mineral water. "You ain't gonna win if you don't," he said softly. "You really want to go home without this prick?"

I raised one palm to slow him down. "You know better than that. But our best bet is to find Blackburn and talk to him for a while. Maybe I can scoop Amadeo without sticking my head into the guillotine."

"How long you reckon to give him?" he asked. "All day? All night? Say he's gone off on a drug trip and doesn't get back for a week. You plan to sit here drinking beer and hoping he'll have news for you?"

"Okay. Let's put some edges on all this. Let's say we'll wait until dinnertime. If Blackburn hasn't come back, we'll get Jesús to point us at García." I kept my voice nice and even, but I was hoping Blackburn would oblige. Seeing García would be a lot less fun than a root canal job.

Thurlbeck checked his watch. "It's twelve forty-eight. What do you say we give him till seven?"

I nodded slowly. "All right. Six more hours sitting around and then the fun begins."

He raised his glass to me, and I matched him, and we both relaxed. And then a young guy with blond hair and a good tan walked through the door, carrying a suitcase. One of the waiters stood up at once and spoke to him in Spanish, and Thurlbeck grinned. "Speak of the angels, hear their wings," he said. "Guess who came home early."

nineteen

The waiter must have told Black-
burn we were looking for him, because he nodded neatly and
went on toward the kitchen, picking up the pace a little, ready
for the now-you-see-him, now-you-don't trick out of the back
door. I beat him to the kitchen by a pace, grinning like a
long-lost army buddy and sticking out my hand. "Hi, Blackie.
Long time no see."

It bought the kids off, but it didn't cut any ice with him.

"Do I know you?" He had the pinched, nasal vowels of the
born New Yorker.

"Sure you do, we sang side by side in the Mormon Taberna-
cle Choir." I kept up the grin until Thurlbeck joined us. He
flipped open his wallet, giving us a quick flash of his gold-
plated badge.

"Adams, FDA," he said.

Blackburn burst out in a torrent of Spanish, and one of the
waiters jumped to his feet, but Thurlbeck smiled at him and
canceled whatever order had been given, in Spanish just as
rapid. Then, for my benefit, he spoke to Blackburn in English.
"This won't take up much of your valuable time, so why don't

you sit down here with us, nice and friendly, and tell the kids to stay where we can see them."

Blackburn came with us to our table. He was still clutching his case and held it on his lap when he sat down. Thurlbeck said, "We're not interested in you, Mr. Blackburn. We understand you're a pillar of the community here, married to a nice girl, running this place. That's fine. Cooperate with us, and things go on just the same as ever, you make your trips south and come back with nose candy, some other sucker takes it up where we have to worry about it. That's all fine and dandy."

Blackburn leaned back, casual as hell, except for his viselike grip on the handle of the case. "I don't know what the hell you're talking about."

"Tell him, Johnnie," Thurlbeck said.

I sat up straight, a Mountie removed from the musical ride and put on a chair instead of his horse. "Rodgers, RCMP," I told him. "I'm in pursuit of one Gregory Amadeo, fugitive from justice."

Blackburn sneered. "What're you guys smokin'? Neither one of you has authority here. Whyn't you finish your beer and go. I'll tear up the check, you can still charge it on expenses."

"Very generous." I matched his sneer. "You want to see some authority that holds good in this place, is that it?"

"Show me." We were like a couple of kids going "Naaah, Naaah, Naaah" at one another in the school yard. I opened my jacket, revealing the Colt. "Guaranteed good anywhere," I said, trumping his ace.

He dropped the sneer but stayed cool. "What are you? Some kind of nut? Pull that thing, and Raúl would have the shotgun from behind the bar and take your head off."

I glanced at the backgammon players. One of them had raised his head when he heard his name mentioned. He was a long way from the bar. "I could drop him before he got there, and we both know it, so cut the crap. Just come along with us like a good boy."

He was starting to sweat. His face was glistening, and his fine white lace shirt was sticking to his chest with it. I studied him, making him more tense. He was handsome in a dated, flower child kind of way, his hair overlong, his face round, his eyes a clear blue. Only now they were narrowed with the most fear he'd shown in a long time, I guessed.

"Come where?"

"To wherever my good buddy Greg Amadeo is waiting for you," I told him. "Only first, you're going to take us all over this place so we can see that he's not out back with *la señora*, drinking a beer and waiting for that suitcase."

He glanced from me to Thurlbeck, licking his lips. "I don't have to show you anything," he said tautly.

Thurlbeck took over, his voice relaxed as morning sunshine. "No, and we don't have to tell you that Amadeo is not only a wanted man but he's got access to a lot of cash. Now us—" he waved his hand at me and then himself—"we get regular paychecks. We don't need any cash. But a businessman like yourself, you probably do. So I'm suggesting that you take us to Amadeo and then we take you to his cash. Fair?"

Blackburn didn't relax, but his eyes narrowed a little in interest. "How much cash?"

"Enough that you could buy Coconuts, or build someplace just as fancy," Thurlbeck said. "Interested?"

He didn't roll over and play dead. "I might be" was all he volunteered.

I took over as the hard-nose. "So you've got a choice. Cash on one hand, pain on the other. Which'll it be?"

He grinned, slowly, as if his face was coming unfrozen after dental work. "Cash sounds good to me."

"Very sensible. Now just show me around this nice place of yours so we know Amadeo's not here, then we'll go outside and my partner will drive us wherever you say."

He stood up, dangling the suitcase casually. "Sure. Come on with me."

"You two go. I'll stay and watch the store," Thurlbeck said. "I wouldn't want either of your *camareros* making any phone calls while our backs were turned." He beamed and raised his glass.

"Yeah, whatever," Blackburn said. He jerked his head toward the back of the restaurant. "Come on, I'll show you around."

I followed him, and he took me out into the kitchen, where two young women were chopping vegetables. He spoke to one of them, the prettier one, in Spanish. "My wife," he said to me, and I smiled and told her *"Buenos días"* and she returned it, without pausing in her work. Beyond the kitchen was an attached single room, simply furnished but with a bed instead of the traditional *hamacas* and with a good big bookshelf, filled mostly with paperbacks.

"That's the whole shebang," Blackburn told me. "Unless you wanna check the bathroom."

"Why not?" I opened the door. The place was the same as the one at the hotel, large and spotless. He'd married himself one hell of a housekeeper.

"Happy now?" he asked. He had set down his suitcase beside the bed and was edging toward the night table. As I turned back from the bathroom, he made a lunge for the table and jerked the drawer down. I dived full length across the bed and slammed him a straight-arm punch in the kidney. He gave a groan and crashed down, pulling the night table over with him. I rolled over the bed and stood on his right hand, then set the night table on its legs again.

His wife appeared in the doorway, still carrying the big knife she was using to chop with. She screamed something in Spanish, and I smiled back at her and said, *"De nada, señora."* It's nothing. She wasn't buying, so I bent down and picked up the gun that lay in the drawer. "Tell her to cool it or this thing could go off," I told Blackburn, and he rattled at her in Spanish and she turned away and disappeared from view.

I took my foot off his wrist and checked the gun. It was a Beretta 9mm, a useful piece. "This thing standard issue for greasy-spoon proprietors?" I asked him.

He sat up, trying to nurse his right hand and his kidney at the same time. "We have a lot of cash on the premises, I need protection, this is Mexico, for Christ's sake."

"And the land-office business you're doing out front, you need a gun? Come on, Blackburn, cut the crap. We know what you are. Smarten up, hand us Amadeo, and we're on our way."

He swore once, then asked, "How do I know you're telling the truth?"

"Look," I said patiently, "if all we wanted was some drug-pushing sleazebag, we could have picked up any of the retailers back home. You're safe as a church with us, once you put us in touch with Amadeo."

He looked up at me as I stood up, back a pace from him where he couldn't swing a sucker punch at my testicles. I could see him measuring the distance and deciding he wasn't fast enough to make it. Then he stood up.

"Right. Now as we go into the kitchen, I want to hear you laughing so the *señora* knows it's all in fun and she doesn't take that cleaver up alongside my head. Got that? Isn't that the funniest thing you've heard since Barney Miller went off the air?"

"Sure," he said woodenly, then he began to laugh. It sounded like a man trying to get a snowmobile started, a rhythmic succession of puffs that got louder and surer over about four seconds. By the time he reached the door, he had it right, and his wife looked up and frowned at us, mystified. He waved a casual hand at her and took me on into the front of the restaurant. I had stuck his Beretta in my pocket, and I kept my hand on it as we passed the waiters. A pale-looking gringo couple had come in and were studying the menu while one of the kids hovered nearby. The other was wiping the top of a table. I hooked my head at Thurlbeck and he stood up, laying a couple of bills on the table.

He stepped ahead of Blackburn and opened the door, then fell in on the other side of him as we walked up the street to the van.

It was punishingly hot now, and the inside of the van was like an oven, but I shoved Blackburn into the front seat and then got in behind him, nudging him in the back of the head with a stiff finger. In his fear he must have thought it was a gun. "Right, now steer us to Amadeo, and no fooling, or you won't be going back to the little woman," I told him.

"Put that thing away. We've got a deal, right? I take you to Amadeo, you take me to his money, okay?"

"Most of it," Thurlbeck said. "This guy's left some debts unpaid."

Blackburn threw up his hands. "What's that s'posed to mean? You guys get the cream, I get the skimmed milk, is that it?"

"He killed a fisherman and beat the hell out of a woman," Thurlbeck said. "We compensate the family and the woman. The rest is doggy doo, for all I care. Now where am I heading?"

Blackburn directed him up the street until we were clear of the waterfront, then across and back down on the north side of the little inlet that runs beside the barracks. The road was rough, and Thurlbeck glanced at Blackburn quickly. "Where exactly are we headed, buddy?"

"He's in my casa, up on the hillside," Blackburn said.

I didn't look up. I was checking the Beretta I'd taken from him. It had a full magazine and one up the spout. I put the safety back on and put the gun in my pocket. Then I handed the .38 to Thurlbeck. He took one hand from the wheel to accept it without comment. I didn't want him to have to do any shooting, but if things went haywire, two guns would be better than one.

"Right here," Blackburn said. I glanced up and saw we were turning up the hillside, following a road that led back and forth through hairpin turns toward a couple of big, opulent places high over the water, the Beverly Hills of Zihuatanejo.

"You're living kind of rich, aren't you?" Thurlbeck said.

"Nothing much else to spend money on," Blackburn said easily. "I don't travel a whole lot, and women cost peanuts."

Thurlbeck glanced at him again. "Women aren't cattle," he said in a cold voice.

"Sorry. I forgot you two guys were on the side of honor and

justice," Blackburn said. I didn't like the fact that he was getting so chipper. It meant he had something up his sleeve. Maybe he had a couple of hungry Dobermans waiting for us at his casa. Ah, well, even the best of dogs isn't bulletproof.

We looped our way up the hill in low gear until we came to a high wall with iron gates set into it. Bougainvillea spilled over the walls, making a scene that would have looked good on a postcard. Having a wonderful time, wish you were here.

"Honk," Blackburn said. "Two long, one short."

"No," Thurlbeck said. "I wasn't born yesterday, son. For all I know, that's your signal that trouble's coming. Get out and open the gate. It's your house."

"Suit yourself." He slipped out of the seat but Thurlbeck put one hand on his arm. "John gets out first, he's gonna have his gun on you, so don't get cute."

I opened my door and stood waiting for Blackburn to get down. He went ahead of me and opened one side of the gate. "Now the other," I told him. "My buddy hates walking."

He shrugged and swung the other gate open. Thurlbeck drove past us and around the circular driveway to the portico of the big white house. I noticed there were bars on all of the windows. Burglar proof, and also a handy prison if you locked a guy into one of the rooms. Maybe Amadeo was penned up inside.

I prodded Blackburn with my left hand, keeping my right in my pocket on his Beretta. He opened the door and called "Carlos."

"No crowd scenes, just get Amadeo out here," I said.

"I guess you've never had servants," Blackburn said, stylishly tossing his hair out of his eyes. He stepped inside, into a tiled entrance hall with open doorways on four sides. "Carlos'll bring him out when I tell him to."

Footsteps sounded on two sides of the entry and suddenly there were two men looking at us, both holding guns on us, one of them a shotgun.

Blackburn laughed out loud. "Which one you gonna kill,

hotshot? Get one, the other'll blow you in half. Now gimme my gun back."

Behind me I could hear Thurlbeck coming in. "I'll take the one on the left," I called, but before I could draw and fire, he spoke.

"Forget it, kid. We've got you."

I spun around, openmouthed. He was standing there, in his feed-store hat, looking like a Norman Rockwell painting, only now he had my .38 pointed at me.

"You mean you're part of this?"

"Give him his gun back," Thurlbeck said. "You got no chance. You'll stop one, the other two of us'll put you down to stay, and I don't want to see that." He was right, I had the Ancient Mariner's chance, I could stoppeth one in three.

Blackburn reached out and took his gun. "There. That's a whole lot better," he said.

The two Mexicans kept me covered, and I stayed close to Blackburn. If either one tightened on the trigger I could still throw him in front of me. Not a big chance of survival, but the best I had. Only Thurlbeck said, "I'm behind you, remember. So don't try anything fancy."

Now Blackburn let his gun dangle casually from his hand. "So, okay. Come on in and meet Don García."

I worked with an actress once, keeping ardent fans from smudging her makeup on location. Later, when I was smudging it for her, she let me in on the secret of all good acting. The best line is silence. I took her cue now. Of all the things I'd thought possible, Thurlbeck's letting me down had been last on the list. He seemed straight as a die. I just walked, obedient to Blackburn's nudge on my elbow, following one of the Mexicans who backed ahead of me down his corridor until we came to a big tiled room furnished in elegant rattan, with plants and statues and, of all things, a miniature shrine of the Virgin. García was in one of the chairs, smoking a cigar.

He took the cigar out of his mouth and smiled at me. "*Buenos días,*" he said.

I nodded. "*Buenos días* to you too, buddy."

He stood up and came forward. Not all the way, not so close I could grab him and play any games, but in that big room he was able to take three of his small paces and still be clear of me. "You give me much trouble, *señor*," he said.

"We aim to please." I was studying him. About fifty-five, just over five feet tall, and wiry. He looked like he might clap his hands together explosively and start clicking out a flamenco on his tiled floor. But he didn't. He looked at me.

"You kill my frien'," he said.

"There was a lot of it going around."

His English wasn't up to that, and Blackburn translated, I guess. His Spanish didn't amuse García.

He ignored me and walked around to shake hands with Thurlbeck. They smiled and exchanged what I took was Spanish for "long time no see."

"Well, old home week," I said. "Birds of a feather."

"Cool it," Thurlbeck said without menace. He didn't need any in his voice, he still had it in his hand. The .38 I'd given him.

My mind was racing. It didn't seem likely that they would let me survive long. On the other hand, they probably wouldn't shoot me here, in García's den. Blood is a bitch to get out of rattan furniture. I decided I would hold off my big effort. If Thurlbeck put the gun away, I would grab Blackburn as a shield and take his Beretta back off him. That still left two men against me, but I'd rather die trying than roll over for these back-stabbers.

García went back to his chair and waved us to seats. I kept standing, but he nodded to Blackburn, who told me, "Siddown. If you try anything, you're dog meat. The *señor* wants to talk to you."

I sat, alone in a big rattan armchair. It was solid and low to the ground, there was no chance of rolling it backward and making a dive for the door. On the other hand, like I said, they probably weren't planning to waste me here.

García smoked in silence for about a minute. The Mexican with the shotgun stood to one side of him, his gun on me.

Blackburn and Thurlbeck had me quartered, one each side and forward, where they wouldn't be in one another's line of fire. They both sat with their guns in their laps. The other Mexican nodded to García and left. No need overdoing things, I guessed. Three of them could take care of an unarmed man.

At last García took his cigar out of his mouth and laid it aside in a big onyx ashtray. "I unnerstan' you're the bodyguard for Señor Amadeo."

"Full marks," I said, and Blackburn translated it as *"Sí."*

García grinned. He had fine white teeth with enough gold in them to show he hadn't bought them in a china store. "You pretty good," he said.

I didn't answer, and he let the grin fade away. "So tell me, what is your plan?"

"I'd like to set aside a little something every payday and retire to Florida at age sixty-five," I said. It was the next best thing to silence.

Again Blackburn translated, and García showed me his gold again. "Funny also. I like that. You are *muy macho.*"

A hell of a thing to put on my gravestone if any of the triggers in the room got pulled.

"An' I unnerstan' that Señor Amadeo has *mucho dinero.*" When I didn't answer, he translated for me, letting his smile die again. "Many dollars."

"Loaded," I said. "I helped him dig it up. He's carrying a fortune."

"How much dollars?"

"Quinientos mil."

He sucked in his thin little cheeks and nodded his head agreeably. " 'Alf a million dollars. You sure of this?"

"It's about the only thing I am sure of today."

He ignored that and spoke to Blackburn in Spanish. Blackburn said, "Don García asks, what is he carrying this money in?"

"You mean you don't know? He came to see you."

"He was empty-handed when he came to see me. I guess he doesn't trust me that well," Blackburn said.

They had dealt me a card, a very small one, but at least I was an active player. Great. I hate being dummy. "Oh, then you don't know what to look for," I said mildly.

"Forget it, kid," Thurlbeck said. "You told me, remember?" He turned to García and spoke to him in Spanish. García nodded.

My actress's advice failed me. "Boy, I sure had you figured wrong, Thurl, baby. Next thing, you'll be telling me your wife's alive and well and you're a big man with the sauce, right?"

"Cool it," Thurlbeck said, and this time there was anger in his eyes.

Blackburn looked amused. "Not working out the way you planned, is it?"

"All part of life's rich pageant." I shrugged.

"And what do you wan' Señor Amadeo for?" García asked.

The old "When did you stop beating your wife?" question. If I said I wanted to take him back to lay the Canadian drug business in an early grave, they would shoot me. Hell, those people were their best customers. "I'm a bodyguard," I said. "Last week I was keeping teenyboppers from beating a rock star to death with their brassieres. This week a drug dealer. Them's the breaks."

García ignored the answer except for the nut of it. "Thees man is your clien', yes?"

"Yes."

"An' when you take him back, he talk to the police an' many frien's of mine go to prison?"

"Now you're getting it." I was still watching all three guns. Blackburn and Thurlbeck were laid back, their guns had drooped. But the Mexican was still earning his pay. The shotgun never wavered.

"This is an evil thing that Señor Amadeo want to do," García said. "He is a man without honor."

"Or scruples, or a good insurance plan."

García ignored me. He took out a leather case and lit another cigar. It smelled good, but then, he could afford the best. When he had it going nicely, he started speaking to Blackburn in rapid Spanish.

Blackburn answered and then García nodded. He stood up. "You will stay here," he said.

"Great. Can I have a beer while I'm waiting?" I wondered what was coming. Why was he keeping me alive? Or was he?

Thurlbeck said, "Cut the comedy. You're only alive as a favor to me. Don't get me teed off."

"I'll put you on my Christmas card list," I said. "What happens now?"

Blackburn answered that one. "Señor García wants to have words with Mr. Amadeo, some serious words."

"You're going to shoot him?"

"Planning to beat the rush," he said. "He wouldn't last a day after testifying against those Canadians. This way we cut out some of the embarrassment that could happen."

"You don't need them. There's a million customers up there, someone else will be smuggling cocaine before Amadeo hits the floor."

"If it ain't broke, you don't have to fix it," Blackburn said. "Listen to your buddy here, don't press your luck. You're alive on his good will."

"And you're going where?"

"To see your boy," Blackburn said. He was cool now, literally. The sweat on his face had dried and he looked easy. I guessed he had opened up to García and was no longer in danger of being taken for a turncoat, trying to run his own sidelines under the Don's nose. He'd be around to feed more customers at his restaurant, instead of feeding the fishes.

"And where's that?"

"You don't need to know," Thurlbeck said shortly. "Now get down on your face and put your hands behind you."

"Not again," I said, but I did it.

Blackburn tied the knots, cranking them up a lot tighter than Maria had the night before. And he looped my elbows together as well, then he cut the rope. That was a relief. But he ended it instantly, throwing a couple of loops around my feet. "We don't want to see you on set," someone said. It sounded like Thurlbeck.

His choice of words made me frown, facedown on the tiles. On set? Were they making a movie? Maybe a snuff movie of Amadeo's last moments, a souvenir to ship up to their good customers in Toronto, a token of goodwill. Who could tell?

García said something short and Blackburn answered him, in Spanish, and then Thurlbeck spoke and I could hear the question in his voice. Blackburn answered tersely and Thurlbeck said, "Ah, sí, el Parthenon."

On set? The Parthenon? I wondered if the ex-police chief who built the place had incorporated a murder chamber he rented out for local events, the way the Knights of Columbus rent their hall for weddings. Then I heard their footsteps receding and the clumping of the front door being shut.

Behind me I heard a match scrape. I gave a squirm and rolled over, face up. It was even less comfortable but it gave me a view of the room and of my guard, who had laid his shotgun on the tiles and was sitting in García's chair, smoking the stub of the big man's cigar. You could see his simple face working. Man, this is the life! it registered.

He looked at me and puffed smoke like a cartoon strip millionaire. If he hadn't been smoking, he might have come over and given me a leisurely kick or two, but it was siesta time and he was sitting down, why rush things. Later he would no doubt have to dig a hole for me somewhere. Now he was going to enjoy the good life. I had perhaps five minutes left.

twenty

I lay and listened for the sounds of other life in the casa. Maybe somewhere a cook was working on the boss's supper, or the other gunny was nodding over his comic book, but if they were, they were doing it silently. It was time to make my move.

"*Señor,*" I said, and he glanced at me and narrowed his eyes, clenching his mouth over the cigar butt. *Muy macho.* I changed the record. "*Amigo,*" I said, "*tengo mucho dinero.*" I have a lot of money.

This time he stood up and came closer. "*Qué?*" What?

"*Tengo muchos dolares para usted.*" That got him. A lot of dollars, for him. He hadn't counted on any bonus. He took another step closer, coming about six inches to the right of my bound feet. Perfect. I pulled my legs up and slammed both heels into his knee. I heard the leg break, and he yowled and fell backward, writhing to hold his shin. I bumped toward him on shoulders and feet and then raised my feet and brought them down on his gut, three times. Advantage Locke.

I listened but couldn't hear any rushing feet. We must have been alone in the house. The other Mexican must have gone with the lynch party, looking for Amadeo. I had a little time.

He was carrying a switchblade. I could see the outline in his right pants pocket. It was tight to his thigh but lying where the handle was in a straight line to the opening of the pocket. I put my heels on the other end of it and forced it out of his pocket, like toothpaste coming out of a tube. It took about thirty seconds before the knife clinked out onto the tile. Then I rolled and grasped it and pressed the opening switch. It flipped open, and I lay and wrestled with the ropes on my hands, praying that he had kept the knife sharp enough to cut under the small amount of pressure I was able to exert. Thank God for machismo. That thing was like a razor. It took only a minute and my hands were free. The loop around my elbows was connected and it loosened as well.

I sat up and slashed the rope off my feet, then picked up his shotgun and checked the action. It was a Winchester pump, loaded with double-0 buckshot, heavy enough to take down a bear. There were five rounds in it, one up the spout and four in the unplugged magazine. I reloaded and went out of the room, carefully, not sure whether any timid soul had heard me and sent for reinforcements. *Nada*. The luck, as Big Ernie used to say, she was running good.

I went silently down the hall, checking in each of the rooms I passed and out to the front door. It swung open and I glanced out. Thurlbeck's van was still parked where he had left it, at the front of the house. There was nobody in sight, but the gates had been closed. That could mean a head-hunting dog loose in the grounds. I stepped out of the doorway, checking all around, still nothing. It didn't seem likely that an ex-cop would have left keys in a vehicle, but I checked the van anyway. Hot damn! More luck. The key ring was dangling from the ignition.

It started, first turn. I continued around the driveway and down to the gate. When I got out to open it, I took the gun. This much luck wasn't natural. There had to be a dog somewhere.

There was, a Doberman lying in the shade of a bougainvillea beside the gate. He launched himself at me in a snarling black arc but the shotgun flung him back against the pillar, spattering blood over the light blue paint. Four shots left.

Discretion was wasted now. I gunned through the gate and down the switchback road, grateful to Thurlbeck for buying a van with a manual gear shift. An automatic wouldn't have held half as well on those curves. At the bottom of the hill I turned back to town and roared back through a cloud of dust, scattering chickens like a whirlwind.

Within seconds I was at Las Tres Marias, the hotel on the beach, and from there on it was town. I slowed and drove quietly through the side streets to the main circle road, then cut around town, at sixty kilometers an hour, keeping up with the other traffic, not drawing attention to myself. Then, at the other end of Zihua, I cut across to the road that led up the hill to Cuatro Vientos and the place Thurlbeck had let slip, the Parthenon.

As I drove I planned my next move. I wouldn't get away with smuggling a shotgun past the armed guard on the gate. Even if I broke it down and wrapped it in a blanket, any serviceman would find it. I would have to get in empty-handed. But how? As I drove up the hill, I flipped open the glove box. There were some maps in there and a couple of letters. I pulled one of them out. It was a businesslike manila envelope, a bill probably, addressed to Thurlbeck in Flagstaff. It had been only lightly sealed and he had opened it without tearing the flap. Perfect. I licked the flap and pressed it down as I drove. It looked official enough to get past even an English-speaker who would read Thurlbeck's name on it.

I planned to flash it at the soldier on the gate and tell him I had a message for Señor García. If I straightened up and adopted the air of a British officer, he would be hard put not to salute me. Perfect.

But at the Parthenon I got the biggest surprise of the morning. The joint was jumping. The steep, washed-out driveway leading up to the side gate was jammed with cars and vans.

218

There was even a Mexican copper on duty there, waving people past the place importantly.

I pulled up next to him and leaned down. *"Buenos días. Qué pasa?"* What's happening?

He grinned and answered in Spanish too fast for me to follow. But the move was made. He was anxious to talk. I got out of the van and slipped him a folded thousand-peso bill. *"Estoy con los otros,"* I told him, I'm with the others. He palmed the bill and grinned again. He was carrying an old automatic, so worn that all the bluing had been rubbed off the frame. For a moment I was tempted to drop him and take the gun, but I didn't know how long I would be inside, and I couldn't risk coming back and finding a posse of locals waiting for me. I had no friends on the inside, it would be good to have some neutrals on the roadway.

I had already shoved the shotgun out of sight behind the seats. Now I left the van unlocked. My *amigo* with the gun and the free thousand pesos would take care of business for me while I went inside. When I came back with the hue and cry behind me, he would question them, not me. If I came back.

I walked up the driveway to the top. Good. García's Continental was parked in the opening to the Parthenon, facing into the gate. As I approached I could see that the driver was behind the wheel. He had the windows open, and his hand was sticking out, the fingers tapping to the rhythm of the tune on the radio. He was smoking, which probably explained the open window. García didn't want his car stunk up with anything except his own Romeo y Julietas.

I came up beside him and slapped my hand on top of the car. He stuck his face out of the window like a little bird, and I hit him a solid left hand on the nose. He fell back inside, and I slid in after him and chopped him in the throat. He gagged and gurgled, and I caught him by the throat and pressed my thumbs into his carotid arteries. He went out like a light.

It wasn't permanent. At most it would buy me a minute of his valuable time, so I did what I had to do, clinically. I chunked him on both collarbones, breaking them both, turning his arms into chopped liver for a few weeks. That would stop him pulling any stunts when he came around. Then I frisked him and took his gun, a Police Special, a .38 Colt with a four-inch barrel. It was loaded in all chambers and was worn shiny but looked cared for. There was a trace of oil on the mechanism, and it was free of the fuzz that accumulates if you don't wipe a gun down regularly. Polishing it had been his equivalent of beadcraft, I reckoned. He'd worn out the bluing with excess care. Good.

I shut the door and got out, the gun in my waistband under my jacket. Then I walked the five paces to the gateway and my first clear view of the big stone veranda that had given the place its name. It was crowded with people, all of them looking away from me, out toward the lip where I had seen the guard standing that morning as I came down the hill. And the bulk of the crowd seemed to be gringos, some tourists, but a lot of them in blue jeans and baseball caps, the semitechnical types you see around film sets. The guard, still holding his M1, was standing behind them, wishing he was tall enough to see over the top. And then I saw why. Debra Steen, wearing a flowered sunsuit, was reclining against one of the pillars, staring up into the sunlight like an ancient Aztec waiting for her cue to cut somebody's heart out and offer it in sacrifice. The client and a photographer were crouching in front of her. The guard turned and looked at me, then came over, bossily. He had that old M1 of his under his arm like a gamekeeper looking after his lordship's pheasants. And he was businesslike. If he couldn't groove on the *gringa,* then he would, by George, be the best bloody sentry in the business.

I could tell that he wasn't going to buy my envelope idea. He had the same look in his eyes you see in postal clerks when they're going to close the wicket as soon as you reach it. And I had only a few moments to get in before the driver came around and started groaning. Then the bread I had cast upon the waters a few nights back returned. Answering some call from the photographer, Debra Steen turned into a new pose that brought her eye to eye with me.

I waved and indicated my chest and then the area behind the sentry. She was working, alert to every signal, and she picked mine out of the air. She excused herself to the photographer and trotted over to me, stopping every male heart in the Parthenon.

I smiled at her and gave her my anxiety through the smile. "I have to get in, Debra, it's important."

"Of course," she said. She turned her charm on to the soldier and he melted like an ice cream in the sun. *"Mi amigo,"* she said and gave me a theatrical kiss. The sentry stood aside instantly and I was in. She led me forward, holding my arm.

"Thank you, Debra." I slowed her down. "It's vital I get into the building. Can you help me?"

"You helped me," she said, and led me over to the big doorway where another soldier stood. He straightened up when she approached and she said, *"Mi amigo"* and pushed me forward.

I grinned at the man and waved my envelope. *"Communicación para el señor García,"* I said, and he frowned, then nodded.

"Donde está?" I asked him. Where is he?

He stepped forward and opened the big wooden door and pointed down the hallway. *"Muchas gracias, amigo,"* I said, and ducked in. So far, so good. My head was inside the same noose as Amadeo's. Wonderful. Now to get the sonofabitch out before somebody tripped the trapdoor.

Inside was an entrance hallway with a floor of the same marble tile as the exterior. At the other side was a doorway that led down a corridor. The soldier watched me as I crossed the room briskly, as if I knew where the hell to go, then turned back to the lightly clad lady. I guessed he would rather see her in a swimsuit than me in my Savile Row three-piece. Ah, youth.

There was another soldier standing outside a tall heavy door at the end of the corridor, and I strode toward him and nodded. He spoke to me, but I frowned at him, a king pestered by a commoner.

"Señor García," I demanded coldly. He nodded and indicated the door. I nodded curtly and pushed it open, shoving my right hand inside my jacket and onto my shiny new *pistola.*

Homecoming week! All four of them were there. Amadeo was sitting in a high-backed chair, shoved as far back into it as he could squeeze himself, while Blackburn and García stood in front of him. Thurlbeck was off to one side, watching the pair of them as they questioned my poor bloody client. From the look of his face, which was streaked with livid finger marks, they had already started slapping him around.

Thurlbeck looked at me and laughed. But he wasn't holding his gun, so I ignored him. Then Blackburn turned. He was holding his automatic lightly in his left hand. His right had been too busy adjusting Amadeo's attitude. I guess inflicting pain makes you feel invincible. He raised his gun at me, and I shot him through the heart. The noise was deafening in that stone-walled room.

Blackburn flipped backward across Amadeo's lap. García scrambled away, and Thurlbeck still stood calmly, looking at me without speaking. "Come on, Greg, time to go walkies," I said.

Thurlbeck spoke then. "How're you planning to explain the bang to our *amigo* with the M1?"

"That's your job." I motioned to García with the barrel of my gun. "Bring the Prince of Darkness and let's haul ass. Any explaining to be done, you do it. And make it good. If I have to shoot you and the other two guards, I'm still taking this guy out."

Thurlbeck nodded easily and turned to the door. "First thing, though, take out your gun and set it on the floor, nice and gentle," I told him.

He reached inside his shirt and drew out the little .38, holding it delicately in his fingertips. "Put it down and scoot it over to me with your foot." He did, and I bent and picked it up, keeping him and García covered the whole time.

"Good. Now open the door and make a joke about the stupid gringo letting off his gun. Okay. I want it to be funny enough for the Carson show."

He opened the door a crack, waving his hand in front of his face as if the smoke were choking him. I could see the anxious face of the little soldier outside and watched it widen into a grin as Thurlbeck explained that *el stupido* had done something or other dumb. Then he closed the door. "Now what?"

"Now we all walk out together and get into the Continental. The driver's got a headache, so you get into the front seat, the rest of us will be in back. And no crap, or you're out of business."

"Okay. It's done," he said. He spoke to García in Spanish and the little guy narrowed his eyes.

"What's he telling him, Greg?" I asked, and Amadeo said, "He just said not to make any fuss, just walk out like we were leaving normally."

"Good. And don't bother picking up that pistol. You don't need one. I want all the guns in here to be mine," I said. I shoved Thurlbeck's gun into my left-hand jacket pocket, my own into my right. It didn't fit too well, the barrel was too long, but my hand concealed it and I could squeeze off at least one round without catching the hammer in the material. After that I would have to pull it out and play for keeps. After that I would have to. There were three M1s between me and freedom.

Thurlbeck was good. He put his arm over García's shoulder and chatted to him like an uncle as we came through the door. I came behind him with Amadeo next to me on my left side. I didn't think he needed any threatening to come along peacefully. I prodded him and he closed the door behind us. Thurlbeck paused for a moment and spoke to me. "Santos here has been taking care of us. I figure we owe him a few bucks."

"Very generous of you. Greg, give the nice soldier boy some cash."

Amadeo was moving like a sleepwalker, but he responded when I spoke and pulled out a roll of pesos and peeled off a thousand, which he handed to the soldier. The guy grinned and told him *"Muchas gracias, señor,"* and Amadeo nodded gravely and patted him on the shoulder. If the soldier noticed the zebra

223

marks on Amadeo's face, he didn't comment. Money has a way of making even the best of us shortsighted.

The hallway seemed longer on this leg. It stretched out ahead of us like the last mile of the Boston Marathon, but we walked down it with Thurlbeck still chatting to García, who said nothing, and with Amadeo breathing like a sprinter beside me.

We reached the end and crossed the entrance hall and walked out into the deep shade of the balcony. And here things got difficult.

Debra Steen was standing in front of us, her back to us, one hand on the shoulder of the guard, the other holding his rifle loosely. Beyond her the photographer was down on one knee, with the fashion-house guy beside him and the mob of spectators behind them, all of them staring at the fair Debra the way good Catholics stare at chocolate during Lent. I recognized Beth and Kelly and Helen from ten thousand years before.

As we came to the door, the client exploded. "For Christ's sweet sake, can't you people keep still, we're working here," he bellowed.

García ignored him and walked on, then Thurlbeck followed, muttering, "Excuse me." The client slapped his hand to his forehead. We walked a few steps, and then I heard the clatter of boots on tile behind me. Carlos had opened that door. I whirled to face him and at the same time Amadeo swore. I snatched a look over my shoulder and saw the driver I'd clobbered reeling beside another man who was carrying a shotgun.

It was a toss-up. I did what the book recommends, slapping a couple of shots in the general direction of the guy with the gun. He dropped, but I didn't think he was hit, and he still had the gun in his hands. Then I spun back and pointed the pistol at Carlos as he pitched through the door, his rifle in both hands. I didn't want to shoot him. He was legitimate, and he was doing his job. So I bellowed at him in a parade-ground voice, *"Alto!"* Stop. Not as direct as "Hands up!" or "Freeze!" but languages come second to survival.

He got the message anyway. He skidded to a standstill and

dropped the rifle. And behind me, only a foot away, I heard the impressive crash of another rifle going off. I spun back and saw the man with the shotgun sprawled sideways, his head leaking blood. Thurlbeck was holding the M1. "Run," he said. "I'll explain later."

The crowd was scattering, screaming in two languages, but Thurlbeck half dragged García, still carrying the M1 in his right hand. I came after them, with one hand on Amadeo's shoulder, the other on my gun.

We tumbled into the car, Thurlbeck throwing García across the front seat and jumping in, keeping the rifle beside him. I had Amadeo in the back and Thurlbeck backed down the driveway and out onto the road. He spun to the right and dived down the hill toward town. I sat and loaded three shells from the little .38 into the big one, not bothering to ask where we were going. I'm like an insurance company. I don't question acts of God.

Amadeo did it for me. "For Christ's sake, which side are you on?" he squeaked at Thurlbeck.

"Same one," Thurlbeck said, whisking around the corner past a burro laden with jerricans of water. "Sorry about the game at García's house, John. I'll explain later. I figured you'd find us."

"That's real big of you," I said. "You and that bastard there as thick as thieves, and you pointing guns at me. I'd like an explanation while you've got both hands on the wheel instead of that carbine."

"Yeah." Thurlbeck almost chuckled. "How about that? Haven't fired an M1 since nineteen and forty-five, but it came right back."

"Okay, so wear your marksman's badge with pride. In the meantime, talk."

"Sure." Thurlbeck nodded as we reached the edge of town and he slowed to a sedate thirty miles an hour. "I met the boyfriend here last year. I was having dinner with the local police chief, professional courtesy. Then García comes over and the chief introduces him as an upstanding local citizen. Gives him my pedigree and all." He paused for a moment and cleared

225

his throat. "At that time, my wife was looking pretty far gone. Traveling was a strain, but she wanted to come down here one last time, loved this place." He cleared his throat, which had become husky. "So we get back to the hotel, we'd taken a room for her sake, she found it hard to be comfortable in the van. Anyway, the room was full of flowers. Like, I mean full."

"García did that?"

"Sure. There was a card there from him. Sweet. It thrilled Fay. Anyway, a day or so later some cute little girl came to see her while I was off birding, brought a piñata that she wanted delivered to her cousin back in Flagstaff. Her mother was with her, looked like a former nun. You get the picture."

"Surely you didn't buy it?"

"I didn't. But Fay did. She said I was just being a cop and the kid was a little angel. And you don't argue with people when they're that far down the one-way track. So I went along, and we took it home."

"And somebody came for it?"

"Yeah, some cute little ankle-biter turned up at the house and Fay gave him cookies and handed him the piñata."

"And that was it?"

"That was it. Until Fay died and I got a letter from the cancer society telling me that somebody called Vasquez had made a one-thousand-dollar donation in my name. That's when I knew for sure we'd been used." He drove without speaking for about a minute, then went on. "So anyway, I knew who García was, and when things fell apart at his house, I put myself on the side of the angels. I figured you'd find some way out. That's why I left the keys in the van and tipped you off we'd be at the Parthenon."

"Cozy," I said. "I bet you'd have been real cut up if you'd come back and found me smeared all over García's parlor."

"García told the kid not to hurt you," he said. "And goddamn it, if they had, I'd still have taken your boy home for you."

"I just love happy endings," I told him.

He drove back past Las Tres Marias and along the shore road to García's turnoff, scattering the same dumb chickens. Then he turned up the hill and pulled up to García's gate. It was still open, and he drove up to the house. Thurlbeck stopped there and turned to look at me. "What now? Can you make your plane?"

"I don't think so. I'd like to phone my contact in Toronto and find out when we can get out. And in the meantime, let's find Greg's money. He's got some unpaid debts down here."

"Right." Thurlbeck grabbed his M1 and nudged García. They got out, and I backed out of the car with my hand on Amadeo's shoulder. He came like a good boy, and we walked into the house and back to García's study.

The room was as I'd left it, except that the gunny I'd hit was lying on the couch, awake now, holding his leg and trying not to groan. And with him, standing behind the couch, was a familiar face, Jesús.

"Hey. Good to see you," I said. "Now the gang's all here."

"Yes," he said without expression, and then brought up the gun he'd been concealing. "Drop that rifle, *señor*," he said to Thurlbeck. "Do not try to use it. If you point it even close to me, you're dead."

Twenty-one

W hat gives?" I asked softly. "I thought you were one of the good guys."

"I am," he said, still watching us all like a cat surrounded by a choice of mice. Thurlbeck set down his rifle on the floor, saying nothing. Then Jesús pointed his gun at me. "Take off your coat," he said. He was taking no chances, his gun never wavered. Jesús saw both pistols as I peeled the jacket. "Two guns," he sneered. "Just like Wyatt Earp."

He said something in Spanish, and García came around behind me and reached around me for the guns, taking them both away and giving me no chance to use him for a shield. Then he walked around in front of us, holding both guns, smiling like the bright boy in kindergarten. He raised one of them, and Jesús shot him right through the smile.

Amadeo gave a little yelp. Thurlbeck and I did nothing.

"I want your money," Jesús said. He gestured at Amadeo. "Where is it?"

Amadeo looked at me and licked his lips fearfully. "It's hidden," he said in a small voice.

"Then we'll go find it," Jesús said.

I was weighing my chances. There were three of us to distract him. If I could get close enough to dive at him, we were home free. And in the meantime, we didn't have García to worry about anymore.

Amadeo said, "Look, if it's just money, we can work this out."

Jesús laughed. "Sure we can. I know that. But I'm not making any deals. I want the whole half million."

Amadeo tried. "That's kinda heavy," he said. "Whyn't I give you half an' put you on the payroll. You'll make that kinda bread over an' over working for me."

"Tell me where it is, or I'll shoot you in the kneecap," Jesús said. "You'll tell me then and wish you'd told me now. Where is it?"

"It's in my room," Amadeo said. I like pragmatic people. "At the hotel. I went back there this morning and put it with my clothes."

I didn't like that. Moving a suitcase was a one-man job. I wondered if Jesús would shoot us all and go for it alone.

"Nice try, Greg," I said. "That's where you left it, but I've been there. I moved it since then."

"Where to?" Jesús whirled to face me. "You been playing games with me, I'll shoot you."

"And you'll still be stuck here in this dead-assed town, warbling out ballads for the tourists. No future in that, Jesús. Placido Domingo you ain't."

He ignored that. "I said, where is it?"

"I'm not telling you until I get some assurances," I said.

Amadeo was staring at me, his mouth partly open. I wasn't sure whether he was marveling at my self-assurance in the cannon's mouth or wondering how I'd found his stash.

"I can shoot your knees off just as easy," Jesús said.

"Yeah. You can kill me, too, but I'm not taking you to the money until I get those assurances. Now why make it difficult? I won't be able to lead you there if I'm on one leg, will I?"

Let's hear it, for sweet reason. He stared at me angrily for a full thirty seconds, then asked, "What's the deal?"

"I want our lives. That's all. You get your money and go

walkabout. We go back home and forget all about you. You still win, only we walk."

He thought about it. "I can make you talk," he said.

"You can try," I told him. "But a big part of the training I took was in how to stand up to interrogation. You could be days getting it out of me. Or you could be wafting out of town this afternoon, humming 'Happy Days Are Here Again.' Your choice."

He swore. "Okay. You can all go. But I want you with me until I've picked up the money."

"Deal," I said, and stuck out my hand. No harm in trying. But he only sneered. "Out in the car."

He walked behind us down the corridor, the other two leading, him at the back, a pace behind me, safe from a leg sweep but close enough to hit me square in the spine if he pulled the trigger. I didn't play any games. Outside, he said, "Locke, you drive. You two, in the back."

They all got in behind me, Thurlbeck sitting next to Jesús, I noticed, and we headed out, at an undertaker's pace, down the hill. My mind was racing, trying to come up with someplace to go that would give me a chance, but where? If I told Jesús I'd moved the money out of town, he would get suspicious, and if I took him somewhere isolated, he would shoot all three of us. He could do it, he'd already proved that on García. No, it had to be somewhere crowded. And then I remembered the pickup truck, standing outside the market. Just in time because he was asking, "Where are we going?"

"You'll see when we get there, Jesús. I wouldn't want you thinking you could go it alone."

"Don't get cute," he said. "I'm losing my patience."

"Relax, Jesús. I don't care about the money. It's drug money, I wouldn't touch it myself, it's all yours," I said. Maybe not the most tactful speech I could make in the circumstances, but a statement of Locke policy, for better or worse.

He said nothing, and I drove back through town and around to the back of the market. I pulled in over the bumpy ground beside the pickup truck, which was still where Amadeo had left it.

"It's in the truck?" Jesús asked incredulously.

"I left the keys with my *amigo* at the diner. Give me a moment and I'll get them back."

"Now just minute." I turned and looked at him. His face was pale and jaundiced under his tan and native color. "You expect me to believe this crap?"

"Go try the doors if you don't believe me." I said.

"Turn your pockets out first. Let's see if you've got the keys." He waved the gun at me, and I obediently emptied my pockets. All I had was some cash, my knife and handkerchief, and the plastic container holding my passport and big bills. No keys.

"Believe me now?" I asked, acting a little aggrieved.

"So go get them," he said. "Forget this trash. It'll be here."

"I need a tip for the guy on the counter," I argued, and picked up my container. A man feels lost without his passport in a strange place.

I nodded to him and got out of the car, unfolding the plastic container to take out some money. He pressed the control to open his window and it slid down silently. "Any tricks, and these two die," he said. His eyes were like flint.

"I know. I've seen you in action."

I walked away over the dusty ground with the sun clanging on my shoulders like a golden gong. God, it was hot. So why was I shivering?

The same kid was at the counter, and he looked up and grinned when I came back.

"*Hola.*" I grinned back. "*Mi jugo de naranja, por favor.*" Hi, my orange juice please. He nodded and reached for the liter of juice I had bought that morning and left there. I like that about Mexicans. I could have left it a week, and it would still have been there. He brought it out from under the counter. It was hot to the touch.

I slipped him a thousand pesos, and he looked at it in surprise. "*Muchas gracias, amigo,*" I told him. "*Tiene usted una caja, por favor?*" Thanks, do you have a box?

231

He frowned, then turned away and dug out a small box that had held some kind of groceries. He held it up tentatively, and I nodded and grinned. *"Sí, es muy bien."* Yeah, that's good. He handed it to me, and I stood the orange juice bottle in the middle of it, then removed the cap. I dug my finger into the top and tasted it. The tasting was for his benefit. I just wanted to check the temperature. It was about the way I like my showers. He looked at me in puzzlement but folded his thousand pesos away and said nothing. I winked at him and turned away.

I walked back to the car and went to Jesús' window, which was still open. "Never take anything for granted," I said cheerfully. "I had it hidden in the market. Wanna see?"

Good old-fashioned greed got the better of him. He craned his head up to look into the box and I jolted it, filling his face and eyes with semiscalding orange juice. He gasped in shock and drew back, but not before I had hold of his hair and had smashed his nose against the edge of the window a couple of times. Then Thurlbeck's voice said, "Nice goin', John. I've got his piece."

I opened the front door and got in. Thurlbeck was holding the gun on Jesús, who was clutching his broken nose between his hands. Blood was seeping out between his fingers.

"Let's go," I said. "Don't let him jump, we need him to do some explaining."

We drove back to García's house. I half expected Amadeo to argue, to want to get his precious money, but he didn't. He was too relieved to have his life. I figured he'd done a lot of growing up in the time I'd been minding him.

I pulled in, past the dead dog, which was a smorgasbord for the local flies by this time, and parked at the door. "Let's go back to García's office," I suggested, and we all got out, Jesús reeling a little, still holding his nose.

The gunny was still lying on the couch, but he had rolled over so he could get a better look at García's body. There went his pension plan, I guessed. I told Jesús to sit in the big chair and he did, after Thurlbeck had patted him down and pronounced him clean. I glanced around. There was a phone on the coffee table beside the couch. "You're the one with the connections," I told Thurlbeck. "Call the police chief and tell him we've got a murderer for him."

Jesús started to say something, but I gazed at him, and he dried up. Then I said, "Nobody says a word about your drug enforcement work. You can use that as you want to. We're turning you in for the murder of García. Any justice in the land, they'll give you a medal."

I doubted that. But at least it promised him some gold at the end of the rainbow, so he sat and held his leaking nose while Thurlbeck called in.

He hung up and said, "They're on their way. Leave the talking to me, he knows me."

"Done," I said. "Now get back on the Don Ameche and get me this number in Toronto, could you, please?—my Spanish isn't up to it."

He dialed the operator, and within a couple of minutes I was talking to Cahill.

"You okay?" was his first question.

"Couldn't be better. But I'd like to get out tonight if possible. Is there a flight, and if so, can you get me aboard?"

He shuffled papers for a moment and came back on the line. "Seventeen-thirty hours, local time there, Holiday Air. They're expecting you and the boyfriend."

"You mean you knew I was coming back today?"

"Dummy." He's Irish, but he never majored in blarney. "I've had a notice out to all of them for the last week, any flight coming into Zihua has seats for you and Mr. Sunshine. Go to the desk and ask to see the captain. He'll put you both aboard first."

"Nice going. That gives me time to pick my stuff up from the hotel. See you around eleven. What's the weather like?"

He told me, and I shuddered. Then the police arrived and Thurlbeck started explaining. Jesús tried to cut in, but the police chief just looked at him, and his voice died. They had

233

him out of there, with handshakes all around, even for Amadeo, before the ambulance had come to collect first García's body, then the wounded man. They do not treat the help well in Mexico.

The last word on the subject came from Jesús. "I'll remember you for this," he said. I'd had the same promise made by a PLO gunman one time, so I took this one with a grain of salt.

"And I'll remember you," I promised him, and they led him away. Nobody had laid a glove on him yet.

"That was some speech you made," Amadeo said admiringly to Thurlbeck. "Shit, you cleaned up the mess at the Parthenon as well." He grinned. "How'd you like to work for me?"

Thurlbeck looked at him straight. "First off, I want that money. We've got to compensate the kid from La Playa Blanca, his family anyway. The rest goes to Maria."

"That dumb bitch!" I thought Amadeo was going to stamp his foot. "Didn't even have enough brains to fill the goddamn boat with diesel. None o' this need've happened except for her."

Thurlbeck came over and stood in front of him, dangerously close, if Amadeo had been dangerous. "I don't like you," he said calmly. "Shut your mouth, and keep it shut until you're on the witness stand. Got that?"

There was no violence in his voice, but Amadeo shriveled. He suddenly found his toe caps as interesting as this month's *Reader's Digest*.

Thurlbeck drove us back as far as his van, then changed vehicles, leaving the Continental alongside the curb. I wondered how long it would stand there. Who would fill García's shoes? And would he want a Continental? Maybe the guards at the Parthenon would bring it inside for the police chief if he ever got out of jail in California.

We drove up Cuatro Vientos and got our keys from the desk. There was a clutter of people there, but I was weary and didn't notice who they were. Gringos, I'd noticed, not dangerous. One of them was Beth. She caught my arm. "John? What happened?"

"Oh, Beth." I straightened up and tried a grin. "Sorry about the confusion up there. Some heavies wanted to talk business."

"I saw what happened," she said, but she didn't look at me, she was looking at Thurlbeck. Then she glanced back. "You hit that man in the arm, but he was still going to shoot you."

"He would've. Except that my friend here is an ex-GI from the big war, and he knows about guns."

Now she turned to Thurlbeck. "You killed him," she said, but her voice was admiring.

He cleared his throat. "I'd rather not talk about it, please. And it's in the hands of the police now, sub judice. We've been told not to say anything."

Beth made her mouth into a perfect O. Behind her a couple more people had recognized us and were standing very still, remembering what they had seen at the Parthenon, wondering whether we were Superman and his team. Beth was radiant. I realized again what a beautiful woman she had been, until only a very few years ago, and how handsome she still was. She was looking at Thurlbeck, who was smiling like Gary Cooper.

I waved at him, "I'm sorry, what am I thinking about, may I introduce you. This is . . ."

"Calvin Thurlbeck, ma'am," he said, and took off his feed-store cap. His hair was still blond over the top. He looked pretty good himself for a guy of sixty.

"Beth Andersen," she said. They smiled and shook hands. You could almost hear the orchestra swelling. I figured I'd better move fast if I wanted a bit part in their drama. "Calvin is staying down here for a while, Greg and I are going home," I said.

"At the hotel?" she asked.

We excused ourselves and went to the room for our gear. Amadeo said nothing. His briefcase was packed among his clothes. I took it off him and gave him my bag to carry. "I'll give this to Cal," I said, and he looked at me and made his last try.

"We can still get away," he said. "You can have half."

"Come on. Grab the bags. We've got a plane to catch."

I left all my change for the housemaid and opened the door. Debra Steen's companion Helen was out there, about to knock. "Leaving?" she asked.

"Yes, mission accomplished, I'm taking Greg home now. Thank Debra for me, we couldn't have done it without her help. How's she, anyway?"

"Fine." She smiled, a nice taut smile, like a TV actress, Linda Evans maybe. "A little shaky in the mornings, but she hasn't had anything for two whole days, and she's working well again."

"That's good. Glad to have been of help." I wanted to go, but she leaned one arm against the doorjamb.

"You're a hell of a guy," she said, and this time I didn't shrug off any of the credit. Thurlbeck was doing just fine where he was.

"I'm sorry about the kerfuffle on your session."

"I want to know what that was all about," she said. "We're in Toronto next month for some commercials. Perhaps we could get together then."

"That would be tremendous. See if you can duck out without the duchess, it's you I'd like to talk to."

She laughed. "That would be a start," she said. "What's your phone number?"

I put the briefcase down and dug a card out from the folder containing my passport. John Locke, Personal Security, and my phone number. "I'm counting on it," I told her.

Amadeo cleared his throat. He wasn't used to being left out.

"Thank you again, John Locke," she said, and reached up to kiss me on the cheek. Nothing splashy, just a promise.

I kissed her and picked up the briefcase. "Next month," I said.

We walked back out to reception. Beth and Thurlbeck were talking, and he straightened up when we arrived. "I'll take you to the airport," he said. Then to Beth, "I'll drop by in the morning. The birds out at La Playa Blanca will carry you away. Terns, gulls, pelicans, you name it."

"Thank you." She reached out to shake my hand. "Good-bye, John. Good luck."

"Good-bye and thank you for all your help, Beth." God! Was I being couth! Noël Coward would have been proud of me.

Thurlbeck led us out to his van, and I shoved Amadeo in the back and got in beside him. "Okay, Cal," I said.

Thurlbeck put his feed-store cap back on and started away. He was whistling. A good choice for a bird-watcher, "A Nightingale Sang in Berkeley Square."

"What about lover boy's cash?" I asked.

"Been thinking about that," Thurlbeck said. "I figure half should go to Maria, half to the kid's family at La Playa Blanca. I'll take care of that part, open an account for them, get somebody to help handle it. It's a lot of bread. They'd have every grifter in the state after it if we don't sew it up."

Amadeo swore. "That's my goddamn money."

"Yeah. An' it was that family's livelihood, never mind about the life of the guy you wasted. I don't wanna hear another word outa you."

I felt in my pocket for the torn thousand-dollar bill. "And one other thing. A guy with his arm in a sling will be at the airport on Sunday looking for me. Could you give him this, please."

"Sure can," Thurlbeck said.

"Think Maria can handle her end?" I asked.

"I'll check," Thurlbeck said. "She won't be up to anything for a couple of days. Then I'll talk it over with her. Probably she'd be better getting it as it is, in cash, if she's got to disappear."

"Good." I left it at that. I knew she'd be as safe with Thurlbeck as if her money was in the Chase Manhattan.

We reached the airport at four-thirty. Thurlbeck parked outside and walked in with us, carrying the briefcase. "Can you pick me up a bottle of Bacardi Anejo and one of Kahlúa, and a big bottle of vanilla, please?" I asked him, and he nodded and peeled off.

237

There was a long line at the gate, people with shiny new tans and sombreros to hang on the walls of their split-levels in Don Mills. I got a few glances as I waltzed Amadeo to the head of the line, but there was a stewardess there, and she said, "Yes, Mr. Locke. I'll bring the captain."

Thurlbeck came back as we waited and handed me the bag with my purchases. I tried to pay him, but he waved it aside. "Most fun I've had in a coon's age," he said. "Think of me when you're drinking it."

"I will. Any chance of you coming to Toronto?"

He cleared his throat, like a schoolkid who doesn't know the answer to the teacher's question. "Pretty good. I'd say," he admitted. "I was talking to Beth. She said you've got a hell of a birder's gathering spot, Point Pelee is it?"

"Right. April is the best time. All the warblers and a whole crowd of others come through then. You can see them all because the trees are still bare."

"Sounds good," he said. Then he cleared his throat. "She seems like a real nice person."

"That's what I thought," I told him, and Amadeo tutted in disgust.

The captain came back with the stewardess, who pointed us out to him. And immediately Amadeo went into his act. He folded at the waist, retching. People shrieked and pulled away. "I'm sick," he said.

I winked at the captain. "I'm a doctor. This is a hysterical reaction. I'll tranquilize him if you'll get us aboard, Captain."

The captain looked doubtful, but Thurlbeck nodded. "I've seen him do this before. Poor guy, that's why he has to travel with his own physician."

I shook Thurlbeck's hand and took my own bag. Amadeo was going to leave his, but the captain picked it up and led us out through the afternoon sunshine to the gangway. I shoved Amadeo ahead of me. He balked, and I stiffened three fingers and prodded them into his kidney. That straightened him up. He tottered up the gangway and collapsed into the first seat inside. The cabin staff were watching him as if he had a leper's bell. I dropped my bag and pinched him under the arm, where the flesh is tender, and gave him a solid horse bite between finger and thumb.

"I can take you back sitting up or lying down. Your choice," I whispered, smiling at him as if we were lovers.

"All right," he said, and I pinched him a little harder. "All right. Where do I sit?"

Twenty-two

The trip was uneventful except for a report that Toronto was snowed in. It was, but not badly enough to get us diverted. We landed at close to eleven, and Amadeo and I were kept on board until all the others had gone. Then they led us down to the RCMP office. On the way there Amadeo said the first words he'd uttered the whole way. "That was some fine speech you made to Jesús," he sneered. "About not touching drug money."

I waited for the other shoe to drop. I was just congratulating myself on a job well done. Going out of a side entrance meant no customs, and I was over my allowance on booze. When I didn't answer, he continued, loud enough that the airport security man who was leading us turned and looked at him oddly. "Where'd you think the cash I gave you came from? The hardware business? You're no different from me, Locke. All you think about is the bucks."

Cahill was waiting for us in the office. He shook hands and turned Amadeo over to two others. One of them handcuffed him to his own left wrist. Then Cahill handed me my topcoat and hat. "You're gonna need this," he said. "Your blood's probably thinner'n maiden's water right about now."

"Nothing a good shot of Bushmills won't fix. Listen. It's too late for dinner tonight. Let's skip it. I'll take you to my favorite place tomorrow."

"Some French place?" he queried. I noticed he wasn't asking about Amadeo. The less he knew, the better, I guessed. The other two Mounties left, Amadeo looking back over his shoulder to sneer, but he said nothing.

"No." I played his game. "My favorite spot in the whole of Toronto is Il Pantalone up on Bathurst. Italian, Venetian, really. Nice no-nonsense place and great food. You should taste their shrimp *al forno*."

"Shrimp?" he queried. He was a corned-beef-and-cabbage man.

The streets were clear, but there was eighteen inches of snow swept along all the curbs. A few hardy souls were out courting heart attacks, cleaning up the last of the day's fall. Cahill gestured at them as he drove. "Glad I live in an apartment," he said. "My ex-wife used to bug hell outa me until I'd shoveled, no matter when the snow fell."

"It was thirty degrees Celsius when I left Zihua," I told him. "Haven't had rain since November. Won't get any before May. Beautiful."

He snorted. "Don't say we never do anything for you."

He looked tired, and when we reached my place, he turned down the offer of a drink. "I gotta lot of paperwork to do in the morning, now we've got Amadeo back. New identity, alla that shit. You know what it's like."

"Yeah. They tell me it doesn't stick. His boys will find him anyway. Is that true?"

He reached over to hold the door handle on my side. "Generally," he said. "That gonna keep you up nights?"

"Couldn't happen to a nicer guy," I said. Then we shook hands, and I got out, into the middle of the piled snow on Clifton Road.

He laughed and then said, "You have to start taking care of yourself, kid."

"Beginning tomorrow," I promised.

241

Then he leaned lower, so he could see me playing king-of-the-castle on the snow pile. "And thanks, eh."

"You're welcome, you smooth-talking leprechaun."

The house was quiet, downstairs anyway. I remembered that it was concert night at the Roy Thomson Hall downtown. The two good friends on the bottom floor had called a truce for the evening and were lapping up Beethoven, side by side. Ah, love.

But on the second floor I stopped and listened. There was a noise I didn't like coming out of the closed door of Janet's apartment. I bent my ear closer to the door and was sure of it. She was sobbing.

I set down my bag and hit the door a couple of slams with the flat of my hand. "Janet? You okay? It's John."

The room went silent for a moment, then a man's voice said, "She's fine, thanks."

"Let me hear her say that."

His voice came back. "I said she's all right. Go to hell."

I stood back and slammed the lock with my right foot. It took two whumps before the door broke and I was inside, looking into her living room. Janet was on the couch, holding the top of her blouse around her. And there was a man with her, fortyish, well built, dark hair, angry. "Listen, prick," he said and ran for me.

You shouldn't do that. I sidestepped and tripped him, and he sprawled headlong down the stairs. Eight of them. He was in his shirt sleeves, and when he got up, there was blood down the front of his shirt. But he didn't stop. He turned and ran back at me, another sucker's trick. I stomped his chest, the way I'd stomped the lock, and he went down the stairs backward this time.

This go-around I went down to him and grabbed his wrist, then I stuck it between his legs, grabbed it again and threw him down the other half of the flight of stairs. He fell better this time, almost managing to catch the banisters. A few more throws and he would have been an expert. But he didn't come back for more. He bolted out the door and into the cold in a staggering run.

I shut the door after him and went back up to Janet's apartment. She was standing now, wiping her eyes with a tissue.

"Are you all right?" a dumb question, but it wasn't the time to lecture her about bringing home strange men.

"I think so." She sniffed and tried to smile. "Thank you, I guess."

"You're welcome, I guess," I said. "Want to talk about it?"

She shook her head. "No." She was definite about that one. "No. I feel dumb enough as it is. It won't get better if I go over it a couple of times, I'll just feel certifiable."

"You're the boss." I picked up my bag. "I brought some rum home. Would you like a little? It goes well with orange juice."

She cried then, but I made her a small drink and steered her up the stairs to my place. The lock was still intact there, and except for being empty, the bed was comfortable. Me, I stayed down in her place. I checked the boyfriend's wallet and found he was a heavy in the investment business. He had a picture of a woman and two kids in his wallet as well. But I've learned never to stick my nose into other people's business, so I left his clothes in a heap and went to the phone.

My mother was still up. We exchanged the usual courtesies, and I told her I had brought some vanilla for her cook, the real stuff, not a synthetic. "Yes, I know where vanilla comes from," she said testily. "You remember, I took you down to Zihuatanejo the first time you went."

"Met some interesting people," I said. I had unfastened my belt and I unzipped the security compartment as I talked to her. The ten thousand dollars Amadeo had given me was still intact, the seawater had not penetrated the leather. You have to hand it to Saks Fifth Avenue, they sell good stuff.

She asked who, and I mentioned Debra Steen, whom she'd

243

never heard of. Then I told her, "Met another rich woman there, a Maria Amadeo."

"Don't say you've become a gigolo now?" My mother does not have much faith in the fruit of her womb.

"No. This one is more of the philanthropic type," I said. "You get the picture, thick legs, homely."

"A gentleman would not discuss a lady in that way," my mother said.

"Well, maybe not. But the thing is, she has a solid-gold heart." I piled my ten thousand-dollar bills into one neat heap and ironed them smooth with the back of my hand. "Yes, when I mentioned that you were raising money for Sick Kids', she gave me a donation."

"Every little bit helps," my mother said condescendingly.

"Ten thousand dollars," I said, and added the kicker, "That's American, call it fourteen grand Canadian."

"My word, that is generous." There, I had bought her undivided attention for only fourteen thousand dollars.

"I thought so, too," I said. "I'll bring it over in the morning."

"Good. That would be very nice. Come around eleven, and we'll have tea."

"Best offer I've had all night," I told her. "Good night."

I hung up and went to the door. It was impossible to lock, but I pushed a chair under the handle and went to bed. Hell, it was only a month until the Debra Steen show came to town and I was taking Helen out for dinner.